With Olivia'[...]
swallowed irritatio[...] [...]
the hallway. She smiled and extended a hand.

He shook it, straightened, and crossed his arms. "I'll tell you up front what I think of Leadership Camp." He glared and shifted.

"I'm interested to hear." Tessa filled her lungs with the power of being in command. "But not right now. My next meeting starts in a few minutes." In a friendly, polite way, she'd let him know her schedule was firm. Refusing to let him intimidate her or direct the conversation, she gestured toward a chair.

Glowering, he ignored her invitation and threw her a confident, dark-as-midnight gaze. Planted in the center of the office, he didn't waver.

A surprising jolt of anticipation sharpened her senses until she could feel his energy reverberate in the still office air. Inhaling sharply, she steadied herself and held her ground. He was clearly not in the right frame of mind for a positive conversation.

"Tell you what." Knees trembling, Tessa flashed her most-winning smile. "Let's rewind and start fresh tomorrow." Mark needed to understand *she* set the ground rules, and she expected him to maintain a courteous tone. She'd show him who was really in charge. Still, frozen by his icy gaze, she felt her heart skitter. His stony presence couldn't throw her off course, or could it?

Love
Leads the Way

by

Margot Johnson

Love Leads the Way

Cover Art by *Kim Mendoza*

The Wild Rose Press, Inc.
PO Box 708
Adams Basin, NY 14410-0708
Visit us at www.thewildrosepress.com

Publishing History
First Edition, 2021
Trade Paperback ISBN 978-1-5092-3478-3
Digital ISBN 978-1-5092-3479-0

Published in the United States of America

Dedication

For my husband, Rick…
Hero of our own, real-life love story

Chapter 1

Mark Delaney beat a steady pace on a treadmill in the HeatNow company gym. He stared out the window at the early-morning Broad Street traffic and counted cars. The habit helped him forget everything else for a few precious minutes before work.

The early rush hour in Regina, Saskatchewan, Canada, hardly compared to larger centers, but cars steadily flowed by, and people bustled across the street to their offices. Jutting into the sky, elm trees waited for spring buds to burst into new leaves, and a brisk breeze whisked dust along the curbs.

The window reflected images of a few other employees, huffing at their own workout stations. Mark's T-shirt dampened around the neck and between his shoulder blades, and he wiped his brow. Upbeat music blared and pumped energy throughout the room, and he breathed the faint odor of sweat and antiseptic.

"I'd like to give you some feedback." Liz Nelson jogged on the adjacent machine.

Liz's breathing rasped, and she spoke in short bursts. Twisting, she ran a hand through her spiky, gray hair and pierced Mark with intense, blue eyes.

"Should I pick up my game?" He chuckled and adjusted the button to increase the incline by two degrees. As Mark's boss, she might offer feedback on his engineering work but not his workout.

"In a sense." Liz glanced over and then out the window.

He frequently nudged himself to stretch his limits and then some. Steeling his chest, he glanced sideways. Liz meant business. As a boss, she was the best he'd had—firm but fair. She was a dedicated mentor who always had his back. They respected and trusted each other. So if Liz had a message, he better listen. "Okay, shoot. I'm ready."

"You like to hear things straight." Liz wiped her forehead with a towel and draped it over a shoulder. "So I won't sugarcoat, Mark. You need to improve your people skills."

"My role is to oversee pipeline projects, not win a popularity contest." Overwhelming warmth he couldn't blame on the workout overtook him, and he jerked calming breaths and guzzled water. Liz could count on him to make sure HeatNow delivered a ready supply of natural gas to homes and businesses. His expertise made a difference. With an engineering degree and over ten years of experience, he was well equipped to handle any technical challenge.

"I understand." Liz stared out the window. "No one knows our business like you. But your brains and talent will only carry you so far. If you want to earn a spot at the executive table, you *must* demonstrate you care about the team."

"I care about customers' safety, not a bunch of people issues." Fisting his hands, he stared at the car lights below. Liz raised the topic at his last performance review, but he interpreted her comments as a suggestion and not a command. Staring at the traffic light below, he needed to slam the brakes on this conversation.

Liz lowered the speed on the treadmill. "We only...get strong results...through...people." She inhaled quick breaths.

"True, but my dad always said it's lonely at the top. I don't expect to be best friends with anybody at work. I don't mix my work and personal life." His dad—Preston John Delaney—jetted to the top of a major engineering firm and expected Mark to follow in his successful footsteps.

Starting his cool-down, Mark slowed his pace. She was the boss, so he shouldn't argue, but an inner voice defended his approach. He focused on the job, just like his dad had taught. Sometimes, he couldn't stand the way people wasted time and socialized instead of worked.

"Mark, you have to pay attention to how you make people feel." Liz darted her gaze toward him.

"How do you suggest I change?" He swiped a wrist across his upper lip.

"I plan to reserve you a spot in the next session of Leadership Camp. Tessa Shore directs the program." Liz made eye contact in the window reflection.

He sighed. He'd heard the course built soft skills for interpersonal connections, but he had absolutely no interest. *Soft* meant wishy-washy and a waste of time. He could serve as a role model without lessons in how to change his personality. The whole idea chilled him like a plunge into a frigid lake.

"I don't have time for leadership games...missing work...people getting all emotional. I already juggle a heavy workload with family demands." He rotated his stiff shoulder muscles. Today's workout was far from the relaxing escape he sought. Mark thumped his runners to the beat of the gym's background music.

He'd never survive without daily exercise to release some of the tension that rode in his upper body. His whole life was a treadmill, hurrying home from work to parent his niece, exercise his dog, and support his mom in the care home. He carved out a few, morning minutes to stay fit and keep stress at bay. Indignation burned in his chest.

"Bree's thirteen, dealing with teenage stuff." Sharpening his tone more than he intended, he glanced over in time to catch Liz's frown. He adjusted down his speed another notch. "I can't just drop everything and head out of town. She's too young to leave alone. I don't have a wife to handle things on the home front. My mom counts on my visits to the care home. They both depend on me." Responsibility stomped on his heaving chest, and he clamped his jaw and shook his head. "Even if I wanted to participate, the timing doesn't work."

"Mark, take my advice, not just as your boss but as a friend. You'll find a way to make time. You don't really have an option." She grabbed the towel and dabbed her neck. "I'm retiring next month, so I won't be around much longer to coach and defend you."

"Already?" He stumbled and grabbed the handrail to regain his balance. Her frank assessment of his leadership skills, topped by her surprise announcement, hit hard. "I'll miss you."

When Liz said goodbye for the last time, she'd leave a giant void. In one swift motion, he'd lose a wise mentor and strong supporter. Why did the most important people in his life always disappear? His other painful losses threatened to shoot to the surface, and he wrestled them deep inside where they belonged.

Digesting the unsettling news, he ran in silence for a couple of minutes. He counted on Liz's guidance and backing. Without her support, a promotion likely wouldn't happen, and now, she'd sentenced him to an awkward learning situation just before she exited.

"I'll think about it." Gripping tight the rail, he lowered his gaze to his glistening arms and legs. What else could he say? For now, she was the boss. His future rested in her hands, at least, for the next month. He bit his tongue against a spout of angry words. The morning gym time was supposed to set him up for the day and not jab a double blow to his gut.

"Good." Liz switched off the machine, grabbed her water bottle, and toweled the back of her neck. "I want to leave you with every chance of success. Have a good day."

"You, too." He doubted he would. Giving her a slight nod and setting his jaw, he spun and charged to the change room. He fired his clothes into a damp heap and stepped under the steamy spray. Liz should understand him well enough not to force him into Leadership Camp. He consistently demonstrated technical excellence. His integrity never faltered. With all the strengths he offered, he didn't need a so-called expert from Human Resources to tell him how to behave.

In the shower, he inhaled the lather's outdoorsy scent and scrubbed so vigorously his head and body smarted. To keep Liz happy, he'd talk to that Tessa woman and at least hear her out. He hadn't formally met her, but he remembered a vague impression of an animated, whirlwind-of-a-person with unruly, reddish hair, wide, curious eyes, and a generous dusting of freckles. If he recalled correctly, she was a little overly friendly. In an elevator, she smiled, joked, and interrupted his concentration on complex pipeline calculations.

He rinsed, dried, and dressed in business-casual wear. The mirror reflected his irritation, and he flicked his hair into place. He'd need a haircut soon to touch up his professional image. Leaning closer to his reflection, he caught a sharp breath. His resemblance to his late father was uncanny. No doubt, Dad would have scoffed at Leadership Camp. He believed the true keys to success meant locking personal issues and feelings into a tight compartment. Definitely, he never would have agreed to a crash course that demanded he examine and expose private emotions.

"Give me a break." Mark stared at his tense expression and huffed bitter words under his breath. In one abrupt motion, he rotated his shoulders and spun to attack the day. If Dad was still alive, he would have bolstered Mark's confidence and counseled him on how to manage the ridiculous work predicament.

On the way to his desk, Mark massaged a brief ache of longing in his chest. He swigged a long, cooling drink from a water bottle and secured any misgivings into his inner vault. Dad always expected him to act like a champ, and he would. He'd show that Tessa woman she couldn't force him to change or reveal anything he didn't want to share.

****

A rustle at the office doorway grabbed Tessa Shore's attention, and she glanced up. Part of the Human Resources Department, she supported an open-door policy. If people needed her, she was ready to help, but she seldom had a drop-in visitor within minutes of arrival.

"Good morning, Tessa. Do you have a minute?" Liz Nelson marched into the office. "I hope you're up for a bit of a challenge."

A vice president didn't need an invitation to enter, and Tessa leapt to greet her. "Definitely. Tell me more." She smiled and swept her gaze over Liz's shoulders. "Excuse me." She straightened the picture on the wall behind Liz.

A quick survey of the rest of the office confirmed the reports and notes sat in neat, prioritized piles on the desk, and the reference books perched on a shelf in a precise, categorized line. Family photos, three succulent plants, and a single grouping of impressionist prints softened the edges and made the space more inviting.

Liz had no idea of the extent of the challenges Tessa managed daily, not only at the office but also at home. She wasn't the sandwich generation caught between her ailing mother, Adele, and her exuberant daughter, Ellie. Tessa was more like stew, with work simmering in a full pot of family demands. Single parenthood was much more difficult than she expected or cared to admit.

"Oh, it'll be interesting all right." Liz raised her eyebrows.

"Would you like to have a seat?" Tessa gestured toward the table by the window and closed her office door. A sunbeam lit a path across the room.

Liz plunked into a chair, leaned forward, and met Tessa's gaze. "I want to place someone in the next round of Leadership Camp."

"Oh?" Tessa widened her eyes. "As usual, the class filled up quickly…" She trailed off partway through her instant reaction. A vice president, clearly, had the final say. Tucking a wayward curl behind her ear, she closed her mouth and waited.

"Mark Delaney. Do you know him?" Liz tapped fingers on the table.

"I know *of* him." Tessa tilted her head and formed her lips into a firm line. She hadn't officially met him, but she'd heard comments about his brusque manner and witnessed his air of detachment. Jaw clenched into a hard line, he barely acknowledged coworkers and focused continually on his phone.

"Exactly. His reputation precedes him." She shook her head. "He can solve any technical challenge we throw his way, but his leadership skills leave a lot to be desired. At best, his peers feel lukewarm." She grimaced. "Last week, he responded in a sharp tone when an executive member asked a question. His approach didn't go over well. That incident was the last straw."

"The last straw?" Mind racing, Tessa tapped a pen on the table. As a participant in Leadership Camp, Mark might challenge her and derail the group.

"I mean Mark's last chance to, well, be himself." Liz grimaced. "He needs to show he cares about people and can build positive relationships, or he'll never get a promotion. Smart as he is, if he can't connect well with people, he can't take charge of an entire division."

"True. I've heard rumors he's difficult to work with, but I always ignore hearsay and form my own opinions." Tessa tilted her head from side to side, weighing whether to continue. "But I admit I've noticed his chill. The last time I encountered him in the elevator and joked about the weather, he didn't even crack a smile."

"Mark doesn't mean to be rude, but he shows so little warmth, he makes people uncomfortable." Liz crossed her legs and flexed a foot.

"What does Mark think of being assigned to Leadership Camp?" Tessa scanned her firm demeanor. Liz must be extremely concerned about his behavior and determined to help her protégé to succeed.

"I told him he didn't have a choice." Liz flapped a hand on the table.

"How did he take the news?" Apprehension twisted in her stomach, and she drew in a deep breath. If she was forced to take on a dissenter, she'd need full executive support.

"As you'd expect." Liz pressed together her lips. "He wasn't thrilled, but he's smart enough to accept my feedback. I've seen the way you transform people. You're viewed as a bit of a miracle worker." Liz made direct eye contact.

"Thanks, Liz." Tessa smiled, and a flush crept up her cheeks. A vice president's praise meant a lot. "I'm really proud of the program, but I usually have the good fortune of working with people who *want* to transform into better leaders."

An unpleasant memory prickled her temples. Five years ago, in the first session Tessa led, she clashed with a difficult participant. The experience shook her confidence, and she vowed it would never again happen. "I can't promise results if Mark doesn't want to be there or won't give the class his full effort." Tessa's office phone rang, and she ignored it.

"I have complete confidence in your approach." Liz slid back her chair, rose, and strode to the door.

"Of course, I'll give him a chance, but I'll lay out the program expectations like I do for everyone. If he doesn't take the opportunity seriously or can't measure up, I'm afraid I'll ask him to withdraw." Searching for full support, she studied Liz's face for a reaction.

Liz nodded and clasped the doorknob.

"I won't allow one unwilling participant to derail the whole group." Tessa clamped together her lips, and the vague, uneasy sensation of losing partial control heightened her senses. The phone rang again, and from a distance, she couldn't read the number on call display. Resisting the urge to interrupt, she flipped her attention back to Liz. "Do you agree?"

"Absolutely."

Liz radiated honesty from clear, blue eyes, and Tessa had no doubt she would keep her word. Then, as if to seal their deal and conclude the meeting, Tessa's personal phone rang from inside a desk drawer.

Tessa stiffened. She needed to be available if the daycare called about Ellie or if her sister, Julie, called about a family emergency. Something must be wrong. Concern swirling in her stomach, she took a deep, calming breath. "Leadership Camp starts next week, so I'll get in touch with Mark right away to go over details."

"Thank you, Tessa." Liz opened the door. "I won't keep you any longer. Someone must really want to reach you. Anyway, keep me posted." She nodded, signaled a thumbs-up, and disappeared into the hallway.

Tessa yanked open the desk drawer and grabbed the phone. Seeing Julie's name listed under missed calls, she breathed a split-second sigh of relief. Ellie must be okay. This morning, her daughter was her usual, bubbly, four-year-old self when Tessa delivered her to daycare, so she didn't expect a problem. But why a call from Julie so early on a work day? Using her personal phone, she punched in her sister's number, clicked shut the office door, and paced.

"The manager of The Benson called. Mom barged into the wrong suite again. Yesterday, she caught a man naked."

Tessa giggled, cringed, and squeezed tighter the phone. She couldn't help her instant reaction, picturing her opinionated mother encountering a neighbor without clothes. No doubt, she sized up his physique and blurted a spontaneous reaction. Mom's behavior would certainly raise more than a few eyebrows at The Benson, the retirement home where she lived.

"Don't laugh, Tess. It's not funny."

"I know. Sorry." Even though dementia was a serious condition, sometimes, it led to humorous situations. Tessa skirted the desk and pictured her one-year-older sister's green-as-grass eyes and springy, reddish curls, so like her own. Taming her younger sister's amusement, Julie would bite her lower lip and bob her head with intensity.

A wave of affection swept over Tessa. Thank goodness, they had each other. Without Julie's support, she couldn't cope with their mother's worsening mental state on top of everything else. She squeezed tight her eyes. Sometimes, the constant demands of work and single motherhood stretched her too far beyond her limit. Controlling everything was plain exhausting.

Tessa bumped the hard edge of the office table,

whirled, and retraced her steps. At this rate, she'd wear out the mottled, gray carpet.

"Wait, let me finish. She slipped into a different neighbor's suite and helped herself to a flowering plant."

"Oh, no." The severity of the situation closed in like an unexpected storm and lurched in her stomach. "Well, Mom did always have a green thumb." Normally optimistic, Tessa tried humor to keep her sister's and her own anxiety in check. Together, they could manage it.

"Tessa."

Julie practically shouted her name, and Tessa flinched. "Sorry. I didn't need more bad news today. What else?" She crossed the floor to her desk and dropped into the chair. Flicking a pen, she glanced at the clock on her computer. Family was her priority, and Julie needed her moral support, but she had a schedule to keep. Like always, when things didn't go as planned, she churned through options to make things better.

"Then Mom wrapped herself in a fuchsia housecoat she found hanging on someone's bathroom door. When she modeled it at morning exercise class, the owner wasn't too impressed. She accused Mom of stealing and created a bit of a scene. The manager says all things considered, Mom needs more supervision."

Tessa sighed and slumped. Tough times lurked.

"Even though The Benson provides assisted living, they expect people to still function appropriately," said Julie.

Tessa sipped water, blinked, and braced herself for the looming ultimatum.

"The bottom line is Mom's state-of-mind has

declined to the point she needs to relocate right away." Julie took a deep breath. "Sorry to be the bearer of bad news."

Tessa wiped a tear that overflowed and slid down her cheek. She had dreaded this day. But now? Today, all of a sudden? "I know Mom's more forgetful and confused, but the situation is worse than I suspected." Trembling, she ran fingers through her tangled curls. Of all the things she could control, her hair wasn't one. "Julie, I'm sorry, but I'm late for a meeting..." She sniffed, dabbed her nose with a tissue, and checked her calendar. "Can you spend the rest of the day with Mom?"

"I guess so. We really don't have a choice. The kids are at school right now, and I can take her along to pick them up. But, Tess, we need to get a plan in place. Soon."

Tessa couldn't miss the unmistakable edge in her sister's tone. "I know. I'll call right after work. I promise." She stood and paced, watching the clock flip past the time of her next meeting. Her mouth dried. She hated to be late.

"Why don't you pick up Ellie and come here for dinner? We can talk with Mom together."

"Okay, I'll see you later." Tessa took a deep breath, blinked away moisture, and stared out the window. Judging by the azure sky, the weather would be as warm as predicted—a perfect spring day—in stark contrast with the clouds lurking over her office. Sure, her mom had always been difficult, but she didn't deserve a life sentence like dementia. Nobody did.

The double dose of bad news—first Mark and now her mom—weighted Tessa's limbs, and she doubted she could run even if the fire alarm blared. After a few minutes to regroup, she forced herself to hurry to the coffee room to refill her water bottle.

"Are you okay, Tess?" Her director, Wendy, paused and narrowed her eyes.

Tessa brushed a tendril off her face and sighed. "A couple of things hit me hard at once like a last-minute, challenging participant in Leadership Camp…and then…" Wendy probably noticed her voice faded into a tremor.

"Oh, I'm sorry to hear. I'm late for a meeting, but let me know if you want to talk later." Wendy refilled her coffee and frowned.

"Thanks, Wendy." She forced a pained smile. Her concerned boss creased her forehead like a worried mother.

Tessa detoured to the restroom and stared in the mirror. No wonder Wendy asked what was wrong. Her green eyes, usually so bright, stared back, faded and watery. Her face was powder white, and her posture sagged. She better pull herself together and act like a leader.

She faked a smile and pinched her cheeks to inject more color. Straightening, she visualized herself as a strong, positive presence, using the same technique she taught her students. Armed with her own best advice, she strode to the meeting room to make a late entrance. Surely, the other participants would view her as busy but not disorganized.

After lunch, she dashed a quick meeting invitation to Mark. She'd lay out clear ground rules and set the expectations for Leadership Camp. Mark would not intimidate her. Drawing on patience and people skills, she'd break through his crusty surface. Maybe his bark was worse than his bite, as was often the case with prickly people.

Seeking a glimpse of sunshine, she spun her chair to face the window. Off on the flat, earthy horizon, a gray bank of clouds swelled, but the forecasted rain likely wouldn't hit for a few hours.

Swinging to her feet, she gathered notes and waved in a young manager. "Good afternoon, Olivia. Ready to talk about positive recognition?"

"For sure." Olivia nodded and took a seat at the table near the window.

Keen to learn skills, she could make significant improvements by applying a few easy tips. For the next half hour, Tessa coached and answered her questions. Then a staccato knock at the door interrupted, and Tessa jumped.

"Mark Delaney asked me to disturb you." Her assistant, Karen, leaned in. "He can't meet later, and he says it's urgent."

Karen's face flushed pink as an eraser. She didn't bother Tessa unless absolutely necessary. "Please, tell him to wait, and I'll see him when this session is over." Heat simmered in Tessa's chest and face. The nerve. She was in charge here, not him.

"Should we wrap up?" Olivia flipped a page in her notebook. "I don't want to delay you."

"First, let's do a quick review." Tessa took a deep breath and smiled. She wouldn't allow Mark to rush her work. "Over the next week, I'd like you to give one piece of specific praise to each of your employees."

"Sure thing. I'll do it and report back." Olivia nodded and headed for the door. "Thank you for your help." As she scooted into the hallway, she nearly collided with Mark.

With Olivia's coaching session complete, Tessa swallowed irritation and waved in Mark from pacing in the hallway. She smiled and extended a hand.

He shook it, straightened, and crossed his arms. "I'll tell you up front what I think of Leadership Camp." He glared and shifted.

"I'm interested to hear." Tessa filled her lungs with the power of being in command. "But not right now. My next meeting starts in a few minutes." In a friendly, polite way, she'd let him know her schedule was firm. Refusing to let him intimidate her or direct the conversation, she gestured toward a chair.

Glowering, he ignored her invitation and threw her a confident, dark-as-midnight gaze. Planted in the center of the office, he didn't waver.

A surprising jolt of anticipation sharpened her senses until she could feel his energy reverberate in the still office air. Inhaling sharply, she steadied herself and held her ground. He was clearly not in the right frame of mind for a positive conversation.

"Tell you what." Knees trembling, Tessa flashed her most-winning smile. "Let's rewind and start fresh tomorrow." Mark needed to understand *she* set the ground rules, and she expected him to maintain a courteous tone. She'd show him who was really in charge. Still, frozen by his icy gaze, she felt her heart skitter. His stony presence couldn't throw her off course, or could it?

Chapter 2

Finally, five o'clock arrived, and Tessa said good night to Carin' Karen. The nickname suited her. Crinkling her brown eyes, she listened and never judged. She was the first to show compassion for others, and if Tessa had more time, she'd confide the issue she was headed to face. With her sister's help, she would calm her concerns and prepare Mom for the changes ahead.

"I hope things work out okay with your mom." Karen tidied her desk and gathered her belongings.

"Thanks. I do, too." Tessa's heart squeezed. She had no idea in what state she'd find her mother and sister. In the car, she lowered the window to sniff the fresh, clean air and clear her head. The drive to Ellie's daycare took only a few minutes, and she barely had time to reflect on the brief meeting with Mark. In their short introduction, she hadn't charmed away his resistance. Overnight, he'd consider his options, and tomorrow, they'd revisit the topic.

At the daycare, Tessa spotted Ellie in a group of other children.

"Come and see the castle, Mommy." Ellie hugged her and then skipped to the cardboard structure in the corner.

Ellie's black ponytail swung from side to side, and excitement danced in her dark eyes. A rush of affection swept over Tessa, marveling at how this bundle of love, born in China, landed in her heart and home. At moments like this, Tessa forgot the thud of responsibility and crush of guilt that, at times, nearly knocked her flat. "Wow, a castle is pretty special." Tessa clapped both hands to her cheeks.

Ellie ducked inside and popped her face out a window.

Tessa laughed at her sweet, animated daughter. "Okay, Princess Ellie, time to go now. I have a surprise about dinner tonight."

"A surprise? What is it? Please, tell me." Ellie bopped out of the castle and squiggled on the spot.

"We're going to Auntie Julie's."

Ellie grinned and tugged one of Tessa's hands. "Will I see Zach and Quinn and Uncle Owen?"

"Yes, and Grandma, too." Tessa softened at the touch of Ellie's warm skin.

"Oh, goody." Ellie beat her mom to the door.

Tessa stopped at home, picked up her golden retriever, Ginger, and then drove the short distance to Julie's place. The cozy, two-story home nestled a few blocks from Tessa's bungalow in the well-treed Lakeview subdivision. She loved living close to her sister in such a desirable area filled with homes dating back to the early 1900s.

All the way, Ellie spouted a running commentary from the back seat.

Her daughter's cheerful chatter wiped away the concerns of the day. "I love you, Ellie Shore." Tessa parked and unbuckled the squiggly pre-schooler in the back seat.

"I love you, Mommy. Oh, I love you, too, Ginger."

Ellie giggled and wiped her face of a sloppy dog kiss. "Hey, we're here." Holding her mom's hand, she jumped out of her car seat and jostled Ginger all the way up the sidewalk.

Julie appeared in the doorway and waved them inside.

Tessa glimpsed a barely-older reflection of herself. Julie's reddish-gold curls were cropped to chin length, and her green eyes matched Tessa's. People often asked if they were twins. As a child, Julie always proudly pronounced she was the big sister, and Tessa strove to be first or best. She'd never be the older sister, but she could be just as accomplished.

A hint of strain, so subtle only a sister would notice, etched across Julie's face. Her tense expression contrasted with her home's casual, happy décor. Off-white walls set off artwork and area rugs in blues, greens, and an occasional pop of orange.

In the entranceway, Tessa sniffed the savory scent of chicken and herbs. "Umm, smells delicious." Her sister's cooking filled her home with the delicious aromas of comfort food.

"Hello, Ellie, jelly belly!" Julie encircled her niece in a combined hug and tickle.

Ellie responded with a tinkle of laughter and wiggled free. "Where are Zach and Quinn?" She peeked around her aunt.

"Waiting in the play room. And Grandma Adele's here, too, in the living room." Julie shuffled aside.

"Grandma." Ellie hollered and flung arms around her grandma's hips. "I like your outfit. You're so bright."

Adele's short hair, dyed tangerine, sprouted the

19

same springy curls as her daughters'. She wore pink jeans and a lime, striped top as colorful as a fruit platter. She dressed like she was ready to shop with a girlfriend and not to have her daughters choose her care facility. Her smile was bright, and only the slightly-vacant sheen in her eyes gave away her deteriorating mental state. Tessa took a deep breath and gathered strength at the disconcerting sight.

"Thank you, Ellie." Grandma Adele hugged Ellie and stooped to kiss her cheek. "How's my favorite, Chinese granddaughter?"

"Mom, no. Please, don't say that." Tessa shook her head and narrowed her eyes. Mom lacked a filter to prevent inappropriate comments, and the results could be quite disturbing.

"What? Well, it's true." Adele threw up her hands.

"Never mind." Tessa pointed Ellie in the direction of her cousins. Although Mom grew to love Ellie, she never let Tessa forget she disapproved of her decision to adopt a toddler from another country and become a single mother.

"What? Not even a hello for your mother?" Adele placed hands on hips.

"Here I come." Tessa hugged her. "Did you have a good day with Julie?"

"My day was fine, as soon as I escaped The Benson. Those people have problems." Mom huffed.

"Oh, really?" Tessa rubbed her mom's arm.

"They have no sense of humor. Your father doesn't like it, either."

"Mom, remember Dad isn't with us anymore. He passed away five years ago." At the memories Mom had already lost, Tessa pressed a hand over her twisted insides.

"Well, he wouldn't have liked living there. I know it." Mom stomped a foot.

"You're probably right." Tessa bit her lip. Her mom flipped like a switch from confused to lucid.

"Let's go to the kitchen." Julie motioned for them to follow. "Owen will be home soon, and I'll put the finishing touches on dinner."

"You girls can cook. I'm going to play with the kids. They're more fun." Adele headed downstairs.

Ginger thumped the stairwell wall with her tail.

The dog was a loyal companion for the whole family. "How was your day with Mom?" Tessa washed her hands at the sink and tore lettuce beside her sister. The activity was so normal she could hardly believe they were in the midst of a family crisis.

"Oh, we had quite a day." Julie chopped celery and scraped it into a pile.

"That bad? Is it possible The Benson manager overreacted?" Tessa gathered a handful of cool lettuce and tossed it into a bowl. Mom's situation threw everything into upheaval. A salad was supposed to be mixed but not her feelings about family life.

"Listening to her prattle and jumble the past, present, and her imagination entertained me for about five minutes." Julie sprinkled chopped peppers into the bowl. "After spending the entire day together, I realize how erratic she's become. She speaks normally one minute and the next, she doesn't make sense."

"I can't believe she stole a neighbor's plant and another woman's robe." As Tessa positioned a loaf of French bread on the cutting board, she couldn't stop her hands from quivering. "Don't they ever lock their doors around there?"

"Apparently not. Probably most of the residents don't bother or would misplace the keys."

"Did you broach the topic of a move?" Tessa flexed her fingers and selected a knife. In the background, the kids' musical laughter contrasted with the serious mood in the kitchen.

"A little. But you know what Mom's like. She might or might not understand." Julie shook her head. "And even if she understands, the memory doesn't stick."

"What a horrible situation." Tessa attacked the bread with brisk, sawing motions.

"Today, she doesn't mind the idea of a new home. You heard her. She doesn't like the people at The Benson. But these days, Mom changes her opinions faster than her nail color." Julie surveyed the table and added the salt and pepper shakers. "While Mom napped this afternoon, I called and found an opening at Heritage Haven." Julie sighed.

Tessa's mouth dried. Was Mom really at the point of needing personalized care? "You mean the place in the south end that specializes in dementia?" She piled bread in a basket.

Julie nodded. "They'll hold the spot for a couple of days until we confirm."

"What about the cost?" Heart tugging, Tessa blinked away moisture. So many factors entered into their decision. She dreaded the conversation they faced after dinner.

"At least, we don't have to worry about finances. The cost is about the same as The Benson, and Mom can afford it. Her income's too high for a government subsidy." Julie rubbed Tessa's back. "After dinner, we'll ask Owen to take the kids to the park and then break the news. Maybe our conversation won't be so bad."

"Mom's always liked variety. Maybe we can sell the benefits of a change." Tessa savored the steady warmth of Julie's touch. They were lucky they had each other. Dealing with Mom's condition would be far worse without a sibling for support.

"My sister, ever the optimist. Mom might like variety, but she accepts everything on her own terms. The situation won't be good. I guarantee it." Julie finished the salad with a scatter of croutons.

The casserole Julie lifted from the oven belonged on the cover of a magazine. Tessa inhaled the aroma of sizzling cheese and pungent oregano. "Smells delicious. Your cooking always puts everyone in a good mood. So, let's hope it helps." Her stomach grumbled, but she wasn't very hungry.

"Hello, I'm home." Owen banged shut the front door.

Tessa smiled at the eager commotion of kids and dog scurrying up the stairs to greet him.

Following on their heels, Adele paused in the kitchen. "Tessa, when did you get here?" She blinked and stared wide-eyed.

"Just a few minutes ago." Tessa glanced at Julie and raised her eyebrows. Mom saw her arrive. They hugged and talked. Mom knew she was here, but her memories lasted only seconds. The sad reality struck, and her throat ached.

Owen chased Quinn, Zach, and Ellie through the kitchen, rubbed Ginger, and kissed Julie, all in one continuous motion. "How are my favorite sil and mil today?"

"Sil? Mil?" Mom frowned. "I'm Adele, and this is Tessa." Mom scrunched her face and huffed.

Owen's affectionate shorthand for sister-in-law and mother-in-law never failed to charm Mom and Tessa but not today. Tessa bit her lip.

Julie shook her head behind her mom to signal Owen not to bother explaining.

"How are you, Adele?" Owen slung an arm around her shoulder.

"Hungry. Is it possible to get a meal in this place?" She paced from the kitchen to the dining room.

Her pinched expression left no doubt she didn't intend her comment as a joke. Tessa opened then closed her mouth. Nothing she could say would soothe her mom's testy mood.

"Dinner is ready, and I'm glad I have a bunch of hungry customers," said Julie. "Go, everyone, wash your hands, and we'll eat."

Tessa was torn. Part of her wanted the meal to stretch forever, so they could avoid the tough conversation ahead, but the other part wanted to rush through the meal and deal with the unpleasant task. "Remember, please, don't feed Ginger from the table." She scanned around the table, pausing on Zach, Ellie, and her mom. They were the most likely culprits.

"We won't, will we, kids?" Grandma Adele smiled, nodded, and blinked an exaggerated wink in their direction.

A surge of hope rushed through Tessa. At moments like this, her mom seemed as lively and headstrong as ever. Maybe now was too soon to transfer her to

Heritage Haven.

"Pass the…" Adele paused and stared at the far end of the table. She huffed and furrowed her forehead.

In slow motion like a video, Tessa absorbed the full impact of the painful scene. Mom struggled to recall a word that formerly rolled off her tongue. Tessa winced. The sad reality stung like a wasp.

"…The… " She flicked an index finger toward the butter. "You know…pass the yellow stuff."

"Butter, Grandma. It's butter." Ellie snatched the dish and passed it.

"Yes, dear, I know butter when I see it."

The instant Adele's tone sharpened, Ellie's helpful smile drooped. "Don't worry," Tessa whispered and squeezed Ellie's leg under the table.

After chocolate-chip cookies for dessert, Tessa shot a glance at Julie. The time had arrived for a serious talk with Mom.

"Hey, kids, how about a trip to the park?" Owen grinned and hooked Ginger's leash.

"I'll come." Adele scraped back her chair and jerked to her feet.

"Owen will take the kids and Ginger while the ladies have tea and visit." Tessa set a hand on Mom's. Much as she dreaded the conversation, she'd take charge and make sure it happened.

"Yes, stay with us, Mom." Julie stood to clear the table.

Mom shook her head and shoved aside Tessa's hand. "You girls take some time to yourselves. I'm going to the park." She ushered the kids out the door.

"Now what?" Julie led Tessa to the kitchen with a stack of dishes.

"Now, we wait until she's back, and then we'll talk." Tessa twisted the tap with more force than needed, felt the warm blast, and sprayed her blouse with a mini shower. "We don't have a choice. She can't live here or at my place. Can you imagine?" Tessa shuddered. "At least, not if we want to keep our sanity."

Sipping tea, Tessa sat on the front porch and leaned shoulder to shoulder with Julie. She was lucky she had a steady sister to share the burden of family issues. Still, the steamy scent of chamomile didn't calm her one bit. The magnitude of her responsibilities with Mom and Ellie knotted her stomach, and the sticky work situation involving Mark didn't help at all.

After the park outing, Owen strolled up the street.

Ellie giggled and skipped behind with her cousins.

"Where are Mom and Ginger?" At first, Tessa murmured under her breath. Sudden apprehension rippled through her. "Where…are…they? Mom and Ginger. Why aren't they with Owen and the kids?"

"I don't see them." Julie stood and peered down the street beyond her husband. "Owen, where are Mom and Ginger?"

"Aren't they here?" He picked up his pace to cross the distance to the front steps. "After about ten minutes, your mom got bored and said she would let Ginger sniff the bushes and then head back. I thought she'd be here by now."

Tessa inhaled rapid breaths. Alarm deepening, she clutched the mug with shaky hands and stared at Owen. She wanted to lash out but bit her tongue. These days, no one could rely on Mom to do anything predictable or responsible. The situation meant trouble but wasn't Owen's fault.

"You let Mom leave with Ginger?" Julie swept her gaze from Owen to Tessa.

"Well, yes, I..." Owen shrugged and threw up his arms.

"You know she's...not right these days. I don't trust her judgment." Julie glowered at Owen and wrung her hands.

Ellie tossed her ponytail and demonstrated a somersault on the lawn.

"I'm sorry, Julie. Tessa, I'm sorry." Owen darted his gaze between his wife and Tessa. "She's come to the park with the kids a hundred times. I didn't think she would have trouble getting back."

"I'll go and find her. I'm sure she won't be far." Tessa blinked and swallowed. "Which way was she headed?" Mom's judgment couldn't be trusted with directions or Ginger.

"South, but she was supposed to circle the park and loop back this way." Owen gestured toward the route.

"I'll take my own car and cruise the neighborhood, too. Call me if you find her first." Julie set her mug on the step and hurried to the car.

"Hey, Ellie, I'm driving to find Grandma and Ginger." Tessa grabbed the car keys and hugged her. "You stay with Uncle Owen, Zach, and Quinn, and I'll see you soon."

Glancing at the gathering clouds, she smelled rain approaching. She jumped into the car, clamped her fists around the steering wheel, and headed in the direction Owen indicated. Jamming a foot on the gas and then brake, she drove like her erratic emotions. Surely, her forgetful mom and beloved dog would stick together, and Mom wouldn't do anything risky like remove

Ginger's leash or worse, tie the leash to a pole and leave her. The friendly dog was such a people pleaser she would welcome attention from anyone and certainly wouldn't scare off anybody who coaxed her away.

Tessa breathed in a rush. Scanning left and right for any sign of her brightly-dressed mom and Ginger's reddish coat, she crawled the streets of the Lakeview area. The pair should be easy to spot. Each time she navigated a corner, she strained to see them. Where could they be? She lectured herself not to jump to dire conclusions, but her throat burned like she swallowed a mouthful of sand.

She passed Julie several times and stopped to confer, but neither of them could think of anything else to do but cruise up and down the streets. Would a kindly neighbor point Mom in the right direction? Ginger was a smart dog. Would she tug the leash toward home? Would the two stay safe? Worries multiplying, she doubled back to Julie's house and parked in front.

"Where's Grandma and Ginger?" Ponytail bobbing, Ellie scooted to greet her.

"Probably taking a nice, long walk." Tessa glanced at Owen, and his downturned expression registered strain. "No sign?"

Owen shook his head. "Julie checked in a couple of minutes ago and then left to drive another loop. Do you want to stay with the kids while I take a turn?"

"Stay, Mommy." Ellie stuck out her bottom lip. "I want Grandma and Ginger to come back."

"Okay, you kidlets. I'll stay here and read stories." Tessa glanced up at the darkening sky, and her heart beat faster. Charcoal clouds swirled above and threatened a doozy of a rain dump.

Ellie chose the first book.

Maybe story time would keep the kids amused and distract her from the alarming situation.

"Mom." Ellie fidgeted and poked her mom's arm. "You're not making funny voices."

"Oops, sorry." Tessa tried harder. As she flipped a page, lightning flashed and thunder rumbled. She paused, swallowed, and cuddled Ellie against the ominous atmosphere. Her stomach churned like the stormy sky. Surely, someone out there would rescue a helpless woman and dog.

****

Glancing at the mounting clouds, Mark arrived home to his tidy bungalow near Wascana Lake and found his niece in her room listening to music and doing homework. The familiar sounds of the dog's clicking toenails and thumping tail reverberated down the hallway.

Rufus burst in, pounced, and rolled on Bree's bed.

Mark rubbed the golden retriever's belly. "How was your day?" He forced a smile he didn't feel. After his encounter with upbeat Tessa, he survived the rest of the afternoon, but the experience left him drained as a bathtub at the end of a long soak.

"Okay." Bree shrugged.

Noticing their similar coloring, people assumed she was his daughter by birth rather than circumstance. Her dark hair straggled from a messy ponytail, and her narrow face rested smooth and serious. "Hungry?" He leaned on the door frame. In contrast with the rest of the home, decorated in muted shades of gray and tan, Bree's room shouted teenage girl. She sprawled on the bed, surrounded by mauve walls papered with posters of popular musicians.

"A bit."

He was not in the mood to extract information, so he left her alone and scrounged in the kitchen for supper ideas. He could better decide what to cook when he was hungry. After hearing Liz's plans, he lost his appetite.

Thirty minutes later, Mark called Bree to the table for ham, mushroom, and cheese omelets, served with sizzling, fried potatoes and juicy, sliced tomatoes. Not fancy, but the combination would pass for a decent meal. "Any plans for your evening?" Mark dragged a potato bite into the ketchup at the edge of his plate.

Bree shrugged.

She never talked much, and if it was possible, she communicated even less since she turned thirteen. He could relate to her introverted style, similar to his own, but he didn't always appreciate it.

Breaking off a generous bite of omelet with a fork, Bree placed it in her mouth and chewed.

"Want to come to the park with Rufus and me?" If he hurried through chores, he could beat the rain.

At the sound of his name, Rufus whined and whacked a table leg with his tail.

Bree wrinkled her nose and stared at her plate.

"Please, come. I have something to discuss."

"Okay, I guess." She widened her eyes and nodded.

Clearly, he piqued her interest. "Tell you what. While you tidy the kitchen, I'll mow the lawns, and then we'll go." An hour later, Mark led Bree and Rufus to his favorite walking route along the edge of Wascana Park and then down a gravel pathway toward the water.

Usually, he mustered the energy to tease Bree or tell amusing stories to make her laugh, but not today. "Remember my boss, Liz? Last summer, she invited us to her place for a staff barbecue."

"Yeah, I remember." Bree rustled her feet through the grass bordering the path.

"She wants me to attend a thing called Leadership Camp." He didn't bother to explain Liz's impending retirement and the possible, negative impact on his career. Bree didn't need to worry about his job situation.

"Is that camp all you wanted to talk about?" The wind whipped her ponytail across her face.

"Yes." By the lake, he steered Bree and Rufus right and headed toward the bridge. He scanned the threatening sky and judged they couldn't circle the lake before the storm hit. The wind huffed through bushes dotting the park, and humidity closed in. He needed to get his niece and dog home before they all got drenched. A prairie thunderstorm was no place for humans or animals.

Spotting a duck in the lake, the dog barked and tugged on his leash.

"Rufus, come." Mark quickened his pace under the murky mix of dusk and clouds. He guided Rufus and Bree in a semi-circle, so they could wind back toward the park entrance. Mark absorbed the scent of rain in the air and a faint rumble of thunder from past downtown across the lake.

"Oh, okay, continue." As the wind picked up, Bree squinted and leaned into it. "Hey, Uncle Mark, we better get home soon. I hate storms." She glanced at the sky and picked up speed to match Mark's.

"Yup, let's motor." He lengthened his strides. "Leadership Camp is not like an actual summer camp with tents and songs around the campfire. The group teaches people how to be better leaders."

"You're a good leader of our family." Bree stared straight ahead.

The wind hissed and muffled her compliment. "Thanks, Breezy. Apparently, Liz thinks I still have a lot to learn about leading people at the office." Above, swirling cloud formations confirmed the reason why Saskatchewan's slogan was *Land of Living Skies*.

"Huh. I guess you have to go to keep her happy."

Her matter-of-fact tone hollered disappointment. She probably expected something a little more interesting than his so-called work opportunity. "Yes, but I need to explain something else."

"What?" She nearly jogged now.

"Leadership Camp, if I do it, will take extra time after normal work hours. I'll probably need to go away for a few nights three different times on what they call a retreat."

"Will I get to come?" Puffing, she scuffed her runners on the loose gravel.

"The bad thing is I can't take you. We would need to find someone who could stay with you."

"I'm not a little kid. I don't need a babysitter." Bree shouted and tilted toward Mark and Rufus to avoid a waving tree branch.

He tensed his jaw. No surprise she resisted. "The person won't be a babysitter. She'll be more like a housekeeper—someone to keep you company, cook supper, do laundry, and make sure you wake up in time for school. Basic stuff." He searched his memory for a parenting tip that might help. When he assumed custody of Bree, he read his share of advice books, but nothing prepared him for every bump along the way.

"Why do you have to go to the dumb Leadership Camp, anyway?" She stared ahead.

"Sometimes, for work, you have to do things you don't like." Thunder rumbled as if to underscore his point. Mark clenched his shoulders and accelerated. Between the sensitive conversation and the threatening weather, he wanted to get to shelter as quickly as possible.

"Maybe Liz will change her mind, and then you won't have to go."

"I doubt it." He tightened his hold on the leash. Liz didn't get into an executive role by backing down on decisions. She even enlisted Tessa Shore to add more pressure. The thought of the perky program leader revved his heart even faster. What was wrong with him?

Chapter 3

"Uncle Mark, I hate it when you treat me like a baby." Bree kicked a stick, picked up a branch, and swatted tree trunks.

"I know you're upset. We'll talk more later. Let's put on the burners and beat this storm home." Mark guided Rufus left and continued down the gravel path toward the street. The air smelled damp. Sheet lightning flashed, and a low rumble thundered across the sky.

Rufus woofed and tugged toward home.

Mark hustled next to his nervous niece and dog. They both depended on him and not just in a storm. If he gave in to Liz's demand, how could he let down Bree? Life as a single uncle turned dad was not easy.

"Glad I came."

Mark chuckled. Bree's sarcastic comment was her way of connecting. "Yeah, you wouldn't have wanted to miss this adventure. We've weathered a lot together. But never a tornado." Her T-shirt flapped like a flag.

"A tornado isn't really coming. Is it?" She swung her gaze to the sky.

"Nah. Just a good, old-fashioned prairie storm. We're almost home." Reaching the street, he spotted another golden retriever trotting toward them and heading in the opposite direction. Grasping the dog's leash was an elderly woman dressed in an outfit that was a rainbow in the hazy evening air. Mark nodded and barely slowed his pace. Why was the unlikely pair out in the threatening weather?

Rufus traded quick sniffs with the other dog.

"Better hurry home." As the first spits of rain hit his cheekbones, he caught a glimpse of the woman's face, partially concealed by a mop of hair the color of a pumpkin. A glimmer of recognition flitted through his mind. Had he met her, or did she remind him of someone?

Bree grabbed his arm. "That lady we just passed was crying."

Mark stopped, spun, and handed over Rufus's leash. In a few brisk strides, he caught up to the woman.

Her golden dog, a mirror of Rufus, wagged a greeting.

"Excuse me, ma'am. Are you doing okay? Can I help you?"

"Yes, please. I'm a little mixed up in my directions." She wiped her damp cheeks. "I left my daughter's house, and I need to get home. Ginger is her dog."

"Where are you headed?" He leaned closer to hear through the wind and thunder.

"Home. Can you point me toward The Ben...?" She swept her gaze from side to side.

"The Benson? Come with us." His pulse quickened. If his mother was in trouble, he'd want someone to help. The woman's confusion reminded him of Mom's dementia. The disease left her confused and distraught, and all he could do was stay strong and stoic in his despair. Since he was seventeen years old, he'd stacked personal losses into an immovable rock inside his core. His mother's illness was just another, painful layer on the pile.

A gust of wind rippled across the lake and scrambled their hair and Rufus's fur. Sprinkles of rain swelled into fat drops and drenched Mark, Bree, the two dogs, and the woman. A whiff of wet fur wafted in the wind.

"Oh, thank you." The woman sniffed. Without hesitating, she clutched Mark's elbow. "My daughter should have warned me about the weather." The woman fished in a pocket for a damp tissue and dabbed her nose, but the rain just spattered it again. "Wait until I tell her what I think."

Like she flipped a switch, she escalated her tone from meek to accusatory. "What's her name? Where does she live?" Mark interpreted the woman's blank expression and didn't expect answers. Her daughter must be frantic with worry. But who and where was she? What kind of woman allowed her confused mother to wander?

****

Raindrops the size of dimes smacked the windows like someone emptied a giant piggy bank in slow motion. Tessa finished the last story just as Julie returned with no good news. The situation would be bad enough on a pleasant evening, but a storm made it worse. They needed to rescue their missing mother and dog.

"I want to find Ginger and go home, Mommy."

Ellie's cheery, daytime voice morphed into her whiny, almost-bedtime tone. "I do, too, sweetie." Tessa hugged her. "Please, cooperate and watch a show for a little while with Zach and Quinn."

"Should we call the police?" Julie wrung her

hands. "Will they think we're crazy to report a missing person and dog when they only disappeared a little more than an hour ago?"

"Mom and Ginger will be drenched by now." Tessa stared out the window and scanned left and right. Water streamed down the pane and bounced off the pavement. Thunder cracked, and the lights flickered.

Clutching her arms around her middle, she peered up and down the street and willed Owen to appear with her mom's curly head outlined in the passenger window and Ginger's black nose smeared against the back glass. But the only cars on the road passed right by, churning up the pond that now filled the street.

"I can't believe Owen let them out of his sight." Julie joined Tessa at the window. "He should have known better. I don't know who hates storms more, Mom or Ginger."

She voiced the fear that drummed in Tessa's head.

Even though the house was warm and muggy, Tessa shivered. "They'll be a sad pair outside in this downpour." Through her strangled throat, she choked out the words. She needed water but couldn't swallow a sip. Another crack of thunder boomed overhead, and she cringed.

"Maybe someone took pity and invited them in," said Julie.

"I hope so. I'll head out again and leave you with the kids this time." Tessa braced herself for the wet onslaught. Poor Mom and Ginger. They didn't need this miserable situation, and neither did the rest of the family.

"Driving around the neighborhood is better than just waiting here. I'll call you the minute I hear anything," said Julie.

Tessa soon spotted Owen, and her breath strangled in her chest. He was alone. She stopped to confer, and the water fell like a sheet between their windows. Rain thunked on the car roof.

"No sign. I've circled the whole area." Owen rubbed his forehead.

"Let's both loop the area one more time, and if we don't find them, we'll call the police." Tessa gripped the steering wheel, and her pulse pounded into each fingertip. "You head north to Regina Avenue, and I'll swing south to Twenty-Third Avenue. I can't imagine them travelling any farther." She raised the window, waited until Owen drove away, and jerked in the opposite direction.

Searching for any sign of her waterlogged mom and dog, she wove along but glimpsed nothing. The sidewalks were deserted, and she passed few vehicles. Her pulse beat so hard in her temples she could hardly think straight.

Where could they be? Where would her mom lead Ginger? Lightning lit up the street like a spotlight on her dread. Where would Mom go? She was about to give up when an idea hit. The Benson was several kilometers away, but maybe in her confused state, Mom headed for home instead of for Julie's house.

Swishing through puddles, she inhaled quick breaths, reasoned, and willed herself to stay optimistic. The weather was just a thunderstorm. Mom and Ginger wouldn't melt in the rain. They were fine. They probably found shelter somewhere. She would find them none the worse for the wear. Still, anger jabbed at the edges of fear. Darn her mother, anyway. Curse the worsening dementia.

As she parked at The Benson, her phone rang. She stopped, threw the gearshift into Park, and picked up the call in one, jerky motion. "Did Owen find them?"

"She's safe."

Julie's whooshed update soothed like a warm blanket around Tessa's shoulders. Sinking deeper into the car seat, she sighed. Her pounding pulse tapered and was replaced by alternating surges of annoyance and exhaustion. Logically, Tessa couldn't blame her mother for the alarming episode. Mom didn't mean to ruin the evening, but that fact didn't make the situation any easier to accept. Dementia caused her to frighten them all and drain Tessa of every ounce of energy. Worse, the disease would only progress and add more stress to Tessa's full load.

"The Benson manager just called to say she's home. She took quite a hike," said Julie.

"I'm in the parking lot. On a hunch, I drove here. I'll check on Mom and grab Ginger. Please, tell Ellie I'll be there soon." She swung out of the vehicle and slammed the door so hard the window rattled.

Racing to the door, she nearly collided with a man who dashed toward the parking lot. "Oh, excuse me." Drawing in a sharp breath, she squinted through raindrops. Why was *he* here? "Mark?" How did he remain so attractive even with hair plastered to his head and shirt soaked? His attitude toward Leadership Camp might leave more than a little to be desired but not his masculine aura. She slowed for an instant.

He widened his eyes and crinkled his expression. A drop of rain slipped off his firm chin.

"Small family emergency." Tessa pointed at the

building. "I can't stop now, but I'll see you tomorrow at the office." Even though the situation was under control, she couldn't wait to see her mom and dog. Not waiting for Mark's response, she scooted past in a wet flurry.

Inside the common area where the residents chatted and played games, Tessa found Mom and Ginger. Relief washed over her with such force her knees nearly buckled. Gray water dripped off Ginger's legs and underside, spattering dirty flecks on the baby-blue carpet. The scent of flowery potpourri mingled with the musky odor of wet dog.

Ginger turned, wagged her tail, and sent a fine spray in a semi-circle.

Oh, no. The Benson had probably never hosted such a soaked, hairy visitor.

A grinning staff member knelt beside Ginger and swiped her furry body with towels.

"Where were you when I needed you?" Mom toweled her hair, shook loose her curls, and huffed.

"Hi, Mom." Tessa gritted her teeth and ignored the reprimand. "We expected you to come back to Julie's, but I'm glad you're safe at home." She wanted to lash back and scold her mom for taking off and worrying the whole family. Instead, she inhaled a deep breath, accepted a towel from the staff member, and helped dry Ginger.

"Did you walk all this way?" Even though she churned inside, Tessa kept her voice calm and gentle. Her mom was nearly impossible to please, long before dementia surfaced. Tessa and Julie labeled their late dad a saint for his patience with their mother. With such a demanding presence in her life, Tessa learned at a young age that life was easier if she controlled any situation that might irritate her mother—or anyone else.

"Well, none of my family helped, so what choice did I have?" Mom clicked her tongue.

"Sorry, Mom. How did you get home?" Tessa squeezed her mother's forearm.

"I don't know." Her mom frowned and shook her damp head. "Let me think. Oh, yes, I met a nice, young man and his daughter. They had a dog like Ginger. The man drove me home."

"You were lucky." Tessa didn't bother to caution her mom about strangers. No doubt, the kind man she described was someone from the neighborhood and not someone who would take advantage of a confused, older woman attached to a large dog. "What was his name?" Perhaps, she should give him a call to thank him for rescuing her mother.

"Was the man's name Mark?" The possibility hit Tessa with a jolt. Of course, he could have just visited a family member, but maybe he was her mother's knight in shining armor. She pictured Mark's tall, slim frame and nearly allowed her imagination to carry her places she shouldn't wander. Why did she allow him to invade her thoughts? Was she losing control of her mind?

"How am I supposed to know his name? It was the least of my concerns, young lady. I thanked him, and he left." Adele flicked the towel and shoved it at the attendant. "I could use a cup of tea after that ordeal. Where's Ellie?"

"She's at Julie's. Now that I know you're dry and safe, I need to take Ellie home to bed." She extended her arms for a hug.

Mom shrugged her off. She shook her head and

glared.

"I'll see you again soon. In fact, Julie and I will see you tomorrow morning." Tessa mentally rescheduled her day, so she and her sister could meet with their mom in the morning. "I'm very sorry about the paw prints." Glancing at the dark-haired attendant, Tessa shook her head and spread wide her arms.

"Oh, don't worry about the mud. The carpet's had worse. By the way, my name is Priya." Flipping back her hair, she smiled and escorted Tessa and Ginger to the front door.

"We'll find a new home for Mom as soon as possible. We know she needs more care." Tessa ran a finger under her moist eyes.

"The decision isn't easy for any family." Priya patted Tessa's arm. "I understand."

On the short drive home, Tessa forced the gas pedal in impatient bursts like she could outrace the difficult choice. She steered through puddles and peered around the wipers. They worked overtime and barely cleared the view.

The evening was a soggy mess and not just the weather. She needed to cleanse her mind of her mother's sad state and, even more so, someone who didn't belong in her imagination. If Mark was Adele's rescuer, then he did have a heart beneath his crusty manner. But he'd need to prove it, and she'd let him know in no uncertain terms.

Skidding to a stop in front of Julie's place, she switched off speculation about Mark's true character. She'd reserve judgment until their next meeting.

"You're back." Ellie shouted out the front door. "Where's Grandma?"

"She's at home, and you need to get to bed, little miss." Tessa scooped Ellie into a hug, promised to pick up Julie at ten o'clock in the morning, and hurried to the car.

The next morning, Tessa cajoled overtired, grumpy Ellie into eating breakfast on schedule.

"I didn't want peanut butter on my toast." Ellie poked a square.

"Finish one more bite, and then you can give a piece to Ginger." Usually, Tessa forbade human food for the eager dog, but today, she allowed an exception just to humor Ellie. In a flurry, she rushed through the rest of the morning routine and delivered Ellie to daycare right on time. Squinting in the bright, morning sun, she tromped from the parking lot on the corner of Broad Street to the office and sidestepped pools of water from last night's storm.

After dealing with her mother's latest escapade, she hated to disrupt her busy day for an unpleasant task. "Good morning, Karen." As she breezed by her assistant, Tessa forced an upbeat tone.

"How's your mom?" Karen clicked keys on the computer and paused.

"Not the best. Thanks for asking, but I won't bore you with the details." Tessa wouldn't let her mother infiltrate the office. Here, she could maintain control, just the way she liked.

Tessa opened the calendar on the computer screen and scanned details. She would need to reschedule a meeting to make time for the family mission. She sent her boss, Wendy, a quick note to explain and then shifted a coaching session to the afternoon.

Scanning the rest of the day, she spotted time for

another appointment in the afternoon. After the rushed, rocky start yesterday, she and Mark needed a calmer conversation. Besides, if he was the mysterious stranger who rescued her mom last evening, she owed him a huge thank-you.

Before she completed a meeting invitation, an email message pinged. The sender was Mark Delaney, and she pursed her lips and sat forward to read his brief note.

I'd like to discuss Leadership Camp. How's ten this morning?

Tessa stared at the words. Email was very tricky because it masked any emotion behind the words, and Mark Delaney offered no sort of hint if his opinion of Leadership Camp changed overnight. He guarded well his true feelings, but until she knew for sure, Tessa would give him the benefit of the doubt.

She pounded the keys and reworded her reply twice before she captured the right professional tone—courteous and welcoming yet clearly in charge. Normally, she dashed off notes without a pause, but the situation with Mark treaded into awkward territory. Based on his curt manner yesterday, the personal question of whether he rescued her mother could wait until she met him later today.

Good morning, Mark! Leadership Camp is a big commitment, and I'll be happy to tell you more. My morning is booked, but I can meet at two. Unless I hear otherwise, I'll see you then in my office.~Tessa

Tessa stabbed the Send key and spun away her chair. Mark didn't scare her a bit. He was no different than any other colleague...or was he?

Chapter 4

The news of Liz's impending retirement spread quicker than dandelions on the prairie. For Mark, the loss of Liz was a possible career blow. For everyone else, it was fuel for gossip and speculation about her replacement. He clenched his jaw and prepared for the worst. How could he deal with Leadership Camp on top of Liz's departure?

Loss of any kind always hit him hard. He had already experienced too much for a guy in his mid-thirties. First, his dad, and then more horrifying, his sister. He shook his head and locked inside his raw emotions, just the way his dad had taught. The memories still burned.

Bree was just six years old when a tragic car accident stole her parents and shattered the family. At the time, his mom's minor memory loss, coupled with profound grief, threw her into a perpetual state of confusion. No one else could care for Bree, so Mark became her legal guardian and an instant single dad.

Coworkers buzzed like mosquitoes outside his office and down the hallway. Apparently, real work would start late today. Clutching their morning coffee, people clustered outside their cubicles.

One guy recounted his favorite memory of Liz, almost as if she died rather than announced her impending retirement.

Liz's plans impacted him more than most. Certainly, he knew her well, but he wouldn't step outside his office and join the melee. He'd never share his feelings the way many did. They treated office news like candies to share. Some of the group out there didn't even know Liz. For them, the topic was just a splash of color in the office routine.

He sipped hot coffee and let it slip down his tight throat. He might as well get on with his day. The office Newsflash memo stated Liz's replacement hadn't been named but soon would be. He doubted he had a chance at a promotion. Now was too early in his career, and judging by Liz's urging him into Leadership Camp, he still had things to learn.

While he listened to everyone else tripping over the gossip that sped around the office, he jotted a note to Tessa. From what he'd heard, Tessa coached leaders into impressive career success. He would see if she delivered as predicted.

Last evening, he was surprised to bump into her—almost literally—at the retirement residence. She scooted past before he could say a courteous hello which was just fine. She was a living reminder of the leadership challenge that loomed. His blood surged at the memory, and warmth invaded his face at his sudden urge to wipe the smeared mascara off her damp cheek. Why did he care, and why did he have so much trouble tearing his gaze from her face?

He hit Send on the email and prepared for his first meeting. As he exited his office, the phone rang, but he ignored it so he wouldn't be late. He'd stick to business as usual, the way Liz and he expected. No-nonsense Liz wouldn't like all the fuss and gossip about her plans.

She had little tolerance for anything that slowed the pace of work. He strode to the elevator, and when the doors opened, he faced Tessa Shore.

Mark nodded and, for the first time, absorbed her appearance. This woman was the ticket to his future. "Did you get my message?"

"Yes, I replied. Sorry, but we'll have to meet this afternoon." She jingled her car keys and held open the elevator door. "I need to attend to a personal matter."

"Oh, I hoped for this morning, but I'll make that time work." He positioned himself on the opposite side of the elevator and examined her smooth and peachy complexion underneath a smattering of freckles. She tucked a defiant, corkscrew curl behind one ear and met his gaze without a waver.

As the elevator descended, the numbers lit and dinged at each floor. He plastered his gaze on the control panel and maintained his outer composure, but his stomach stayed up on floor eight.

"What a surprise about Liz. What's the mood in your department?" Tessa adjusted her purse strap.

"Interested. Curious about their new boss." Mark clamped shut his mouth. He didn't need to provide analysis about a topic that shouldn't concern her. She was just like the rest, compelled to talk about the change even though there was little to say. The elevator glided to a stop.

"I'll see you later." Mark exited, and the doors closed. Only when she disappeared, leaving a trace of her fresh scent, did he realize how her presence unsettled him. Back on solid ground, he regained his equilibrium, and his composure fell back into place. Odd, he both dreaded and anticipated the meeting later today.

****

Tessa brainstormed until her mind bulged with strategies of how to handle her mother this morning and Mark this afternoon. As she sped down College Avenue, she skimmed by the greening grass and budding trees. She'd allow herself time after work to enjoy her favorite season.

Mark Delaney's attractive looks and brooding expression simultaneously attracted and repelled her. She glanced at the clock on the dashboard and upped the radio volume. Tapping a hand on the steering wheel, she buzzed with nervous energy. The cause must be her mother's situation. It couldn't be the potential addition to the next class.

Mark's intensity would be touchy to manage but the kind of challenge that energized her. She ran Leadership Camp the same way she raised Ellie—with clear expectations, consistent rules, and minimal flexibility. A little structure was good for everyone.

Tessa braked in front of her sister's place. "How will Mom take the news?" She spewed the question before Julie even climbed in and closed the car door.

"Good morning to you, too." Julie raised her eyebrows.

Wearing a crisp, white shirt and faded blue jeans, she was fresh and ready for the challenge ahead. Still, Julie probably looked more relaxed than she felt. "Oh, yeah, good morning." Tessa laughed. "Don't mind me. I have a lot on my mind today."

"When I hear what you deal with at work, my days as stay-at-home mom suit me just fine." Julie tapped her thighs.

Arriving at The Benson, Tessa sent Julie to retrieve Mom, and she poured coffee for all three. The scent of fresh-baked, blueberry muffins wafted at the snack station, and she added two to a plate. Mom and Julie might appreciate a treat, but she felt slightly sick.

Tessa settled in a quiet section of the lounge with comfortable seating and a table. Gripping the arms of the chair, she waited for her mom and Julie to appear. The knot in her stomach strained. She couldn't predict her mother's mood, and if it was negative, the morning would be torture.

A few minutes later, Mom stomped ahead of Julie and dropped onto a chair opposite Tessa. "You should visit more often," Mom huffed and glared.

Breathing deeply, Tessa ignored her barbed tone and surveyed her appearance. Mom's hair stuck out in an asymmetrical halo, and her lipstick stretched beyond the borders of her mouth. Her illness transformed her into a different person than the fashionista who raised them. She still flashed signs of her former fireball self, but more personality changes loomed like a scary intruder. Tessa sighed. Life would never be the same for Mom or the rest of the family. The future would not be smooth.

"Where are the kids and Julie's husband?" Mom grabbed a cup and peered over the rim.

"Zach and Quinn are at school, Ellie's at daycare, and Owen is at work." Tessa sipped steaming coffee. "Julie and I need to tell you about an exciting plan."

"A holiday? You want to take me on a holiday?" Mom leaned in.

"Uh, no..." Julie twisted a napkin. "You said you don't enjoy living here."

"What?" Mom widened her eyes. "What do you mean? I love it here! This place is my home. Where are the kids and Owen?"

Tessa inhaled a deep breath. "Mom, we'd like you to live in a place where you'll get better care."

"Care?" Mom stiffened.

"Yes, more staff to help you with...well, anything you need. You can enjoy different activities and make some nice new friends." Tessa grimaced at Julie. This conversation wasn't easy, and it was just one of the difficult situations they'd face.

Julie set down her mug. "Mom, The Benson doesn't offer the services you need. They said you've been...uh, helping yourself to other people's things."

"So, now a person can't borrow something from a neighbor? What has this world come to?" Mom clunked down the cup and threw up her hands. "Where are Owen and the kids?"

"They're at work and school." Julie glanced at Tessa and widened her eyes.

"Maybe a change will be good." Tessa imitated Julie's low, slow tone and touched her mom's arm. The muffins sat untouched. The conversation didn't help anyone's appetite.

"No, I don't need a change. I refuse to go anywhere." She bumped her mug and sloshed coffee onto the table.

Tessa soaked up the spill with a napkin. "Tell you what. Julie found a place we think is perfect. Let's go and tour it together." With Julie's help, Tessa coaxed Mom into a short ride to Heritage Haven. The small care home was located in south Regina in a pleasant neighborhood filled with well-kept, modest homes.

When they arrived, a sturdy, compact woman with graying, auburn hair appeared in the doorway. Wearing a dotted sweater set and crisp, navy pants, she conveyed an image of comfort and efficiency.

"Welcome, ladies." She held open the door, stepped back, and waved them inside. "I'm Irina, the manager here, and I'm very pleased to meet you."

A soothing lobby, decorated in soft pinks and sage green like a flower garden, greeted Tessa.

"You must be Adele, Tessa, and Julie." Irina extended a hand.

Adele narrowed her eyes, paused, and shook her hand.

"What lovely shades of blue." Irina smiled and gestured to Adele's multi-colored blouse.

"Thank you." Mom smoothed the front. Staring at Irina, she narrowed her eyes. "Do I know you?"

"I make sure this home is a nice place to live." Irina squeezed Adele's hands. "Do you like to shop? We take a bus to a mall twice a week."

Mom widened her eyes.

Tessa glanced at Julie. Shopping piqued Mom's interest. She could have hugged Irina for setting a positive tone and making an immediate connection. With any luck, the surroundings and company would impress Mom.

Already, the atmosphere felt serene and welcoming with the aroma of banana bread floating down a hallway. Within minutes, Irina charmed her into a relaxed mood. Obviously, she had plenty of experience setting residents' and families' minds at ease.

"I'd like you to meet Rose." In the extended lobby area, Irina extended an arm toward a tall, striking woman whose gray hair was styled in a sleek bob. "I think you'll find a lot of things in common. Rose enjoys shopping, too."

"Hello." Rose smiled and surveyed the trio of visitors. "I could use a new friend."

"She's right," said the manager. "Rose's best friend just moved to Vancouver to be closer to her daughter. Now, let's show you your place."

When Mom didn't resist, Tessa mouthed to Julie, *So far, so good.*

Julie flashed a thumbs-up sign.

Tessa relaxed her tight chest muscles just a smidgeon. She could survive this step just like she dealt with all the other challenges she faced as a busy mother, daughter, and business leader. After viewing the apartment and touring the rest of the center, she confirmed details with Irina. Mom would settle in on the weekend.

"I'll see you soon." Mom smiled and waved. "What did you say your name was? Oh, yes, Rose. I'll see you soon, Rose."

As Tessa drove back to work, she basked in the upbeat mood, even if temporary. Her mom might forget what she agreed or change her mind, but the decision was made. At least, for now, one problem was resolved. Her stomach fluttered. Now, she just had to charm aloof Mark Delaney.

****

After a meeting, Mark weaved through coworkers who still loitered in the common area and speculated about Liz's replacement. Did they have nothing better to do? He swung shut the door to his office with a satisfying bang. Maybe they'd get the hint.

The light on the phone signaled a message, and when he recognized the president's voice, he straightened and listened twice to the confident request. "Mark, it's Don Reilly. I need to speak with you. Come and see me in my office."

Mark attended group meetings with Don Reilly and occasionally bumped into him in the cafeteria or elevator. A summons to the president's office was a first. Why today? Did a major engineering issue need his expertise, or could Don possibly want Mark to replace Liz? Was he about to get his big break? If so, he'd cancel his meeting with Tessa Shore in a heartbeat. Obviously, if the president would promote him without Leadership Camp on his resume, his leadership skills didn't need a tune-up.

Mark's heart rate picked up as if he sprinted up seven flights to Don's tenth floor office, overlooking downtown. In reality, he only climbed two.

"Go right in." Don's assistant ushered him to the door.

"Good morning, Mark, although good might be the wrong description when we've just announced the departure of a strong leader like Liz."

Don's brown hair and complexion matched his earth-toned office. Even his large stature left plenty of space to spare in his plush surroundings, furnished with thick, beige carpet, dark, wooden desk, and subdued, modern art. The hushed décor swallowed excess noise and suggested important decisions happened here. "Good morning, Don."

Mark shook a large hand.

"Sit here." Don gestured toward a round table beside the window.

Mark sat forward and cleared his throat.

"You probably wonder why I called you. I wanted to let you in on my plans before I announce them."

Judging by Don's lead-in, he wasn't about to offer Mark the coveted position. Mark waited to hear more. A promotion would have been a long shot, but the disappointment stung.

"Liz spoke very highly of you, and she had high hopes you'd become her successor. Of course, her retirement date was supposed to be a couple of years from now."

Long lines cut Don's expression, and a shadow darkened his eyes. He must have a serious message to deliver. Mark shifted and took a deep breath.

"I really respect her views on things. She always speaks highly of your skills. Says you're one of the top technical people in the company, and she believes you could become an executive-level leader, too." Don placed a palm flat on the table and raised and lowered it. "Here's the kicker, though. Vice President of Engineering is one of the biggest jobs in the company. I can't take a chance on an unproven guy."

Keeping a neutral expression, Mark stiffened his back. As if he agreed, he nodded. He didn't like the message, but he understood.

"At least, not yet. You're just not ready, and promoting you wouldn't be fair to the team or you."

Don stared and blinked.

Staring at the president's bulgy eyes, Mark sat immobilized in the hushed surroundings. He might be a superstar engineer, but he didn't measure up as a leader. The situation was so annoying and unfair.

"I won't appoint a permanent replacement for Liz

right now. Greg Phillips plans to retire in six months, so I can arrange to slide him into a temporary assignment in Engineering and backfill his position in Customer Service." Don drummed the fingertips of one hand on the table.

What did Don's plan mean to Mark's career? His heart raced and mouth dried. He should have carried his water bottle to the meeting.

"I'll make a decision later on the permanent head of Engineering. Nothing's a given. You're not the only one who has his or her sights set on the job. But I'll give you six months to grow enough to put yourself in the running."

"Thank you. I appreciate the opportunity, Don." Mark's heart pumped a celebration through his body, and he squared his shoulders. His dad would have been proud.

"Don't thank me. Show me I'm right. Demonstrate people skills. Build some bridges and not just pipelines, so to speak." Don chuckled and riveted his gaze on Mark. "I see your potential, but you need to make some changes before you're ready for an executive chair. Expand your network. Make some friends. I'll wait a few months before I make a final decision." He leaned forward and bumped a fist on the table. "Are you interested?"

First, Liz, and now, Don. The senior people in the company sent him a strong message his engineering skills weren't enough. He didn't measure up, and he hated to fail at anything. Doubt pricked the back of his neck. They expected him to be a technical whiz and Mr. Nice Guy. Was he even capable of delivering what they asked?

Mark remembered the way his father's voice boomed across the dinner table. Dad described a tough day at the office and summed it up with a resigned assessment. He always said, It's lonely at the top. Dad counted his success in dollars, not friendships. He worked hard and separated his personal and work lives. When he fired somebody, he shook his head and said, That's why they pay me the big bucks. When he believed workers showed too much emotion, he called them weak and prided himself on keeping a stiff upper lip.

Mark coveted the post, and he needed to convince Don he delivered the right skill set. Six months to transform his personality. Could he do it? Did he have the desire? Whether he wanted to or not didn't matter. Liz said he didn't have a choice, and Don just confirmed it. Mark swallowed, gave a tight, closed-lip smile, and nodded. "I will do whatever you recommend, Don."

"You remind me a lot of myself when I was your age, which is not entirely a good thing, but it means you have potential." Don shifted and gave the table a final tap. He stood and shook Mark's hand. "Do you know Tessa Shore in Human Resources?"

"Our paths have crossed." Slight annoyance jostled his stomach. Definitely, she left an impression of someone on a mission both at the office and in The Benson parking lot. Her untamed hair was hard to miss, too.

"I suggest you go straight to Tessa's office and bond. If anybody can help you with this challenge, she can."

Heat crawled underneath the collar of Mark's shirt

and up his neck. He nodded and charged out of the office and down the hallway. He didn't have a choice. When he heard the company president speak, he listened, but how much could a total stranger really help him change? Could he stand taking orders from Tessa? How would she react when she disliked his opinions? His heart thudded. He couldn't possibly click with her, or could he?

Chapter 5

"Come in, Mark." Tessa extended a hand. "This meeting feels like déjà vu, but let's pretend yesterday didn't happen." Inhaling deep breaths, she offered a wide smile as a peace offering. Despite the shaky start, she'd do her part to make a positive connection.

A few dust flecks floated in the air, and behind his shoulder, a book tipped sideways on a shelf. She would straighten it the minute he left. With a serene and orderly environment, she could manage anything because she controlled the agenda.

"Hello, Tessa." He shook her hand but didn't return a smile.

Mark's handshake was firm and warm, and without warning, Tessa flushed. The trouble with her fair coloring was the way it lit her feelings with a spotlight. Fighting an inclination to place a hand over both cheeks to conceal the evidence he rattled her more than a little, she gestured toward a chair at the table by the window and opened a desk drawer to retrieve a pen and notepad.

She ordered the burn in her cheeks to quit, but the heat only intensified. She shouldn't be the one on edge, but the way Mark shot a gaze from his navy-blue eyes jolted her like she jumped from the safety of a dock into a very cold lake. This meeting revealed an up-close and personal view of the guy with a reputation for being difficult to know and harder to like. She expected to be the one in charge instead of floundering for composure. Arms tingling, she swung shut the office door and joined him at the table. Silence hung in the air.

"Your work comes highly recommended." Mark sat straight.

"You mean by Liz? I still can't believe she'll retire so soon." Tessa adjusted her chair, and it clunked on a table leg. Maybe some office small talk would help him relax. His hunched shoulders practically touched his ears.

"By Liz and our president. Don recommended I get to know you."

"He did?" A pleasant warmth hugged her middle. Positive feedback made her day. "Well, here we are." She leaned forward. "What's your favorite color?" The fizzy sensation in her arms intensified and spread. Why did he have this uncontrollable effect?

Mark widened his eyes and jerked back.

He reacted as though she poked his chest. Tessa laughed. "Sorry, I scared you. I'm just kidding. Hey, before we start, tell me. Did you rescue my mom last evening?"

"If your mother is the woman I drove home." He blinked and sucked in his cheeks.

"Thank you, very much. You probably realized she suffers from dementia. When I heard she disappeared, I panicked."

"No problem." He shrugged. "I just helped the way anyone would."

He closed the subject and didn't show interest in continuing the conversation. Clearly, he preferred to stick to business. She couldn't miss the direct signal. His attitude scolded. "Okay, tell me why you want to be part of Leadership Camp." Tessa picked up a pen.

"I don't."

She wanted to raise her eyebrows but maintained an even expression. So far, he lived up to his curt reputation. "Then why are you here?" Ready to jot highlights of their conversation, she clicked and poised the pen. His intensity nearly jumped across the table to grab her. Behind him on the wall, the soft, impressionist prints contrasted with his sharp body language.

"I want to compete for the top engineering job the next time it opens. I've been told I need to pick up my leadership game."

"Do you believe Leadership Camp will help?" Tessa tilted her head and examined Mark's expression. His face remained stony as a wall, but the alluring scent of spice, so subtle she barely detected it, hinted he was human.

"So I've been told." He clamped his teeth.

"How do you feel about the idea?"

"Doesn't matter how I feel. I don't have a choice." He glared and squared his shoulders.

"Tell me what you know about Leadership Camp." Tessa worked down the list of standard questions she always used to screen candidates for the program. Just because Mark earned executive endorsement didn't mean he could skip the usual selection process. She remained alert for signs of his infamous, clipped attitude.

"I'd rather you describe it." He gripped the chair arms.

"I'll get to the details." Tessa sipped water. His abrupt tone was just short of snappish. With a full hour booked, she wouldn't rush through the process. "I always like to hear what people know about the program. If *your* learning expectations are way off *my* expectations, we have a challenge on our hands." She plunked a palm on the table and flipped it for emphasis.

"I really have no expectations. Liz and Don recommended it."

"You must have picked up things from the class alumni?" She took time to breathe and examine his expression. Staring out the window, Mark's eyes were icy pellets.

"People say the course is a big time commitment and starts with a retreat for a few days at an actual camp. The group meets four days a week for three weeks."

Tessa nodded. "Yes, what else?" She fixed on his blue eyes.

"I gather you play games. Sometimes, people cry." He raised his eyebrows. "I heard the class produces results. The people who participate are often the next ones to get promotions." Mark swept a hand through the front of his hair.

"Oh, I see." Tessa sized up his commitment. He appeared more human with a few hairs out of place. She had yet to see him smile. Under the surface, he either held a natural reserve or a trace of arrogance. Whatever the cause, no doubt, he was anything but excited. She clamped fingers around the pen, and anticipation spiraled into her stomach. In a shocking way, his resistance attracted her as much as his clean, masculine scent. What was happening?

"Well? How did I do?" He tapped a foot.

Tessa caught no trace of a twinkle in his eyes. He was serious. He must know she judged him by his answers, and his question was no joke. "You did well. You passed the first test." Tessa would make him smile if it killed her. She accepted his scrutiny and smiled, but he still didn't crack his somber expression.

"What's next?" He clasped a hand over a fist.

"The information you've gathered is all true, and I'll tell you more. But first, let me see if I understand." Tessa rested the pen on her chin. "If it were up to you, you'd skip Leadership Camp, but you're willing to enroll for the sake of your career."

"Fair assessment." Mark leaned forward. "Now what?"

"If you needed to select a team for your next, big pipeline project, what kind of people would you choose?"

"Bright. Committed. Passionate about their work."

Mark left unsaid *of course*, but his tone spoke the words. He demonstrated the exact, curt mannerism Liz described. Annoyance pinched inside Tessa, but she tossed her head and retrieved patience from an inner pocket. "Thank you. Now, which of those words apply to your qualities in relation to Leadership Camp?"

Rolling back the chair a few inches, Mark narrowed his eyes. "Right now, I'd say bright. Obviously, I need to work on the committed and passionate part."

"Thank you for not pretending. I'm a pretty good judge of character, and I sense when someone's heart isn't in something." At least, he was honest. She might not like what she heard, but she could work with the truth. "The program will tear you away from the office for days at a time. Evaluations and other tools will give you honest feedback that might be difficult to accept."

He nodded.

"I expect visible teamwork at all times, and above all, you need to show an obvious openness to learning." She wouldn't miss a single detail. He couldn't claim any surprises. Occasionally sipping water, she talked for half an hour. As she described each segment of the program, Mark's flat expression never changed. "The first session starts on Tuesday morning at Valley Camp." She held these interviews all the time. Why did her heart jump?

"You mean next week? I have a lot to digest." Mark gripped tight his fists. He shifted, and the chair creaked.

His reaction was hardly typical. Blinking, she took a calming breath. From the street below, the honk of a car horn broke the silence. Usually, participants would do practically anything for the opportunity. He didn't even attempt to sell himself. Something was wrong. Tessa was supposed to evaluate him and not the other way around. "Yes, and you'll need to pack your commitment and passion." She smiled and studied his reaction.

"I take it none of the segments are optional." He glowered and leaned back.

"All the pieces combine to give you a full, leadership-immersion experience. You can't pick and choose the elements." Excitement and pride jetted through her. She designed a topnotch program, and it worked.

"I see." He gave a single nod.

"Well, how do you feel now? Are you ready to take the plunge? You're standing at the edge of a pool, and I'm about to elbow you into the deep end." Tessa splashed Mark with a water image and crinkled her eyes. She didn't give up easily. Surely, she could do something to loosen his expression.

"The deep end doesn't worry me a bit. I was a swimmer. A qualified lifeguard, actually." He quirked an eyebrow.

"Okay, poor analogy." Tessa tossed her head from side to side.

"No problem. Anyway, I consider the program one of the tools I need for the future. A life jacket to equip me for the rapids ahead." He pursed his lips.

"If you choose to swim, I'll coach you all the way. If you decide to let go and sink, I'll throw you a few lifelines, but I won't let you weigh down the rest of the group or me." Tessa studied his reaction, and her heart beat a little faster. Why did his blue eyes affect her this way? She had never seen anything so icy, yet hot, and a very confusing and alluring mix.

"I understand." He blinked and stared.

"Leadership Camp is built on clear expectations. If you don't know where you're headed, how will you know when you get there?" She scratched another note in her book and willed her heart to slow. She was in control, so why did it pound at such a crazy pace?

"What happens now?" He leaned forward.

"You need to tell me the commitment and passion part of the equation won't be a problem, and then I tell you you're in." She dropped the pen, clapped together her hands, and pointed at his chest.

"Right now?" He shook his head. "I need the night to decide."

"Hmmm. Usually, people clamor to hear the news they earned a spot. You're a very unusual client, Mr.

Delaney." She waited for a hint of a smile, and at the same time, a flush tingled and warmed her cheeks. She couldn't believe her own tone, and her heart jolted. If she overheard another woman interact the same way, she'd accuse her of flirting.

Long ago, she imposed a rule for herself to keep professional relationships businesslike. A romance with a colleague didn't break a company policy, but it treaded into uncertain waters. She didn't need anyone to suggest an improper personal relationship influenced her success or interfered with her results.

Others could do what they wished, but she wouldn't let innuendo or gossip tarnish her reputation. She'd worked hard to build it and wouldn't do anything to jeopardize it. Participants in Leadership Camp were the most off-limits of all. She was their mentor and guide, and she needed their respect.

"Well, Miss Shore, it is *Miss* Shore, isn't it?" He flickered the corners of his mouth.

If she wasn't mesmerized by his gaze, she would have missed the nanosecond change of expression.

"I may be unusual, but I'm realistic. My dad taught nothing worthwhile is ever easy, and I'm not making a promise I can't keep. So, I'll make you wait until morning. I need to consult someone before I make it official."

This approach didn't feel right at all. Instead of Tessa determining whether he was in or out, he would tell her in the morning. "I understand." But did she? "Maybe you want to discuss the commitment with your wife."

"I'm not married." He glared and set a fist on the table with a thump.

Tessa's heart jumped, and she scolded herself. His marital status didn't matter. She was interested in his leadership skills and nothing else. She shouldn't care who he needed to consult, anyway. His personal life was none of her business. As long as he informed her of his decision by tomorrow morning, she could ready the materials and exercises for Tuesday.

Mark's expression and tone slammed closed a door. "You can take the night but no longer." Tessa snapped shut her notebook and sprang from the chair. "I need to know by nine. Deal?" She flashed him her best smile and stuck out a hand. If it was moist, maybe he wouldn't notice.

He shook her hand. "Deal. Thanks, Tessa." He stretched to his full height and strode to the door. Peering over his shoulder, he squinted and grabbed the doorknob. "You smeared ink on your chin."

She clapped a hand over the spot and flushed under his critical gaze. "Good to know. Blue's my best color." If he thought he could intimidate her, he had another thing coming.

****

Mark strode down an empty hallway and stifled a grin. Tessa showed spunk. The way she swooped her hands like a traffic cop, he was surprised she didn't smear herself with more ink. The faint, blue streak took nothing away from her pretty, fair coloring and perfect, white smile. Soon, he'd decide whether to join her at Leadership Camp.

If he wanted to date someone, she might be a prospect. But with work, Bree, and his mother, he had little time to think about a woman. Besides, she might act similar to others he had dated. They probed for his

66

innermost thoughts and, when he refused to share, labeled him cold and unfeeling.

He climbed the stairs two at a time to the eighth floor. On the way to his office, he nodded to a couple of colleagues who loitered near the coffee area. The murmur of their banter and laughter followed him down a hallway, and he clicked shut his office door for some peace and quiet.

The meeting with Tessa ate more time than he expected, and a pile of pipeline drawings waited for his review and approval before five o'clock. Peering out a window, he rubbed the back of his neck and rotated his shoulders. With a heavy workload to jam his thoughts, he shelved the decision about Leadership Camp until after dinner.

That evening at home, he knocked on Bree's bedroom door, cracked it open, and stuck in his head. "Want to walk with Rufus and me?" Music blared, and clothes trailed across the floor. She was a teenage girl, all right, but if she kept the noise and clutter contained, he could live with it. He swallowed and rubbed a fist over his chest. If only her mother could see her now.

"No, thanks. But I'll watch a show with you later." She lifted her gaze from a book.

He nodded and flashed a thumbs-up. He didn't have the energy to coax her outside so left and headed to the park. If he was expected to spend a good chunk of next week at Valley Camp, he needed to make arrangements for Bree and Rufus. His mother would survive without a visit for a few days, but who would agree to stay with a thirteen-year-old girl? She didn't need a babysitter for short stints, but an absence of several days was another matter. His lack of family support hurt like a pinched nerve. He had few people he could really rely on, and Bree needed him. They seldom parted.

Mark led Rufus toward the lake and drank in the clear air. The steady hum of traffic faded, and water lapped ahead.

Rufus lunged at the Canada geese that overran the paths and grassy areas.

The gray-and-black birds squawked, flapped, and cleared the pathway.

"Good job, Rufus." Mark leaned and petted the dog's side. As he headed toward the bridge, he reviewed child and dog-care options. A couple of married friends were parents of toddlers. Bree would never agree to stay at their places, and he couldn't ask them to look after her *and* a large retriever. Only a dog lover would welcome big, furry Rufus.

Who else? He couldn't ask his cousin, Paul. His busy life didn't allow time for kids. Perhaps his next-door neighbors, Mr. and Mrs. Sawchuk, might agree. They were kind, youngish grandparents who enjoyed Bree and Rufus. They always stopped for a chat on their driveway, and sometimes, Mrs. S, as Bree called her, delivered fresh-baked cookies for a dessert treat. He couldn't think of anyone else.

Mark rounded the lake in record time, and when he got home, he left Rufus in the back yard and knocked on the Sawchuks' red front door. From the step, he admired their yard. It was always groomed well enough to fit in a gardening guide.

Footsteps tapped toward the door, and Mrs. Sawchuk swung it open and grinned. "Hello, Mark. Come in for cookies and lemonade. Where's Bree?"

She dusted her hands on an apron tied around her waist.

The scent of chocolate drifted and teased Mark's taste buds. If he had more time, he'd take her up on the offer.

Mr. Sawchuk followed her into the entranceway. "Mark, good to see you."

The small, gray-haired couple, as similar as a pair of salt-and-pepper shakers, linked arms.

A pang shot his heart. Next to their togetherness, his aloneness magnified. "Thank you for the offer, but I won't stay for a snack this time. I wanted to ask a big favor."

"Hey, what are neighbors for?" Mr. Sawchuk dropped his arms to his sides and glanced at his wife.

"I have an opportunity at work. But I need to go away for a few days next week..." Mark shifted. Asking for help felt weak.

"And you need somewhere for Bree to stay?" Mrs. Sawchuk intertwined her fingers.

"You're always so nice, and you even like Rufus." He offered a smile. "I hoped maybe..."

"Oh, Mark, normally we would love to." She flipped her gaze toward her husband and back to Mark. "But next week we're visiting our daughter and grandchildren in Calgary. I'm sorry."

"Any other time." Mr. Sawchuk nodded and leaned on the doorjamb.

"I wish we could. You don't have much family." Mrs. Sawchuk crinkled her forehead.

Mark's stomach muscles contracted, but he masked his disappointment and forced a neutral expression. "Thanks, anyway." His best prospects were busy, and he had no backup option. He clenched his jaw so hard it ached.

Bristling at the twittering birds, he crossed the driveway to his yard and surveyed the lawn. The downpour last night and the sun today would help transform it to lush and green. He rounded the house to the back and chucked Rufus's ball until the dog was exhausted.

In the morning, he'd brief Tessa. He didn't need the class as much as everyone thought. Family was his number-one priority, and he wouldn't allow anything to interfere. She probably wouldn't approve of his decision, but her reaction didn't matter. Why should he care what she thought? Would she pressure him to change his mind? He would stand firm, but what would she say?

Chapter 6

Joined by Julie and the kids, Tessa spent the evening at Mom's, packed her belongings, and marked boxes. The family would help her to relocate on the weekend.

By the time they arrived at The Benson, Mom already changed her mind several times.

Her usually tidy suite overflowed with cardboard boxes and rustling newspaper. The tweedy, blue sofa and chair displayed a selection of ornaments waiting to be wrapped.

"That nice lady, Rose, can't wait for you to arrive, Mom." Tessa wrapped dishes.

"Who's Rose, and what are you doing with my glasses?" Mom huffed and jammed her hands on hips.

"She's the friendly woman we met at your new place. We're packing for your move." Tessa bit her lip and widened her eyes at Julie. Mom tested her patience to the limit, even more than in the past when she was healthy.

After Ellie bored of helping, she played a card game with her cousins and Grandma. If Grandma Adele slipped on the rules, Ellie guided her.

"One more evening will finish the job." Tessa flopped onto a chair. "Let's call it a night."

"I'll pour cola." Julie wiped her hands on the back of her jeans. "We made good progress."

After a quick refreshment break, Tessa drove home with Ellie.

"Why does Grandma have to move?" On the way, Ellie called from the back seat of the car.

"Grandma has a sickness called dementia. It means her brain doesn't work right. She forgets things and gets confused." Tessa scanned the light traffic and giant trees overhanging Angus Street. Soon, they'd create a leafy canopy and provide her and Ginger a shady route to a walking path along a nearby creek.

"In the matching card game, she forgets where the pairs are." Ellie swung her feet and tapped the back of the driver's seat.

"Yes, I know." Tessa glanced in the rearview mirror and smiled at Ellie's furrowed forehead. "Last night during the rainstorm, she took Ginger to The Benson instead of Auntie Julie's house."

"Was Grandma lost?"

"Maybe a little. She didn't know which way to go," Tessa explained at a four-year-old child's level. She found her mom's behavior difficult to understand, too, and didn't want to alarm little Ellie. "Sometimes, Grandma needs help to make good choices. Without asking, she borrowed some things from neighbors. So, she'll live at a place where people know why she acts confused. They will look after her."

"Oh."

The explanation was a lot for a four-year-old to digest, but the problem was too big to hide.

"I can help Grandma when I get bigger."

"Aw, Ellie, you're a sweet girl. You can even help her now...like tonight, when you played the card game." Tessa swallowed a lump in her throat. The sad and overwhelming fact was now poor Mom would need assistance from the whole family.

Lying in bed after a refreshing shower, Tessa sank under a heaviness as thick as the quilt that covered her. She had decorated her gold-and-cream bedroom as a tranquil cocoon, but tonight, the space closed in and smothered. She drew in long, deep breaths to slow her whirling mind.

With the right medication and strong support from Heritage Haven, perhaps her mom could enjoy a decent quality of life. Dementia affected the whole family, and Tessa balanced a tough act between Ellie, work, and Mom's increasing needs. She rolled, rubbed Ginger's soft ears, and stared at a wall adorned with family photos.

Ginger groaned and nestled close.

Tomorrow would be another busy day, and she reviewed her long to-do list. She would hear from Mark Delaney before nine o'clock, and then she could finalize plans for next week's Leadership Camp kickoff. She was lucky because when she travelled for work Julie cared for Ellie and Ginger.

Surely, Mark would grab the opportunity. At least, if he was smart, he would. When she met him, she kept an open mind and didn't dislike him just because others did. But others might judge him right. Mark was abrupt to the point of rudeness yesterday, and from their brief meeting today, she understood why he wasn't the most popular guy in the HeatNow office. He didn't exactly ooze warmth and humor, but at least, he was a straight shooter. He was open and honest about his feelings toward Leadership Camp, and she respected his transparency. Stretching, she relaxed her tense arms and stiff legs, and a surprising attraction tingled along her spine. With his curt manner and striking appearance, he definitely left a lasting impression, but what was happening? She couldn't possibly be attracted to a potential student.

Who did Mark need to consult to make his final decision about enrolling in the program? If he chose to participate, coaching him would not be easy. She popped open her eyes, bolted upright, and leapt to stare out the window. The peaceful neighborhood contrasted with the commotion in her brain. She cracked open the window and breathed the cool, dry air. If Mark joined the class, what challenges loomed? Should she hope his answer would be yes or no? If yes, then what?

****

This morning, Mark would deliver his final decision to Tessa, and he couldn't relax his tight back muscles. He didn't mind breaking the news, but even though he shouldn't care about her reaction, he did. Why was her opinion so important?

Squinting, he adjusted the blind on the window over the kitchen sink. Sunlight flooded in and paled the beige walls to nearly white. Surrounded by the aroma of toast, he ate breakfast with Bree and packed her lunch.

Sometimes, he marveled his niece was so much like him she could have been his daughter. She was smart—too smart for her own good, sometimes—and a bit of a loner. He fully accepted his own need for solitude, but he sometimes worried about the same characteristic in Bree. "Any plans after school?" Mark scrubbed the counter, wiped the fridge door, and scanned the floor for crumbs. He always left the room clean and tidy.

"Just homework." Bree opened the dishwasher and added her cereal bowl.

"Will you take Rufus out to play?"

"Yup."

"Do you want to invite over a friend?"

"Not really."

Mark sighed. "We should visit Grandma tonight." He gathered his lunch and work laptop and grabbed keys from a hook near the back door.

"Do we really have to?" Bree picked up a book and headed to a favorite reading chair in the living room.

"You know we do." Mark followed. "Hey, give me a fist bump. Have a good day." He would tell her the news about the program at dinnertime.

Settled at work, Mark checked his calendar. His first priority was to catch Tessa. She was so proud of the program and set such high expectations for participants she would likely question his decision.

Positioned along two walls, his desk accommodated multiple projects, and he prioritized a collection of reports spread across the wide workspace. Coworkers' banter in the hallway already interrupted the quiet environment. Shortly after eight o'clock, he typed an instant message on his computer keyboard.

I decided. Are you free to talk?

Her reply took a few minutes.

Good morning, Mark. Give me five, and then come see me.

Exactly five minutes later, he arrived in her office. He didn't notice yesterday, but a cute, dark-eyed little girl peered from a photo on a shelf. If she was Tessa's daughter, she didn't resemble her. Next to the picture, books and mementos rested in precise lines. He entered and nodded. He'd make the conversation quick. Facing Tessa, he inhaled a sharp breath. He shouldn't notice, but she wore her hair in a loose knot, and her fitted, green dress skimmed her trim shape. She widened her eyes, as though she expected good news to start her day. Not a speck of ink dotted her chin.

"Well, what did you decide? Are you ready to jump in and join us?" She flung up a hand, motioned toward a chair, and closed the office door. "Let's chat."

Dropping to a seat, he was almost sorry to break the news. "I need to pass." He delivered the message without a smile and landed his gaze on her face.

Smile fading, she arched her eyebrows.

She reacted the way he expected, and the invisible band around his chest tightened.

"Oh? Can you share your thoughts?" She clasped her hands and tapped a thigh.

He didn't owe her an explanation, and he needed to cut short this probing conversation. His decision was his business. "The program has a good reputation. It might help my career." He clenched his jaw.

"But…?" She flicked a stray hair off a cheek.

He'd rather not explain but shifted under her scrutiny and cleared his throat. "I can't for personal reasons." He leaned back, crossed his arms, and forced them apart. No doubt, Tessa analyzed body language, and he didn't want to send any unspoken messages. "I have custody of my niece. She's thirteen. I can't leave her alone."

"Oh, I see." Tessa nodded. "You've explored all your child care options?"

"Every one." He refused to answer more questions. He didn't need to share details of his personal life.

"This time, I can't participate."

"I'm sorry to hear." She twisted a lock of hair around a finger.

"Can't be helped." Mark shrugged. Missing Leadership Camp wasn't the end of the world. Anyway, he still wasn't convinced a program would transform him.

"I understand the challenge of suitable child care. Sometimes, my sister helps."

At the mention of Tessa's sister, he rubbed a stab of pain that never fully eased. Did she know how lucky she was to have a sister? "Thanks, anyway." Mark thrust out of the chair, strode to the door, and twisted the knob. Glancing over his shoulder, he narrowed his eyes and snapped his gaze to her tight smile. "I appreciate the offer. Maybe another time."

His chest closed tight on a sliver of regret. He should attend, but Leadership Camp wasn't essential. Not compared to time with Bree. She needed him. She had no one else, and he promised his sister long before the deadly accident that if anything should happen, he would always take care of her child.

"I'm sorry the opportunity didn't work out this time." Tessa followed him to the office doorway. "If you ever want to talk about leadership, let me know."

Office conversations floated along the hallway. As he retreated, his back burned from her gaze, but he resisted the urge to turn and catch her. He couldn't fault her dedication to the program and understood how her enthusiasm could be contagious—for the right person. But even though he might adjust to Tessa's bouncy personality, she represented an experience he'd rather avoid.

By the time he hit the stairwell, he steered his mind to his challenge of the day. He would design a solution for installing pipelines where the geographic terrain caused risky ground shifting. Technical work was much more important than Leadership Camp. Besides, he'd prove to everyone he could become a better leader without Tessa.

Back in his office, he stared out a window at city streets and the wide prairie beyond. Sinking into a chair, he massaged a temple. Why did the image of her glowing aura linger, and what could she teach that he couldn't learn on his own?

****

Alone in her office, Tessa grabbed a moment to lean her forehead against the cool glass, peer out the window, and clear the conversation with Mark. A sure sign of spring, leaves burst on the trees below. Mark's decision about Leadership Camp disappointed her. She didn't want him in the group until she met him. In person, she bumped against his rough edges, but if he let her, she could smooth his image.

Tessa sighed, and her structured mind organized random thoughts into a line so straight it pointed to an answer. She could change Mark's mind. Scrolling through messages on the computer screen, she scanned for priority items. A company Newsflash, a note from the president, was the first item on the list.

I'm pleased to announce Greg Phillips accepted a temporary appointment as Acting Vice President of Engineering.

No surprise, Mark Delaney wasn't the successful candidate, but the president made a temporary appointment. He left the door open for another candidate to assume the permanent post within a few months.

Tessa flipped through emails, sorted, deleted, and responded, but she couldn't free her mind of Mark's child care dilemma. A pang jostled her stomach. If she couldn't rely on Julie, she would struggle to get away. But child care aside, Mark needed her help. If he could develop his leadership skills quickly enough, he could take a shot at the top engineering job. No doubt, Leadership Camp was his best chance to grow and buff his reputation.

Greeting coworkers along a bright hallway, Tessa bustled to the coffee room to refill a water bottle. The scent of strong coffee hung in the air. When she returned and passed her assistant's desk, she stopped. "Hey, Karen, do you have a minute to come to my office?"

"Of course. How were your meetings with the infamous Mark Delaney? You were a little frazzled yesterday, but now you look happy." Backing away from her desk, Karen bobbed her head.

Tessa read concern in Karen's crinkled expression. "I'm glad I have an office mom like you to keep an eye on me." She laughed. "I'm fine. Really."

"First, should I grab a notepad?" Karen stood and straightened her skirt.

"No, you won't need it." Tessa led her to the office and motioned to a chair. "Come, and sit here." She slid into the spot opposite and leaned forward. "Do you think your daughter would stay for a few nights with a thirteen-year-old girl as sort of a live-in nanny?"

"Probably. She's always eager to earn a few extra dollars." Karen propped forearms on the table.

At least, she could hope. "Listen to my crazy idea. Mark wanted to join Leadership Camp, but he couldn't find someone to stay with his niece. If I found him a sitter, he could participate, after all."

"You must really want him in the group." Karen smiled and winked.

"I don't have a personal reason. Believe me." Tessa wrinkled her nose, yet inside her middle, a butterfly fluttered. Karen would never know Mark was an intriguing package waiting to be unwrapped. "I just think he would benefit even more than most."

"I'll call Nicole right now and see what she says. Stay tuned." Karen hustled to complete the request. Five minutes later, she appeared at the office doorway. "Nicole is willing. At least, she's open to hearing more details. You can give him her email address and phone number." Karen crackled a piece of paper with Nicole's contact information and handed it to Tessa.

Should she call or email Mark? Maybe a quick, in-person chat would be best. Tessa dashed an instant message.

Hi, Mark, Didn't expect to talk again so soon, but I have an idea to share. Can I pop by your office in a few minutes?

In seconds, his reply pinged.

OK, if you're quick. Leaving for a meeting in ten minutes.

Tessa lifted a mirror from a desk drawer and examined her face. She applied a touch of lip balm, climbed the stairs to Mark's office, and tapped on the door.

He hunched over a diagram that covered the desk. The office walls displayed maps of different areas of the province, but the space was all business with no photos or other mementos on display. It revealed nothing except his work focus. "What's up?" Mark straightened.

She couldn't read his expression to learn whether he was at all happy, annoyed, or neutral about her interruption. Once he heard, he might be grateful. "I found a solution." A tendril of Tessa's hair fell forward and tickled her cheek, and she brushed it away.

"Can I come in and sit for a minute?" She didn't wait for an invitation and dropped onto the chair opposite his desk. The visitor chair was lower than his, and she perched like a child asking for a privilege her parent would deny. Only the thermostat click broke the silence.

"I can't participate in Leadership Camp." He sat and leaned back.

"If someone stayed with your niece, you could." Palms forward, she signaled *stop*. "Just listen for a minute. My assistant, Karen, has a very responsible daughter who's twenty and attends university. I asked Karen to find out if she'd be willing to stay with your niece, and she said yes. So there you go. I arranged an option."

"You did what? You took it upon yourself to find a caregiver for my niece? Without my permission?"

Color sped into his cheeks, and his eyes darkened. He turned into a thundercloud ready to burst. She narrowed her eyes and straightened. No way would she show him his strong reaction shook her.

He tensed his entire body and fisted both hands.

Tessa stared, blinked, and swallowed. She couldn't withdraw the offer now. Her intent was to help, not anger Mark.

"You took leadership a bit too far." Mark leaned forward and thudded a fist on the desk. "I never want to be the kind of leader who interferes in other people's business."

"I only tried to do you a favor. Obviously, I made a mistake." Tessa shot to her feet and backed away. "If you don't join us for this session, you'll miss a great opportunity." She tossed a paper onto his desk. "Her name's Nicole, and I'll leave her contact information."

"Fine." Mark stood and jammed his hands on hips.

"Do what you want. It's your career. But if you plan to show up, let me know by tomorrow." Quivering, she threw up an arm in a dramatic wave. "Oh, and have a nice day."

Tessa threw open the door, exited the office, and sped along the hallway. What a grouch. She didn't expect such a strong, negative reaction to a helpful gesture. Would he cool down and consider her generous assistance or stick his stubborn feet in the ground? She flew a shaky hand to her chest. Why did she wish so hard for his change of heart?

Chapter 7

The woman displayed nerve. She overstepped her bounds by a giant leap. On his way home from work, Mark clamped fists around the steering wheel.

The rest of the day had passed in a blur, and he didn't steal a moment to think about Tessa and the child care solution until he sank into his car and took a deep breath. She needed to understand nothing would change his mind. He glanced at the clock and zipped along the parkway. After a long day, the polished-leather smell of the car interior always soothed.

When his last resort for a companion for Bree wasn't available, he ruled out Leadership Camp. His niece was sensitive and a little prickly, and he couldn't leave her with just anyone. As a mother and the leadership whiz Tessa was reputed to be, she should know better. He couldn't invite a total stranger to stay with Bree. The arrangement would be plain awkward and uncomfortable. He honked at a driver who paused a fraction too long at a light.

A few minutes later, he rushed in the door at home. "Sorry, I'm late." The swift air stream puffed stray dog hair ahead to announce his arrival. Fortunately, tan area rugs and furnishings concealed some of the mess. Keeping up with housework, along with everything else, was a never-ending task.

Rufus circled and whacked his tail against Mark's

legs.

Lounging on the sofa, Bree peered over her book. "Hey, Uncle Mark. When you get home at the same time every day, you're acting normal. You're not late."

He laughed. With her sharp observations, she was his niece, all right. "Hungry? I'll throw burgers on the barbecue, and we'll eat pretty soon."

"Okay. After I took out Rufus, I had a snack." Bree set down her book and followed Uncle Mark out to the kitchen. "I'll make a salad."

"Thanks. See you in a minute." In his bedroom, Mark exchanged work clothes for jeans and a T-shirt. Bree would be happy to hear he wouldn't need to leave for Leadership Camp, after all. Returning to the kitchen, he grabbed meat from the freezer and barbecue sauce from the fridge. "How was your day?"

"Okay." Bree rinsed lettuce under the tap.

She didn't sound convinced. Ever since her best friend moved away, she spent most of her spare time with books and Rufus. "Your teacher suggested you run for Grade Eight Graduation Committee." Balancing the barbecue supplies, Mark paused. "What do you think?"

"Maybe." Bree shrugged and patted dry the leaves.

He strained to hear her response and then dropped the topic. She'd only clam up. He'd try again to draw her out, but conversation was never easy.

A few minutes later, he served a plate of sizzling, charbroiled burgers. His mouth watered at the savory scent. Seated at the kitchen table, dotted with jars of condiments, he passed Bree the ketchup. "I decided I won't join Leadership Camp." Mark took a large bite, chewed, and waited for her reaction.

Rufus nuzzled his head on Mark's lap.

He petted the begging dog with a free hand. "None for you, boy."

"Why?" Bree stopped chewing, dragged a carrot stick through ketchup, and swirled it around the edge of the plate.

"I have too much work at the office and, besides, I'd rather spend my free time with you. Doing ketchup art." He scrunched his face at the red streaks circling her food.

Bree furrowed her brow but giggled. "Oh, Uncle Mark." She chomped a giant bite of burger and talked with her mouth full. "Don't stay home cuz of me. You should go if..."

Were teenage hormones responsible, or did Bree strive to be unpredictable? Yesterday, she dug in her heels about the possibility of being left with a caregiver. Now, she seemed resigned to the idea. "If what? You didn't sound so sure yesterday."

"Yeah, well, I didn't want to get treated like a baby. But you should do what your boss says. If someone cool can stay here...not to babysit...just to cook and keep me company, you can go."

Mark shifted forward and rested his forearms on the table. He smiled at his niece's narrow, pinched face and deep blue eyes that matched his. With her dark hair gathered into a loose ponytail, she could pass for younger than thirteen, but her mood swings suggested otherwise. Time flew, and she'd grown quickly in the seven years since she dropped into his fulltime care. His chest burned at the shattering memory.

"How do you like the sound of a young woman named Nicole? She's twenty. A university student. Her mom works at HeatNow."

"Well, maybe." Bree slipped a piece of meat to Rufus.

"Hey, no wonder he begs at the table." He shook his head. They both loved their pet, bad habits and all.

"You feed him, too."

"I can't argue." He chuckled. Nothing slipped by Bree. She was right. Rufus was so much a part of the family he earned frequent treats just for tilting his soft, golden head and batting his velvet-brown eyes. "Are you sure you don't mind about Leadership Camp?" He searched her expression for clues. She didn't always let him know how she really felt.

"Sort of." She chewed another bite and let Rufus lick a sticky finger.

"Bree, you need to be *very* sure before I tell the organizer I'll come."

"I'm pretty sure." She shrugged. "When can I meet Nicole?"

"Very soon because the class starts Monday." He swiped a paper napkin across his mouth. "I'll arrange something."

"Okay. Can we go to Cool Cones for dessert now?" Bree smiled and stared.

She caught him in a weak moment, but the popular ice cream stand on Victoria Avenue tempted him, too. This early in the spring, the line shouldn't wind around the block. "If you help load the dishwasher, yeah, sure." He stood and cleared the table.

Drooling, Rufus stuck close.

Thank goodness, some things never changed. The peaceful scene nudged his heart. Bree's presence, a loyal dog, and a comfortable home encircled him. A predictable life and neutral surroundings struck others as bland, but they were his sanctuary.

Humming a popular song, Bree rinsed and loaded the dishes.

Mark wiped the table with extra vigor. He didn't expect Bree's flip-flop or his own. At the sink, he gripped and twisted much harder than necessary to wring the cloth and thrust it onto a hook. Even with Bree's support, he still shunned the idea. But she was right. First, Liz and then the president urged him to participate, so he better do whatever they required for his best shot at the top job.

Gambling he and Bree would like Nicole, he'd let Tessa know first thing in the morning he would participate. Dad said the path to the top wasn't easy, but he didn't mention how many irritations would litter the way. How would Mark navigate the route without stumbling over a certain woman?

****

The next evening, Tessa and Ellie took Ginger to the park and met Julie, Zach, and Quinn for playtime. Pushing a swing for giggling Ellie, Tessa drooped her shoulders. "This week drained me." A whoosh of air breezed into her face. She craved her sister's support.

"I agree." Julie rolled her eyes and petted Ginger.

"Not just Mom's situation. Her issues are bad enough, but work has its share of challenges, too." Tessa threw wide her arms to demonstrate the magnitude. She filled her lungs with the mild spring air, scented with grass and earth, and scanned for signs of budding lilacs in the bushes at the perimeter of the playground.

"Higher, Mommy. Please, make me touch the sky." As she swung, Ellie's black ponytail sailed and flipped against her face.

"Please, don't forget your patience, Miss Ellie," Tessa gently chided and pushed with renewed vigor.

Ellie giggled and swung her legs. "Whee, you can't beat me." She grinned at Zach and Quinn, flying high on their swings.

"What's up at work?" Julie swooped both kids in a giant arch and swiveled to face Tessa.

Julie always listened with interest and gave insightful feedback, even though her current role as stay-at-home mom was a world away from a busy office. Tessa recapped the last-minute addition to Leadership Camp. "Mark is the mystery man who rescued Mom."

"Really? What a small world." Julie widened her eyes. "I hope you thanked him on behalf of the whole family."

"I tried, but he brushed off the topic like he swatted a fly." Tessa tilted her head and shrugged. "I can't wait to see his stony face melt into a smile." The image sent her slightly off-balance, and she straightened before Julie noticed. If Mark followed her advice, she could mold him into an amazing leader.

"He must have a heart, but he's a human statue with one hard, unreadable expression." Tessa thrust the swing and, inside, rode along. He had a very unsettling effect. She raised her eyebrows. "Mark's boss plunked him into the class, so I could teach and fix him. He's the company's leading expert in gas pipelines, but he, apparently, doesn't have a single personable bone in his body."

"You can't resist a challenge." Julie tapped Tessa's shoulder.

"I agree, but he won't make my job easy." Tessa ruffled Ginger's fur. "Yesterday, he declined to participate, and I didn't know whether to cheer or groan. But today, he changed his mind."

Mark had appeared in her doorway even before she switched on her laptop computer. His cheeks radiated a slight flush, probably from an early-morning workout, and his hair still glistened with dampness. "Change of plan."

"Oh?" He didn't waste words. She jumped and swooped around the desk to face him. She wouldn't let him tower above. He needed a reminder she was the one in control.

"If Nicole will stay with my niece, I'll participate."

"Excellent. I'm happy to hear." She didn't expect to cross paths with Mark again and, definitely, didn't expect this news at all. A slight tremor landed in her knees. She clapped once, locked on his cobalt eyes, and stuck out a hand. She would show him who set the rules. "Welcome to the group."

He hesitated and then shook her hand. "I'll book Nicole. Send me the agenda and any other details I need."

Tessa stiffened. Did he know the words thank you? The sudden warming effect of his presence upped her temperature, but she tugged her lips into a smile. His eyes glinted deep and cool as the ocean, yet clear and hot as a summer sky. She had refused to be first to glance away.

"Hello, Tessa. Are you still here?" Julie waved a hand to grab her attention.

Tessa snapped back to the present and took a deep breath. "Oh, sorry." She shook her head to clear it of the distracting images.

"You were thinking about Mark, weren't you?" Julie laughed. "Caught you."

"Maybe, but only because he needs help." Tessa smirked and slowed Ellie's swing. Sometimes, Julie read her mind. She tucked away the details of his brooding good looks for another time. Harboring such mixed feelings, she didn't need Julie's teasing.

"Hey, let's go and slide." Ahead of her cousins, Ellie sped to the next attraction.

Strolling beside Julie, Tessa rustled through the grass to the red, yellow, and blue play structure.

Ginger flopped and rubbed her sides and back on the gravel.

"If he gives you any trouble, he clearly doesn't know who he's up against." Julie circled a finger and pointed at Tessa. "I'm sure you'll take charge as usual and keep him on the straight and narrow."

"I plan to." She hurried to the foot of the slide and laughed at Ellie's wide eyes and open mouth. Despite its daily challenges, motherhood offered plenty of fun moments.

"Throw in a little of your feminine charm, and he won't know what hit him. Just a little advice from your equally-charming sister." Julie cupped her face and exaggerated a smile.

Demonstrating her allure, Tessa pretended to primp her hair.

Julie laughed and slung an arm around Tessa's shoulders. She drew her close and squeezed. "If anyone can tame the beast, you can."

Ginger circled and wagged her tail.

The beloved dog never failed to make everyone

smile. Stroking Ginger's soft ears, Tessa checked the time. "Ellie, after two more slides, we need to go home."

"Aw." Ellie protested but glanced at her mom and stopped.

Tessa furrowed her brow in a don't-argue-with-me expression and swallowed the slight lump in her throat. Even though single parenthood burdened her more than she believed possible, she never for a moment doubted her love for this bundle of energy and joy. They were a family of two and probably always would be. When exhaustion struck, she might second-guess her decision to prove she could parent alone, but no one needed to know the secret that sometimes kept her awake in the middle of the night.

"I hope you're right. I do know for sure I won't let him sabotage the class—or my success." She waved Ellie toward her. "Oh, one more thing." Trepidation tiptoed into her stomach, and she rested a hand on Julie's arm. "I'll meet you at Mom's at nine Saturday morning, and we'll kidnap her."

Later that evening, after she tucked Ellie into bed and brewed a soothing cup of tea, Tessa mapped the next few days. Settled on the sofa, she rubbed her feet along Ginger's furry back and jotted notes to keep her busy life organized. Raising her mug, she breathed the steamy scent of camomile and savored her comfy surroundings. The cream leather furniture was easy to wipe clean and the small, quaint home with well-worn, wood floors was perfect for a busy mom, pre-schooler, and dog.

The next two days at work, she would initiate Mark's formal feedback from the president, peers, and team so evidence of his current approach formed a baseline for improvement. The opinions might shock him. She sipped tea and scribbled more notes. Saturday morning, she would load Mom's boxes and relocate her to Heritage Haven. Biting her lip, she clicked the pen on and off. Fingers crossed Mom would have a lucid day and cooperate. Then Monday evening, she would drop Ellie and Ginger to stay at Julie's place during Leadership Camp.

Mind whirring, she made a few more notes of errands and chores and reviewed the long list. She'd find a way to make all the moving parts run smoothly. She always did. "C'mon, Ginger. Time for bed." She yawned, stretched, and switched off lights. Then the phone rang. "Who's calling so late?"

Ginger cocked her head.

Call Display revealed who was on the other end of the line, and she hesitated before she picked up. "Hi, Mom. I'm surprised you're still awake."

"I have a problem, Tessa. A big problem. I called your sister, but the message machine answered, and I needed to talk to someone right away."

Mom's urgent tone suggested a major catastrophe. "What's wrong?" Tessa kept her tone even. Mom's emergencies were seldom worth a panic attack.

"My place is full of boxes. Where on earth did they come from? Housekeeping here isn't what it used to be. I can hardly squeeze by, and I need to remove these boxes right this minute."

Mom's voice screeched into Tessa's ear. Tessa flinched but drew a deep breath and gathered patience. She'd calm her before the situation escalated. "Those boxes hold your belongings. Julie, you, and I packed most of your things. You're ready to move to a new home."

"Move? What do you mean?" Mom huffed and clucked her tongue.

"We found a nice, new place for you to live, where the people will treat you well." Tessa paced and stopped to peer out the kitchen window at the twinkling stars overhead. If only a wish upon a star could clear Mom's mind and resurrect her coherent self.

"I need you to come now."

Mom's tone escalated until she nearly shouted, and Tessa chose a soft tone to calm her. "Sorry, I can't right now. Ellie's asleep." Of course, Tessa couldn't load her sleeping daughter and rush to Mom's side. With any luck, now that Mom aired her tirade, she'd relax for the night. By morning, she might remember the purpose of the boxes or, at least, forget why they bothered her. Tessa searched for the right words. "You need those boxes to hold all your nice ornaments and pictures."

"I don't know what you mean. This place is my home, and I'm not moving anywhere. I will wait by the door until you come and remove every one of these darn boxes." She banged down the phone.

A dull pain throbbed in Tessa's temples. In Mom's agitated state, she didn't care about the late hour or Ellie's rest. Day by day, dementia peeled away her judgment and self-control. Wide awake and vibrating with nerves, Tessa returned to the living room, flopped onto a cushy chair, and cradled her head. The confusion that swirled in Mom's brain must feel terrible. Never the most tolerant or understanding person, now she couldn't help her behavior. Conflict was never pleasant, but, surely, Tessa would find a way to manage Mom's fits. She'd done it all her life.

The newest participant in Leadership Camp was another story. She shivered. No doubt, he wouldn't hesitate to challenge her, but she'd figure him out and teach him things he needed to learn. She was an expert in her field, and he was a student like any other. So, why did excitement dance in her stomach every time he ventured near?

Chapter 8

Saturday morning, the sun shone bright, and a brisk wind whipped up dust and crisp leaves left from autumn. Yard work tempted, but Mark needed to deal with other priorities.

After a quick, early circuit of Wascana Lake, Mark arrived home, unzipped his windbreaker, and hung Rufus's leash on its hook. In the park, he had breathed chilly, refreshing air scented with damp earth. Seagulls swooped and cawed overhead, and Canada geese paddled below. Still, as he jogged, the implications of Leadership Camp distracted him from the scenery, and he failed to clear his mind of the impending experience. He'd far rather stick with engineering work.

"Do you want to visit Grandma this morning or afternoon?" Mark flung open the living room windows to rid the house of stuffiness. He tidied magazines and newspapers into a pile on the ottoman, straightened toss cushions, and ran a finger along the top of the TV.

"Um, neither." Sprawled on the sofa opposite the front window, Bree flipped a page of a book.

"I didn't list that option." Mark sighed. He loved his niece, but where had the agreeable little girl gone? Reclining in a rumpled T-shirt and cotton pajama pants, she didn't respond. Parents always moaned about the teen years, and apparently, he wasn't immune to the challenge.

Fortunately, when Bree met Nicole last evening, she clicked with her potential companion. He breathed easy he could leave Bree in the care of the poised university student. With studious glasses, blonde bob, and bright smile, Nicole definitely oozed confidence and responsibility. Sipping lemonade at the kitchen table, she had been in no hurry to leave.

"What kinds of books do you read?" She shifted to face Bree.

"Fantasies and mysteries." Bree glanced up and then at her glass.

"Me, too." Nicole grinned and nodded.

Eventually, Bree relaxed her tight expression. The situation could work. Mark sucked on an ice cube and listened.

"I hope you don't mind I'll have a lot of homework." Nicole peered at Bree and blinked.

"Nope, I don't mind. I have stuff to do, too." Bree gulped her drink. Her cautious smile revealed her top braces. Mark pushed back from the table and unloaded the dishwasher. Bree's reaction was better than he hoped. Maybe he could leave with peace of mind.

Rufus plodded from a spot near the back door into the room.

"Oh, I love dogs. He's so cute." When she finished the last swallow, Nicole dove and encircled him in a hug.

The dog thumped his tail and nuzzled right back.

Nicole's affection for Rufus sealed the deal. A rush of warmth pumped through Mark, and he wiped away a smile with the back of a hand. Leadership Camp would produce its share of stress, but at least, the caregiver situation had gone well.

Shaking his head, he focused back on Bree and the immediate challenge. He wouldn't think about the retreat for a few more days. Right now, he just needed to get Bree off the couch. He furrowed his brow and stood firm. "We always visit Grandma on Saturday. Your pick. Morning or afternoon?"

Bree dropped her book and scrunched her nose. "Afternoon, I guess."

He could live with her choice, so he did chores for the rest of the morning. After lunch, he drove to the care home and followed Bree inside. In the lobby, he sidestepped a pile of flattened boxes, probably ready to recycle. A new resident must have moved in. Even though Mom suffered from dementia and her conversation was repetitive, she still enjoyed social contact, so she'd soon make a new friend.

Bree zoomed ahead and tapped on Grandma's door. "Guess who."

Sauntering behind, he breathed a mix of pine cleaner and chicken noodle soup, still wafting from the dining room. The meals were decent here, but he could do without the lingering reminders of the residents' last meal.

Mom opened the door and grinned. "Breezy and Champ...my two favorite people."

Mark half-smiled at his childhood nickname. Dad christened him Champ as a reminder to hide his troubles and act like a winner, no matter what happened.

"I haven't seen you in ages. Let's go have coffee," said Mom.

She was well groomed, as usual, with smooth, gray hair tucked behind her ears. "I visited you just a few days ago, Mom. I left the magazine." He pointed to a table in the corner.

She paused, furrowed her brow, and frowned. "Are you sure you paid me a call and not some other old gal?" She giggled and swept him into a hug. "I missed you. And my goodness, Breezy...you're so grown up. I bet you're old enough to chase boys."

Bree's expression flickered between a smile and a frown. Mark suppressed a chuckle. Mom's dementia was no laughing matter, but sometimes, it caused some mildly-humorous situations.

"Let's go for coffee." Mom waved in the direction of the lounge.

Shrugging, he didn't resist. He reminded her every week he and Bree didn't drink coffee, but she always proposed her favorite beverage. "Sure, Mom." He winked at Bree. He understood why the visit drew on her patience. He could relate. Beside Mom and Bree, he sauntered down a hallway to a spacious area where soft music played and sunshine flooded the pastel décor.

Bree led them to a table and helped select beverages from the snack station. Then she slumped in a chair and slurped pop.

"Tell Grandma Rose about your science mark." Mark leaned forward and tapped the arm of Bree's chair. The information wouldn't stick, but it might give Mom something different to think about. In her better days, she was interested in every detail of his life. If she was her old self, before dementia robbed her attention span and memory, she would dote on every word her granddaughter said.

"I got ninety-eight percent." Over the rim of the glass, Bree rolled her eyes.

"Very nice, dear." Mom scanned the room. "Who's that woman?" She widened her eyes and pointed.

Bree glanced over her shoulder. "I don't know. Probably another lady who lives here." Then she tugged Mark's sleeve. "Hey, isn't she the lady we helped in the storm?"

"You're right, but I bet she doesn't remember us. She must be a new resident. I noticed a pile of empty boxes near the front door." He was about to suggest Mom could meet the woman later, but he didn't have a chance.

"Well, I'd better go and say hello." She set down her coffee mug, and leaving Mark and Bree alone at the table, she crossed the room.

"I told you I didn't need to come." Bree downed the last few drops of cola.

"We won't stay long." Mark didn't blame her for feeling a bit exasperated. Mom's condition wasn't easy to take and demanded plenty of understanding. An ache in his chest twinged.

After several minutes, Mom dragged over her new friend. "Breezy and Champ, when did you arrive? I told Adele she should come and join me at my table for coffee, and here you are, too."

Adele hesitated and set down a half full mug.

Mark stuck out a hand. "Hello, I'm Rose's son, Mark. This girl is my niece, Bree. I think we met. You got caught with your daughter's dog in the rain." Just what he needed. With Adele living here now, at some point he'd probably encounter Tessa.

Adele clasped his hand, peered at his face, and shook her head. "No, you must have me confused with someone else." She slipped into a chair. "My daughters left me here, but I'm sure they'll come and take me home soon."

"Oh." He didn't know what else to say. How could he explain to a woman with dementia this place was her new home? At least, he presumed she was the newest resident. He glanced at Bree, studying the ice in the bottom of her glass. "Very nice to meet you, Adele. We'll excuse ourselves and let you ladies get better acquainted."

"Give me a kiss." Mom tipped up her face.

Mark bent, kissed her cheek, and touched Bree's arm to encourage her to do the same. "Bye, Mom. Bye, Adele. See you soon."

"Oh, you won't see me soon." Adele clunked her coffee mug on the table, and the brown liquid sloshed over the edge. "I won't be here the next time. My daughters will take me home."

Mark raised a hand in a slight wave and followed Bree to the door. Things could be worse. Rose might not engage in normal conversation or remember where she hid things, but at least, she recognized home.

"Do you think Grandma and her new friend will remember each other tomorrow?" Bree furrowed her forehead.

"Good question." He couldn't predict how his mother's illness would progress. He'd just bear the pain. The pressure in his core intensified, reminding him of everything he wanted to forget.

When Mark arrived home, he checked work emails, and one message jumped out.

Mark, I look forward to our time at Leadership Camp. The experience will change your life—if you let it. I challenge you to open your mind, embrace the learnings, and practice new behaviors. Get ready for fun, too. See you there, Tessa

His pulse jumped. Her vivid, green eyes must have stared at the screen, and she might have flashed a broad, white smile as she keyed. He couldn't tell if the note was personalized or a group message with individual, participant names inserted. One thing was sure, she dedicated extra hours to her job, sending out work correspondence on the weekend. He reread it and then hit Delete. He'd give the class his best shot, but nobody said he had to like it. If he didn't, how would he feel about the instructor?

****

Leaving Ellie in Owen's care, Tessa strode with Julie and Ginger to Wascana Park. After the morning with Mom, she needed to burn off a little steam and enjoy the serenity of nature. She also needed to regroup for the tough week ahead. "How are you?" Striding briskly and gripping the leash, Tessa swung her free arm and inhaled deep breaths of the mild air. The scent of damp earth and new growth teased her nose and hinted of the warmth and foliage to come.

"Drained." Julie stared out across the water. "How are you?"

"Relieved." Tessa's eyes welled, and her throat ached. Moving their mom to a care home was not easy, but they had no choice. "Mom doesn't know yet what hit her. Who knows if she'll ever understand?"

"We can only hope she'll soon make a new friend to help her feel more settled." Julie quickened her pace. "Lucky you get to take a break for a few days."

"These days, a business trip feels almost like a vacation. I can't thank you enough for taking care of

Ellie and Ginger. And Mom, too. I'll visit her Monday evening before I leave."

"Thanks. We're in this turmoil together, for better or worse." Julie patted Tessa's back.

"You make us sound like a married couple." Tessa laughed and drank in the view. "Believe me, you're the only partner I need. You're the one person I can always count on."

Next to Julie, Tessa circled in front of the imposing Legislative Building where rows of flowerbeds were still just dirt awaiting a planting crew. In a few weeks, the black patches would bloom bright with a multi-colored array of flowers, attracting locals and tourists for evening strolls. The promise of spring, with a prairie summer soon to follow, instilled hope in everyone.

"While you're away, don't worry about a thing." Julie brushed Tessa's arm.

A wave of guilt struck Tessa at her readiness to leave Julie to contend with Mom and Ellie. "What can I ever do to repay you?"

"Let's see. Flowers, wine, chocolate...I like them all." Julie laughed and poked Tessa's shoulder. "Just kidding. I'm happy to help. But next time I entice Owen on a date, I might call in a favor."

"It's a deal." Gratitude filled Tessa until she almost ached. Julie's company brightened the day and eased her load.

Monday evening, Tessa left work and picked up Ellie a bit early, so she could visit Mom before dinner. At Heritage Haven, she found her relaxing in the lounge beside another woman. She squinted at the pair perched on a loveseat like a mismatched pair of bookends. Adorned with a mass of wiry, orange curls, Mom wore a pink-flowered blouse that didn't quite match her red, gauzy skirt. Her companion complemented a sleek, silvery hairstyle with a tailored, black-and-white pant suit.

"Hi, Grandma. Surprise, I'm here." Ellie bounced across the room, batted her eyelashes, and swung her ponytail.

"Well, if it isn't my Chinese granddaughter." She hugged Ellie until she wriggled free. Twisting toward her friend, she waggled a finger. "My daughter adopted her. This little girl needs a father."

"Hi, Mom." Tessa ignored the comments. Nothing she said convinced Mom otherwise. "Hello, I'm Adele's daughter, Tessa." She reminded the woman who she was and extended a hand.

"Hello, dear, I'm Rose. Who is this little sweetie?" She wiggled fingers at Ellie.

"Her name is Ellie." Tessa ran a hand over her shiny hair. She smiled at the pair. "Did you have a good day, Mom?" She scanned the serene surroundings. Sage carpet and floral upholstery muffled footsteps and conversations.

"I always enjoy a nice hotel, so I found the day pleasant enough." She crossed her legs and swiveled toward Rose. "How long will you stay?"

Tessa blinked and swallowed the urge to fix the situation. Could she even begin to explain? She glanced at her mom's bright expression. She'd leave well enough alone. Mom believed she was on vacation and had no idea she was settled in a new home, but she was content for now, which was the main goal.

Rose paused and tilted her head. "I don't really know. But I enjoy the place, so I don't plan to rush away." She patted Adele's hand. "You stay, too."

"Well, I guess I could." Adele shrugged and pursed her lips.

"Where is the little girl's daddy?" Rose pointed at Ellie.

"Her birth parents live in China." Surely, Rose would drop the subject after a simple explanation.

"I live with my mommy but not a daddy." Ellie jiggled in place.

She delivered the simple, matter-of-fact response Tessa taught and skipped across the room to flop down with a stuffed toy from a basket in a corner.

"Oh, the poor dear." Rose frowned. "Where's her daddy?"

"I raise Ellie on my own." Tessa smiled and racked her brain for a new topic. Sometimes, the absence of a father for her daughter pinched on the surface, but right now it stung deep inside. Single parenting was not easy, but she coped, and most of the time, Ellie didn't know what she missed. "What did you ladies do today?" Tessa clasped her hands.

"You need a husband, dear." Rose tutted her tongue and shook her head. "You should meet my son, Champ. He's very handsome and very polite. He would make a lovely father for your daughter."

"She has a point, Tessa." Mom nodded.

"I appreciate the offer, Rose, and I'm sure your son is a charming man. But I'll tell you a little secret." She lowered her voice. "I don't need a husband, and Ellie is just fine without a dad. I'm quite capable of handling everything on my own." Still, she'd underestimated the magnitude of the task. Parenthood demanded endless love, patience, and energy. More than once, she cried over the loss of her ordered life.

She dragged over a chair and sat across from the women. Why did she bother to explain her situation to a woman she just met and wouldn't remember a thing she said? She sighed and slid her gaze to Ellie, playing out of earshot.

"Now, where is the little girl's daddy? He must be Chinese." Rose pointed at Ellie.

Tessa pretended not to hear the question. "I need to travel for work, Mom. I won't see you for a few days, but Julie will visit, so you'll have company."

"Rose keeps me company, but okay. Where will you go?"

"Away on a business trip." Tessa took a deep breath, and a murky mix of sorrow and peace rose in her chest. Despite Mom's obvious mental decline and confusion, she still conversed easily and stayed physically strong. Unaware of her losses, she found contentment for today, anyway.

"Come and say goodbye to Grandma. We'll go home for dinner." Tessa motioned toward Ellie. The savory scent drifting into the lounge suggested Mom's meal would soon be served, too.

Ellie squiggled into a hug and then backed away.

"Goodbye, Mom. Goodbye, Rose. I enjoyed meeting you." Tessa guided Ellie toward the hallway. The conversation floating between Mom and Rose followed them, and she clasped Ellie's hand, squeezed, and accelerated.

"Where is the little girl's daddy? Her mom needs a husband. She should meet my son, Champ," said Rose.

"I agree," said Mom.

Tessa rolled her eyes and sighed. Already, she

juggled a full load. Despite pressure from her mom, Tessa long ago decided a man would only complicate everything. Dating a guy named Champ was not in her plans, now or ever.

Chapter 9

Tuesday morning, Mark rose earlier than usual and exercised Rufus along the open space behind the art gallery in Wascana Park. Greening grass stretched like a carpet for blocks, and sparrows flitted and chirped in bushes. Back home, he dashed into the house just long enough to grab his suitcase and say goodbye to Nicole, already on duty as Bree's temporary nanny.

Last night, he had said goodbye to Bree in case he departed before she woke for school. Leadership Camp beckoned.

"See you later, Uncle Mark. Make the most of the opportunity." Bree consented to a half hug.

His heart panged. His sister would be so proud. Bree sounded older than her years, and her words echoed advice he had delivered somewhere along the line.

Now, driving east from Regina toward the nearby Qu'Appelle Valley, he yearned to curve in another direction. He headed to spend four days at a camp on the shores of Katepwa Lake. The setting was picturesque and far more pleasant than the purpose of the trip. While he could commute for an hour every morning and evening, he wasn't allowed.

He tightened his grip on the steering wheel and absorbed the hard, cool texture. Tessa insisted all the participants stay together, well removed from work and family distractions. She might dictate the agenda but not his attitude.

He scanned the wide road and open fields to the horizon. The soil rested black and ready to nourish the wheat and canola crops that would soon sprout green, before transforming to rich golds and yellows later in the season. The cycle of life continued. He stayed alert for deer leaping across his path. No doubt, the peaceful drive was the best part of the day.

Tessa's note said she looked forward to time together. He would connect with the group over the next several days, and the intense interaction was exactly what disturbed him. She'd pry and prod him to share his feelings, and already he stretched way beyond his comfort zone. Clenching his jaw, he peered ahead and steered around a bend in the road. He didn't care to share personal details with anyone, let alone coworkers he barely knew.

Mark's dad taught him well. By example, he demonstrated how to shield himself from pain and criticism by wearing an invisible vest that kept threats out and emotions in. He insisted that big boys don't cry.

Mark never forgot the firm expectation, and he squirmed, remembering how much he struggled at age seventeen to contain his grief over the death of his adored dad. If he knew CPR then, maybe his dad would still be alive. Teenage Mark bit the inside of his cheeks and didn't cry, except a little in the shower where no one could hear.

Leaning forward, he blasted the radio to catch the morning news and distract himself from morbid images.

"A serious car accident on Regina's Ring Road last evening sent two local people to hospital with critical injuries." He punched the Off button. Staring at the road, he blocked the horrific scene that roared back, in contrast with the sunny morning. Ten years after Dad's death, he lost the next-most-important person in his life. He never stopped missing his sister or hating the drunk driver who smashed his brother-in-law's vehicle.

Shaking his head, he breathed deeply until the pressure that radiated to his throat and temples subsided. Just in time, he spied the turnoff sign. He was almost there. His thorny past secured inside, he faced a troubling future that loomed all too soon.

Behind a couple of other cars, he slowed into the parking lot. He selected a spot away from the laughing, chatting carpoolers who jumped out of other cars. Obviously, unlike him, they were excited to start their demanding leadership class. He didn't consider sharing transportation with anyone because he didn't need the company of strangers. Raising a hand in a brief wave, he strode into the retreat center. He'd settle in and unload his suitcase later.

Mark paused just inside the door to get his bearings, and warm air swirled with the musty scent of an old building mixed with strong coffee and sweet cinnamon. A ring of wooden chairs filled the center of the room, and worn, burgundy sofas and faded, lumpy chairs framed the perimeter in casual groupings. Near the entrance, Tessa acted as morning greeter, dressed casually in khaki pants and olive jacket.

"Good morning, Mark. Welcome to your home away from home." She smiled and stuck out a hand.

She wore her hair tied back, containing all but a few wayward curls, and energy radiated from her entire being. "Good morning." He returned the handshake, and warmth spread up his arm and threatened to flush his face. He needed to get an immediate grip on his rogue emotions. Why did she cause such a dramatic reaction? He hardly recognized himself.

"Help yourself to coffee and a cinnamon bun, and we'll start in a few minutes." Tessa swept a hand toward the refreshment table.

"I don't drink cof..." He shook his head and didn't bother to finish his explanation.

She scooted away to greet others.

Left alone, he strolled to the refreshment table and filled an insulated water bottle, selected a bran muffin, and savored the sweet tastes of molasses, sugar, and raisins. "Hey, Samir." He greeted a peer he met last year on a project and downed the rest of his morning snack.

"I was so pumped about this course I hardly slept last night." Samir bent an arm and raised a fist.

"Yeah, lots of people would give anything to participate." Always true to his word, Mark found something positive to say without suggesting he shared Samir's just-won-the-lottery enthusiasm. He rubbed a temple. If he relaxed his tight shoulders, maybe the tension squeezing up to his brain would ease. He shifted and glanced around.

Out of the milling group, Holly from the Marketing Department joined them to form a triangle. She peered over the rim of the coffee mug. "Isn't this a fun experience?"

He nodded. "Interesting, anyway." Fun was the farthest thing from his mind, but he couldn't burst Holly's bubble. Her dark eyes and rich complexion radiated excitement he could never match. He would force himself to meet Tessa's standards but only because the bosses insisted.

"Please, take a seat, everyone," Tessa called and raised a hand.

Her voice rose above the anticipatory buzz in the room, and Mark's mouth dried. The formal part of the program was about to begin, whether he was ready or not.

"Refill your coffee and join the circle." She pointed to a ring of chairs in the center.

Mark chose a seat between Samir and a guy he didn't know, set down his water bottle on the floor, and waited for instructions. He took a deep breath and scanned the other twelve participants. They all vibrated energy and were more animated and eager than he imagined possible. Clearly, he was the thirteenth participant and the odd man out.

Tessa positioned herself in the center of the circle and waited until conversation dwindled to a murmur and then complete silence. She scanned the group and made brief eye contact with each participant.

Her face shone light pink, the color of a prairie sunset. Unblinking, Mark caught the fierce glint in her emerald eyes. Ready to analyze her opening remarks, he propped hands on his thighs to brace himself for a challenge. The muscles underneath his palms hardened into stone.

"Welcome to Leadership Camp. I'm very excited about the adventure we embarked on. First, I'll explain ground rules, and then we'll start our first exercise." Tessa flipped up her hands and smiled. "I expect full participation, and please, switch off your phones." She rotated and pointed. "Some of the experiences might feel awkward or uncomfortable, but leaders work through every challenge."

He clicked off his phone. Did he imagine the pause, or when she glanced his way, did she hesitate for a split second? She enunciated each word with an energetic lilt and almost spun him into her colorful web. Her constant motion grabbed his attention. Still, he held back and gulped water.

"I expect everyone to stay here together to interact. Just because the formal sessions end, do not run off to your rooms. Stay in the lounge area, play games, socialize, and use the opportunity to learn more about each other. Leaders build and nurture their networks." Tessa spread wide her arms.

At no time did she mention leaders perform to high standards or provide in-depth, technical expertise to their teams and peers. A slow burn smoldered in his chest. His best qualities didn't make the list of opening pointers. Everything she stressed involved connections with people. But what good were they when people just slipped away from your life? Liz's impending departure was a far cry from losing a beloved family member, but her absence would be a loss just the same.

"Now, time for introductions. Please, share your name, your role, who you are outside of work, and a fun fact. I'll give you an example." She clapped her hands into a clasp. "You know my work role. I'm also the mom of a four-year-old daughter. And...let's see...as a teenager, I won first place in a provincial figure-skating championship, and I can still land a double toe-loop."

"Ooh, impressive."

Mark couldn't identify who commented first, but a murmur and mild applause rippled around the circle.

She swooped in an exaggerated bow. "Okay, your turn. Who's next?"

He studied the floorboards and racked his brain for a suitable fact to share. His pulse rushed in his ears. A long and trying week confronted him. Tessa meant well, but how would he endure her over-the-top energy and strict demands?

****

Tessa couldn't miss the message Mark shouted through his stiff body language. He wanted to speak last. She let him off the hook this time, but soon, she'd demand more. To increase his success, he needed to break out of his shell.

"Thanks for volunteering, Samir." She swung a hand toward the accountant seated next to Mark. "You start and pass the baton counter clockwise." She spun to demonstrate the direction and sensed a subtle relaxing of Mark's jutting jaw. He must realize she orchestrated the exercise to give him last spot.

The group were good sports and contributed an eclectic mix of family information and little-known skills—everything from singing and playing guitar, to sports and performing magic. Frequent laughter and good-natured teasing filled the room and set a relaxed tone, exactly what she hoped to achieve with the opening exercise.

"We could hold a full-scale talent night with all the musicians in our midst. Last, but not least…let's hear from Mark." Tessa smiled and pointed.

He cleared his throat. "Mark Delaney. My day job is Director of Engineering Services. I'm legal guardian of my thirteen-year-old niece." He paused and glanced left and right. "So if anyone has any tips on dealing with teenage girls, let me know." At the sound of chuckles, he hinted at a smile.

Still, his stiff back and shoulders left no doubt he disliked the opening exercise.

"For my fun fact, keep in mind I'm an engineer and specialize in math. I can multiply triple digit numbers in my head." He leaned back and lowered his gaze to the floor.

"Wow, a human calculator. Maybe we'll test you later." Tessa laughed along with the rest of the group. He'd shown a glimmer of humor which was an encouraging sign. The next challenge might prove a little tougher.

"Now, please pair up and discuss a topic with a partner. Talk about a leadership highlight and low point you experienced and what you learned. Then I'll ask you to return to the center and share thoughts." She scanned smiles and nods, confirming the group was ready to delve deeper. Everyone, except Mark.

Frowning, he shook his head and jerked from his seat.

"Since we have an odd number of people, I'll partner with someone." She gazed across the circle to the tough participant. "Mark, you and I can pair up this time." Her heart quickened. Somehow, he grew more handsome every time she ventured near. His blue jeans and denim shirt, rolled to just below his elbows, showed off his muscular and fit masculinity.

The group settled with partners, and the murmur of conversation escalated.

She poured coffee at the refreshment station, rearranged a chair, and sat opposite Mark. "How are you?" She scanned his tense posture and searched for a way to set him at ease. If he would just relax, he would find the whole experience so much easier.

"Making the best of the situation." He rubbed his chin, gulped water, and set the bottle on the floor next to the chair.

"I'll win you over." She flashed her most engaging smile and flushed. Sure, she persisted, but her intent was purely business. Or was it? She only needed to convince him of the value of the course, but why did she want him to like her, too?

He raised one eyebrow and half smiled with tight lips. "I appreciate a challenge, too, so I'll see where this experience leads me."

A flutter unsettled her stomach, and she sipped coffee, sending warmth to calm her from the inside out. Was his tension contagious, or did something else unsettle her? She was the one in charge here, and she wouldn't let his arresting appearance and cool attitude interfere with the goal at hand. "Let's get started. Tell me about a personal leadership highlight." She tilted her head and focused. If necessary, she would also coach.

"I completed a resort project ahead of schedule and under budget." He tapped a fist on a thigh.

The motion was a muffled drumbeat emphasizing his intensity. "Impressive accomplishment. What role did you play?" She clasped her mug and steered the topic to the people side of the work.

"I was the project coordinator which meant I made sure everyone understood their assignments and delivered." He raised both hands and thrust up his palms.

Tessa nodded and waited for him to continue but

struggled to maintain steady eye contact. She stared at the carpet and bit the tip of her pen. His tone suggested the answer should be obvious, and she bristled but didn't let her irritation show. "How did you engage the team?"

"What do you mean? I gave detailed instructions, and people followed them. Pretty simple." He slid back. "What are you getting at? I didn't hold their hands or follow them around and pat their backs. They were all adults and understood their roles."

Through inky eyes, he flashed defiance, and she was tempted to persist but paused. Remaining in control meant choosing her battles, and she didn't need an outward clash this early in the program. "What did you learn from the experience?" She again tested a winning smile.

Arms crossed, he stared across the room and flipped back his gaze. "Honestly, not much. Everyone focused on the deadline and budget. I contributed what I always do—expect and deliver results."

She swallowed. He deserved his reputation as a star achiever with prickles where a softer coat should lay. The situation was clear—he defended his position and blocked new ideas. Well, at least she wasn't afraid of a test. The hum of multiple conversations bounced off the walls. No one else was finished with discussion, so she signaled to continue.

"Next question." Mark ran a hand through his hair.

She made eye contact, swallowed, and refused to allow him to intimidate her. His unblinking eyes stared as threatening as a stormy sky. "Talk about a leadership low point and what you learned from the experience." Suddenly, she needed to escape and cool her warm face. She rose and raised a palm, signaling he should remain. "While I circulate and pour a glass of water, I'll let you think for a moment." She scurried away.

He left his spot and strode to a window.

She wasn't concerned. Maybe the scenery would calm him enough to continue the discussion. After checking on the others, spread in pairs throughout the room, she joined him and drank in the rolling terrain and sprouting leaves. The peaceful and therapeutic setting was the reason she chose this location.

Flicking its tail, a chubby squirrel scooted across the pathway and climbed a tree.

Planted at the glass, Mark's attention floated away, far from the beautiful nature that surrounded them. He probably concentrated on a gripping topic like a pipeline dimension and, in keeping with his fun fact, calculated details in his head. "Time to get back to work." She waited and then cleared her throat, but her broad hint didn't speed his response.

He stared out the window, rotated, and sauntered back to his place.

"Well, give me your example." Seated opposite him, she encouraged a response. No other student resisted assignments the way he did. Did his approach demonstrate arrogance or determination? Either way, he disrupted the flow.

"I don't dwell on lows." He flipped his gaze to the window.

Pulse jumping, she clasped her hands and squeezed hard against his pushback and her own frustration. "Describe a time when things didn't go as planned, or you appeased an unhappy team. With people issues, we all experience tough moments." Surely, he didn't think he was above typical challenges.

"Nothing jumps to mind other than the recent news I won't get an immediate appointment to head the Engineering Division." He picked up his bottle, swished the remaining water, and stared at the motion.

He didn't exactly answer the question she posed, but at least, he volunteered something. "When you reflected on the president's decision, what did you learn?" She fixed her gaze and waited.

"He wants proof I can handle the top job." He shrugged.

"What skills need the most work?" She crossed her legs. A shadow crossed his face. He wasn't pleased with the decision or the directive to improve.

"I believe in my ability. But I need to convince Don I can lead a team." He rubbed a temple.

He refused to acknowledge his deficiencies. "What do you most want to learn?"

"I didn't ask for this opportunity." He scowled and furrowed his forehead. "Excellent quality work should speak for itself. I want to convince you and others I can be true to myself and still build success." He angled back and the chair creaked.

Warmth brushed Tessa's cheeks. How could she explain he needed to open up and show more empathy? A strong leader demonstrated to others he was human and cared about them as people and not just workers. Clearly, she hit an impasse on the assignment. He must feel more emotion inside than his composed demeanor conveyed, and she would find a way to unlock his inner vault. Now, she better check with the rest of the group and stick to the agenda.

"I can't tell you what goals to set, but I suggest you

think further about what you want to achieve through the class. Leadership needs followers. If you don't treat people right, they won't follow." She raised both hands, flipped over her palms, and shook her head.

He glowered and shifted in his chair.

Even a sour expression didn't mar his handsome features. With so much to teach, she shouldn't notice his good looks. She should focus on his progress in class and nothing else. The unsettling combination of his attitude and appearance complicated everything. A jumpy sensation flickered through her stomach. Why did he toy with her feelings this way? "Tell you what. We'll revisit the topic later. First, I'll call back the group and debrief." Flushing, she jerked out of the chair and left him behind.

Plastering a smile she didn't feel, she instructed everyone to join the circle. The sound of chairs rubbing along the worn wood floor signaled their cooperation. "Please, explain what you discovered in your conversations. We learn a lot from each other." She scanned for reactions.

When she landed on Mark, she paused to encourage him to make eye contact. Avoiding the invitation, he hunched and stared past her out the windows and didn't even pretend to be fully engaged. "Mark, I need a helper. Please, capture the key ideas on the whiteboard." She threw an extra-large smile in his direction.

He hesitated and then sauntered to the whiteboard. "Sure, but I can't guarantee anyone will decipher my writing." He picked up a marker and flipped it in the air.

"Thank you." She never met anyone she couldn't

grow personally and professionally. Clasping her hands, she inhaled a calming breath. Hard as he might resist, he could not derail her objectives or tarnish her successful record. She'd teach him a thing or two. Still, he already demonstrated he wasn't the average participant. Would he react the way she hoped? How could she remain objective when she practically melted in his presence?

Chapter 10

After lunch, waiting for the afternoon session to begin, Mark popped outside for a breath of fresh air to blow away the tension that bombarded every muscle in his body. Returning, he surveyed the room. The scent of chicken fingers and fries lingered from a satisfying noon meal, and clusters of classmates framed the space.

Much as he wanted to ignore Tessa the whirlwind, he couldn't. Flitting around the room, her toned body drew his attention like a magnet. Her animated gestures and expressions jolted him into high alert. Earlier, just to refocus, he drank in the wide, blue sky outside the window.

This morning, she irritated him. She dared choose him as her partner and then narrowed her eyes at his views. Mark also didn't appreciate her enlisting his help with the mundane task of recording the group's insights. He wasn't anybody's administrative assistant. How would he survive the next three days?

Tessa smoothly circulated, talked, and laughed with participants. She tossed her head and, when the motion didn't work, brushed a stray springy curl off her cheek.

He muffled a chuckle at the mild aggravation her hair caused. The way she ran the class, obviously she took command of everything.

"Let's start." She clapped three times. "Please, take

your seats." She paused. "This afternoon, you'll review feedback from your boss, peers, and team members. Then based on everything you've learned, you'll set formal learning goals."

Mark could handle the afternoon's plans. The feedback might confirm he didn't need to change as much as she predicted, and setting goals was his forte. He adjusted his shoulders and straightened.

"But first..." She grinned and paused.

At the word *but*, he stiffened. What now? Her impish expression signaled trouble.

"First, we'll do a short exercise to warm up." Tessa rolled to her toes. She scanned the group and swung forward her arms.

Afternoon sun sneaked in the windows and lit her green eyes. Of course, she'd hit him with an activity he'd rather avoid. Her enthusiasm might excite his classmates but not him. He huffed a breath and contained an eye roll. *Exercise* was the corporate term for silly learning activity. He heard rumors of the games participants played in these sessions, and he had better things to do with his time.

Numbering off the participants, she formed two groups of four and one of five. "Take turns, blindfold someone and, using words only, guide him or her through a chair maze."

Obviously, the objective of the exercise was to show the way clear instructions and specific feedback determined success or failure. Pretty elementary. Still, he forced himself to clap, cheer, and shout guidance and encouragement, and his team finished first. He joined in the excessive high-fives and then grabbed a seat. Even though the experience wasn't exactly rocket science, it woke him for the afternoon and prompted a laugh or two.

Waiting for his turn to meet with Tessa, Mark read a few handouts and outlined goals and action plans. At her waving signal, he joined her at a round table and steeled his core where feelings hid. "What's the bottom line?" No sense beating around the bush. "What did people say?"

"I always deliver honest feedback, but I sprinkle in diplomacy to help the recipient understand and accept it better." She smiled and laid the report on the table.

Shifting his gaze between Tessa and the stapled stack of paper with his name at the top, he breathed her subtle, fresh scent, as delicious as a summer day. He caught his breath and released it in a rush but couldn't relax his tight jaw. Her reference to the importance of diplomacy inferred he should work on the same approach.

"First, I'll give you an overview, and then I'll explain the details." She scraped away her chair and fixed her gaze on his eyes. "Basically, the information confirms what Liz and the president told you. People see you as a skilled technical expert."

He nodded, and a hint of pride flowed up his spine. His talents were well recognized. He sat straighter.

"At the same time, people see you as somewhat distant from others. While they respect you, they don't necessarily feel comfortable in your presence." She pursed her lips. "Should I continue?"

He nodded. No surprise, the comments echoed Liz's feedback, both positive and critical. "My skin is thick. Nothing surprises me." He didn't strive for popularity, but the hard fact that people would rather avoid him squashed the air from his lungs. He inhaled a deep breath of stale, warm air.

"Is it *thick* skin or a full suit of armor?" She raised her eyebrows. "Your comment summarizes the feedback. You don't let people past the surface, so they can't read you and aren't sure they matter."

Tension grabbed his throat, and he cleared it. He flipped pages, jammed an index finger onto a chart, and leaned back. "People are too sensitive." Others weren't schooled by a strong father on how to stay tough and keep messy feelings out of sight.

"Feedback is a gift. If you choose to listen, you'll learn to build on your strengths and minimize your weaknesses." She spread flat her palms on the table. "You get to choose what you do with the information. How do you feel?"

"Slightly annoyed." He adjusted the chair. Murmuring voices swirled, and he wanted to swat them away like a bug. "I never trot out my so-called weaknesses for all the world to see. I prefer to focus on the positives. Leaders seek solutions."

"Exactly. Effective leaders grow possibilities into accomplishments." She leaned elbows on the table and propped her chin on clasped hands. "But leaders don't just focus on the hard-core projects. They improve themselves and inspire others." She examined his expression.

Whipping over the report pages, he scanned the comments. Indignation filled his middle and climbed to his temples. He breathed, but the pressure in his head only intensified. He'd better escape before he said or did something rash. "I need fresh air." Slapping shut the booklet, he shoved it away and jumped to his feet.

"Go ahead." She scraped back her chair. "If you promise to reflect on what you just read, you can leave." She tapped a forefinger on the wooden surface. "Be back here in thirty minutes for your next assignment."

He locked his jaw and narrowed his eyes. Tessa demonstrated some nerve to order him around. "Whatever you say, boss." He saluted.

She widened her eyes and dropped her jaw.

Instantly, he regretted his impulsive action. He intended to keep his tone light and camouflage his extreme irritation, but his retort burst out more belligerent than teasing. Pressure mounted like rocks in his chest. Apology catching in his throat, he bolted to the door. He didn't back down, but neither did the demanding instructor. Would the growing tension build to a breaking point?

****

The next day, Tessa delivered strict instructions for another small-group assignment and paused to catch her breath. She insisted on group progress. Brushing back a tendril of hair, she surveyed the trios and a foursome scattered around the room. As she strolled the perimeter and wove among tables, she noted questions and observations to share.

Yesterday, she assisted participants in decoding their feedback and gave them a framework to develop action plans for individual improvements. Twelve dove right into the exercise, and the thirteenth…well, he still hung back.

Participating in today's discussion, Mark clustered in a group of three. "Give me time to think of a good example."

The others probed further with good, open-ended questions.

He pursed his lips and remained silent for a full minute.

Tessa refilled a water bottle and monitored activity around the room. Mark hunched as if he waited for a dreaded dentist appointment. She hadn't yet converted him to a fresh leadership style, but she'd find a way. By now, he should know she didn't take *no comment* for an answer.

Yesterday, after he had burst out the door to digest—or escape—feedback, she paced and calmed her simmering frustration. Although his uncooperative behavior irritated her, he was entitled to understanding, and she couldn't overreact. Candid comments could be painful to accept, so she granted him a brief time to gather his composure. The other keener participants deserved her attention, so, at that moment, she ignored his resistance.

A few minutes later, cool air announced his return. He presented a calm demeanor and blank expression. If he was bothered by the feedback, he refused to show anyone. "Welcome back." Strolling closer, she brushed an upper arm. "Did you consider taking a dip?" She shivered. The water would still be far too cold for swimming.

"I needed fresh air but not a total shock to my system." He quirked an eyebrow and sauntered to the table where he abandoned his report. Breaking the quiet, he frowned and had rattled pages.

Tessa cut him some slack yesterday, but if impromptu breaks continued, she would intervene. Circling the room, she strolled through another snatch of conversation.

"I'll pass on the question." He shook his head and tapped fingertips on the group table.

She paused, narrowed her eyes, and wove toward the next group. She wouldn't embarrass him in front of others, but she made a mental note to remind him she expected full participation. She didn't mind if he listened more than he spoke. Introverts could be strong leaders, too.

Mark gravitated toward Samir in discussion groups and during breaks, so he wasn't a total loner within the group. She really hoped he'd fit in and absorb the teachings. New insights could transform him. Even if he wasn't convinced, his career and her reputation depended on success in the class.

"Hello, everyone." She held up a hand to grab the group's attention. "Come back to the circle and share your biggest developmental goal. By stating it aloud to your peers, you'll reinforce your commitment and increase your chances of achieving it." She motioned them toward the center of the room.

A hum of comments and laughter reverberated off the walls, and she savored the familiar satisfaction of a well-run agenda in action. Overall, the session flowed as planned with no major bumps.

"We'll start again this time with Samir and proceed clockwise." Sweeping her gaze for reactions, she paused on Mark, and a shadow crossed his face. No doubt, he wasn't pleased she placed him second in line to speak. She wasn't sure he'd selected his goal, but she'd soon find out.

"My goal is to share a stronger vision with my team." Planting hands on knees, Samir tipped forward.

"At times, I assume people know what to do, and then I'm surprised if they don't measure up."

"Excellent goal." Tessa flashed him a thumbs-up. "Next." She pointed at Mark.

"Can I pass?" He tensed his shoulders.

"I'll let you off the hook for now but not for long." Catching a few participants exchanging glances, she flushed. She expected him to go with the flow and not veer from her plan. She tapped a hand on the outside of a thigh and then pointed toward the next person.

"Time's up." After she listened to the others' goals, she returned to Mark and forced a smile. "We've all waited for this moment." She faked a drumroll in the air, but the second she teased him, she regretted it. She never intentionally, embarrassed anyone.

The lines along Mark's jaw tightened, and he lowered his gaze to the floor.

Rolling her lips inward, she waited and clasped her hands. Now she wanted to hug him with an apology, but her impulse was inappropriate and impossible.

"My goal is to continue to strive for excellence." He squeezed both fists and gave a single, firm nod.

"Thank you for sharing. Can you elaborate on how you'll motivate others?" Tessa strode across the room, and heaviness followed. She dragged every word and example from Mark's brain.

"I didn't mean the team. I'll challenge myself to produce excellent results." He shifted and straightened his back. "My work sets the standard. The higher the bar, the better everybody performs. Plain and simple."

How could she help him see true leadership demanded he develop others and not just his own skills? She rarely met anybody with so little self-awareness. His driven approach produced the exact opposite effect than he expected. This week, she'd make the best of a less-than-ideal situation, but she'd soon demand a change in his perspective. She'd never met a participant she couldn't win over. Surely, Mark wouldn't be the first.

****

On Friday afternoon, class wrapped for the week, and Mark stayed as long as he tolerated his classmates recounting highlights of the week. Outside the retreat center, he filled his lungs with mild, clean air. Squirrels rustled in the trees, and birds chirped above. The peaceful surroundings eased a little of the tension that rode in his back and shoulders.

He couldn't wait to escape and regroup. In the parking lot, he excused himself as soon as he could depart without appearing rushed and rude. Striding past Tessa, Samir, and a few others who chatted in a cluster, he raised a hand in a quick wave.

"Hey, want to join us for a drink at the new pub on the east side?" Holly smiled and motioned.

"Thanks, but not today. Time to deal with things on the home front." When he called Bree each evening, he discerned very little from the one- or two-word answers she shared. In person, he could better gauge her state of mind, although Rufus would probably show more enthusiasm at his arrival. The crazy dog never failed to brighten a day.

"See you Tuesday in Moose Jaw for week two." Tessa squinted and parted her lips into a broad smile.

"See you next week." Bright sunbeams lit her face and hair, but he snapped away his attention, shook his head, and slid into the car for the short ride back to

Regina. When he slammed the door on the week, sniffed the leather interior, and headed to the open road, he relaxed stiff muscles. He lowered the window and inhaled deep breaths of prairie air. Sun glinted off the hood of the car and into the front window, and he slipped on sunglasses. At the signs of approaching summer, a surge of optimism buoyed his spirits. For three whole days, he could act like himself without Tessa pestering him to change.

Along the way, he blared upbeat music to replenish the energy drained by the week's sessions. Constant discussions and probing for deeper meaning exhausted him. What mattered about how he felt? Why should he concoct long explanations of how past experiences influenced his current actions? How could Tessa expect him to share details about his personal challenges and weaknesses?

He squeezed and loosened his hands on the steering wheel. Why couldn't others allow him to trap his feelings safely inside where they belonged? Scanning the highway and ditches for wildlife, he continued toward Regina. The tires hummed on the smooth stretch of highway.

He passed a rusted vehicle, and the vivid color rivalled Tessa's shiny curls. With a jolt, he jumped his focus to the black road and blue sky. Right now, she was the last person who should fill his brain, but she made an impact. As instructor, she lived up to her reputation as someone who always demanded complete commitment from the group. She juggled numerous details and ran a tight ship.

His heart quickened. The combination of her full mouth and trim figure teased his senses. She wore her sandy freckles like the perfect accessory. If he had any room in his life for a companion and confidante, he might chase the teacher. But the idea was beyond impossible. His hands were full with supporting Bree and his mom, and he didn't need someone to fill his scarce free time and mess with his heart. Judging by the way she insisted he expose his inner self at work, in an actual relationship she would drive him crazy.

Steering around a curve, he slowed to let a flock of blackbirds clear. Even though he disliked her pointed questions, he admired her facilitation skills. If he wanted to explore and share his inner voice, he would appreciate her efforts to make the learning environment comfortable and confidential.

The trouble was he still didn't see the value of dredging up painful memories and linking them to success in his current role. He contained his issues very well and forged ahead, no matter what. Dad had taught him the best way to approach everything. One week down. Two to go. He whooshed out a breath, flushing the last remnants of the week's tension. A weekend away from nonstop leadership jargon and exhausting assignments would rejuvenate him for a fresh start on Tuesday.

The geometric silhouette of Regina's compact downtown appeared in the distance. Soon, he'd arrive home to Rufus's frenzied greeting and Bree's distant demeanor. Everything wasn't perfect, but warmth still filled him like sunshine in a park. Along with Mom, his niece and dog enriched and grounded his life. Strong family, combined with a demanding career, equaled busy and content. A guy didn't really need much more.

He rolled into the driveway, parked, and grinned at

Rufus, panting and wriggling at the window. He'd start the weekend with a brisk hike and dinner with Bree. Tomorrow, they'd visit Mom as usual. The evening stretched ahead with the prospect of some welcome quiet time. He swung open the front door and lunged to rub the dog's reddish-gold body. "Hi, Rufus-boy." Inside, he left behind the cooler outdoor air. A faint, not unpleasant smell of dog wafted and confirmed he was home. He'd air out the place later.

"Hi, Mark. Bree's in her room." Nicole greeted him at the door and straightened her glasses.

"How'd it go?" Mark set down his suitcase and surveyed the living room. Sunlight filtered in, and the sofa beckoned. After dinner, he'd relax in the neutral, restful surroundings.

"Ask Bree, but I think we had a pretty good time." She gathered a large backpack and shoved a laptop and papers inside. "She's a smart girl. Quiet, but nice. I'll just say goodbye and head out." She retreated down the hallway and returned a moment later. "See you next week."

Breathing a sigh, he shut the door behind Nicole. She clearly took the role in stride and didn't get concerned about his niece's reticence. Over a thick, gooey pizza, delivered from Mario's on Hill Avenue, Mark savored the quiet familiarity of home. "How was your week?" He extracted Bree's take on the days with Nicole. The spicy aroma of pepperoni hung over the kitchen table and enticed him to eat more.

"Nicole's okay. Actually, I like her. She's cool. She convinced me to enter my name for the grad committee. She said I don't have to be the most popular kid to win."

He leaned forward and flashed a thumbs-up. "Hey, I'm not the most popular guy, either." He grimaced. "You don't need to be everybody's favorite person to do well."

"I guess not." She chewed on a large, cheesy bite.

"I'm proud of you, Breezy." He patted her hand, and a realization jolted him. The way he praised her was exactly what Tessa expected for his colleagues. But coworkers shouldn't need the same encouragement as a teenage girl.

All things considered, she had adjusted pretty well in the past seven years since she'd moved in, and he'd taken over as surrogate dad. Right now, she missed her best friend who moved to Calgary, but she never pined for her parents. He showed her how to plow past anything.

"I didn't get picked yet." Half smiling, she jutted her chin. Sliding away her hand, she lifted a slice of pizza and studied it. "The vote's next week."

"I'm proud you'll try something new, even if it's hard." He pumped a fist. Funny how often he offered encouragement at home but held back at the office. "You're strong." He hated to desert her next week, but he'd call as often as he could. If the kids elected her to the committee, maybe she'd make a new friend. "Remember what Grandpa taught. No matter what happens, you'll handle it like a…"

"Champ." Smirking, Bree finished his sentence. "I know. You already told me." She tilted her head and grinned. "That's why Grandma calls you Champ."

"Yup." He chomped a mouthful of pizza and forced it past the ache in his throat. He worked hard and did his best to be a good substitute parent. He liked to think his dad and sister approved, but he'd never know for sure.

Later that evening, he settled on the living room sofa and rubbed Rufus's velvety sides. The dog's coat matched Tessa's coppery curls. Stiffening, he shot to his feet and paced until he banished the alluring image. He had no choice but to interact with her at Leadership Camp, but he would not allow her to invade his free time and spark his feelings. No way.

Hustling to the kitchen, he popped a huge bowl of popcorn and doused it with melted butter. A treat might take his mind off everything. The savory scent followed him down the hallway to Bree's room, and he tapped on the door. "If you want a bedtime snack, come and help yourself."

"Be right there," Bree called.

Back on the sofa with Rufus's head on his lap, he munched a mouthful of salty popcorn and exercised his tight jaw. Three days of relief from the class and Tessa stretched ahead. He shouldn't wonder or care one bit, but a single question burned. What did she like to do on weekends?

Chapter 11

Tuesday morning, Tessa waited for participants to gather at the Prairie Spa in Moose Jaw, the site of week two of Leadership Camp. Settling into the hotel meeting room, she sniffed the faint scent of natural minerals floating from the spring-fed pool. The upscale location gave the group a dash of luxury to soak away weariness from long, demanding days.

Her dark jeans, white shirt, and denim jacket were crisp but casual and comfortable. Energy pulsing in her limbs, she paced around the room and checked lighting, refreshments, and seating arrangements clustered around scattered tables. She planned every detail and checked off a precise list to create a positive learning environment.

"Good morning." First to arrive, Mark entered and paused.

"Hello, Mr. Delaney. I trust you're ready for round two." Something about his stiff posture made her tease him with a formal name. Anticipation and apprehension hurdled in her middle. On the weekend, she practiced the right words and visualized a private and sensitive conversation.

"Ready as I'll ever be." He shifted and scanned the room layout.

"I'm glad we have a few moments alone." She tapped the smooth fingertips of one hand over her lips and flushed. Her choice of words sounded suggestive. "At least, I want to share some feedback."

"*More* feedback? You mean I didn't get enough last week?" He lifted an eyebrow, planted apart his feet, and crossed his arms.

"You're one tough customer." She raised her eyebrows and smiled. "Good thing I like a challenge." She rocked onto the balls of her feet.

"Hey, I'm honest." He unfolded his arms and shook his head. "I won't pretend to turn cartwheels over uncomfortable assignments."

"I understand you hold true to your values. We all do. But please, make a stronger effort to dig deep. You experienced things in your past that shaped the person you are today." The lines of his jaw hardened into stone, and she paused. "The better you understand yourself, the more you grow as a leader."

"I got the message last week." He cleared his throat. "Some things are meant to stay buried."

Tessa blinked and waited. Wishing she could shrink away, she drew forward her shoulders. His eyes shone like moist glass.

He glanced away and stepped back.

She swallowed. Had she trod too far? "Try something new, Mark, even if it's a foreign concept. You'll be surprised how much you learn by searching inside and sharing with others. I want you to succeed, so please, try harder." She invested in every student, but he cried out for extra attention. No doubt, his outer shell covered deep-seated pain. He couldn't possibly hold past experiences so close without a reason. A shadow crossed his face. From the hallway, the sounds of lively banter and shuffling feet approached, signaling she'd soon be interrupted.

Mark gave a single nod. Then he backed away, sidestepped a group that spilled into the room, and hurried to the refreshment table.

"Good morning, class." Tessa smiled and delivered her best teacher-voice impression to the newcomers. The scent of coffee and fresh-baked muffins welcomed them.

"Good morning, Miss Shore." Samir grinned and straightened.

"Long time no see." Holly clutched a notebook and pens. "Did you miss us?"

"While I played with my daughter, groomed my dog, cleaned my house, and visited my mother, I missed you all weekend." Counting activities on her fingers, she laughed. Heart jumping, she swallowed and slid her gaze toward the refreshment table where Mark poured water. All joking aside, throughout the days off, she daydreamed of one participant in particular.

What activities filled his free time? During class, as soon as she probed for the roots of his rigid leadership behavior, she ran into a wall. His blue eyes clouded, and his confident persona faded. He was probably more caring and sensitive than he ever let on. Parenting his teenage niece must demand buckets of compassion. Still, Tessa couldn't continue to give him the benefit of the doubt. Like every other participant, he needed to demonstrate new behaviors and measure up.

"Come in...join the fun...you've come to the right place." She bantered with participants, reveled in their energy, and monitored dynamics in the room. Conversation and laughter buzzed.

Samir, joined by Holly, strolled over to chat with

Mark.

Mark bent his head to listen and then tipped it back and laughed.

Tessa relaxed her shoulders. Seeing him fit in released a nagging concern. For a few moments, her tension floated away like a helium balloon. He didn't mingle easily, but he took his time and, eventually, interacted with others.

Tessa checked her watch. "Let's start, everyone." She waited until the group settled. "Last week, you explored what leadership means and received individual feedback to show your strengths and areas to improve." Scratching sounds of scribbled notes drifted over the tables.

Scanning the room, she paused on Mark and met his scrutinizing gaze. His blue eyes were clear, focused, and bright, which was an encouraging sign. A sliver of hope tickled her spine, and she tucked a wayward curl behind her ear. She paced across the front of the room, picked up a marker at a flipchart station, and printed, *What is leadership?* "Anyone? Mark, help me out. Give us the definition."

He cleared his throat and stared at the poster. "I paid attention. You taught us leaders create a clear vision and motivate people to achieve results."

Her difficult student spewed facts the same way he multiplied math equations, but his flat tone held no hint of passion. He listened well, but theory hadn't lit a fire. "You don't sound convinced." She tapped the marker beside the question. How could he remain so resistant and restrained? He tested her, but he couldn't divert her from the session goals.

"I'm convinced you know your stuff." Mark

clicked a pen on and off. "But a leader has to forge his own way, in his own time, and apply his own style." He jabbed the point onto a pad of paper and clamped shut his mouth.

"Let's hear some other ideas." Considering her next tactic, she twisted and squeezed the marker. He resisted without hostility, but he dug in his heels all the same. She couldn't allow him to influence the rest of the group in a negative direction.

"Leaders stay open-minded and are willing to change." Holly bobbed her head.

The group then spring-boarded off Holly's comment and bounced ideas in a lively discussion.

As others spoke, Mark darted his gaze from person to person.

His stiff body language didn't in the least exude leadership behavior. For a few minutes, Tessa allowed the conversation to volley and then noted on the flipchart in big, block letters. *Week Two: Self.* "This week, you'll get to know yourself better."

"Samir, meet Samir." He shook a hand with the other one.

A ripple of laughter lightened the mood in the room. Tessa chuckled, and while the reaction to Samir's humor subsided, she underlined the word *Self* and stuck the cap on the marker. "You'll do quizzes and exercises to examine your beliefs and values—the important factors Mark mentioned—but you won't stop there. You'll see your core values and beliefs in a new light. I expect you to build on your best qualities and clean up bad habits that threaten to derail your career." Gauging readiness, she scanned the room.

Mark slouched, gripped a notepad, and stared at a

blank page.

A hard ball lodged in her stomach. She took a full breath, heavy with scents of coffee, ink, and the hotel mineral pool. So far, his progress didn't appear any greater than last week. If he thought he could win a power struggle, he was mistaken. In the classroom, she ruled. "We'll talk about values first." She sauntered around the perimeter of the room. "Write three non-negotiable values you hold." She waited for everyone to stop writing. "Now give me examples. Call them out. What do you hold sacred?"

"Honesty."

"Family.

"A strong work ethic."

"Passion for what I do."

"Community."

"Self-control. Independence." Mark raised an index and then a middle finger.

Tessa nodded encouragement. He participated in the discussion, so he met the criteria for the exercise, anyway. His succinct answer explained his restrained temperament and why change might prove difficult.

"Now, examining what's really important, how can you meet those needs and still become the best leader possible? How do your values line up with the critical qualities we discussed?" She scrawled across the flipchart: *How?* Underneath, she stroked three lines, and the marker squeaked.

Mark stared at the chart and shifted. He picked up a pen, jotted notes, and stopped occasionally to stare into space.

The room fell quiet except for people shifting and shuffling paper.

Tessa circulated and stayed accessible in case participants wanted to ask questions or float ideas. Soon, she'd announce a coffee break, but for now, she'd leave the group deep in reflection. Passing Mark's table, she glanced in his direction.

He jerked back, stood, and gestured he wanted to say something.

She backed up and breathed his faint spicy scent. "Yes?" Her heart fluttered, and she flushed.

"I need a short break," he murmured toward the side of Tessa's head near an ear. "I'll grab some fresh air, and see you in five or ten minutes."

Stiffening, she jammed a hand on a hip. He didn't even pretend to seek her permission. He spoke in a low, respectful tone, but he set his own agenda. Even though she led the program, she couldn't stop his determined choice. Similar to last week, he disappeared when self-reflection grew intense. Before she could comment or promise a group break, she faced the back of his lean body striding toward the door.

One step forward—and two steps back again. He contributed to the group discussion but bolted before the official break. Internal angst or not, he must comply with class requirements. How would she show him and the rest of the class she set the agenda, no matter what? He was nobody special...or was he?

****

Mark arrived back to the classroom just in time for the break. Inhaling the scent of strong coffee which didn't tempt him and buttery croissants which did, he sauntered to the refreshment table. Now, he might even survive the day.

"Where was the fire?" Samir nudged Mark with an

elbow.

"Found some cool air to clear my head." His quick exit did not go unnoticed. He rubbed his jaw. Nobody else dared veer from the planned agenda.

Samir popped his dark eyebrows toward a receding hairline.

Mark tipped back his water bottle and guzzled. His cheeks and forehead burned. A few minutes outside only slightly eased the stress of constant chipping at his inner self. "Not sure Tessa appreciated my impromptu break, but I can only dissect my inner workings for so long." Through a locked jaw, he forced a chuckle.

"She probably didn't appreciate a deviation from the plan." Samir chomped a bite of pastry and scattered flaky crumbs. "Tessa rules with an iron fist. Don't land on her bad side, or you might get detention." He laughed and swiped a napkin across his mouth.

"Yeah, I figured." Mark shrugged and loaded his plate. At this point, he didn't care what Tessa thought. He protected his private core. She couldn't chase him out of his comfort zone, and classmates' chatter didn't give him a true break. Returning to his place, he set a plate and water bottle on the table.

At the front of the room, Tessa sorted and organized materials.

Before he could change his mind, he strode across the room. "Excuse me, Miss Shore." He lilted a teasing tone and stopped. Maybe his exaggerated formal address would hint sometimes that her air of authority stretched too far.

She jumped and straightened. Running a hand through her hair, she moistened her lips. "Yes, Mr. Delaney. How can I help?"

"Forgive the brief interruption. I finished the assignment." Breathing her light, fragrant aura, he shoved his hands into pockets and shifted. Was his apology sincere, or did he dredge up an excuse to ease close enough to absorb her captivating presence? He didn't understand himself. One minute, he wanted to escape, and the next, he drew near.

"We need to talk, but later." She pointed at a pile of handouts on a table. "I'm ready to start the next session."

Blinking, she flashed green sparks that lodged hot in his chest. "Yes, ma'am." He tipped forward his head, spun, and sped back to his seat.

"Back to work, everyone." She tapped a couple of shoulders and shushed conversations. "Please, think of a leader who heavily influenced you in any aspect of your life. Reflect on what made the person special. What did you learn? How do you apply those learnings today?" She wound among the tables. "After you've selected someone and gathered your thoughts, pair up and share with a partner."

Mark stifled a groan and set a fist on the table. She never granted a reprieve. Every assignment banged on his private door and tested the lock. He gulped water, gripped a pen, and settled into the latest challenging task. The image of his father's confident stance and chiseled features leapt to mind, appeared, and faded in a persistent, pulsating rhythm.

His throat closed, and he swallowed cool water. Dad's teachings still dominated, nearly twenty years after his awful sudden death. But did Mark's classmates really deserve to know? How could he describe everything his father meant to him and still keep a torrent of emotion contained?

Mark scribbled angry geometric patterns on notepaper until the sharp pen tip tore a jagged line. His feelings for Dad were personal and would stay that way. Instead, he forced his mind to his boss's lined face.

Liz was a mentor but only in a professional sense. He took a deep breath, and the tension eased in his throat. Sure, he dreaded her impending departure, but if he shared what she taught him, he still could manage his disappointment and mild sense of loss. He swallowed and gripped the pen. With Liz as acceptable selection, he made quick notes and scanned the room for an available partner.

He jumped his gaze from one participant to the next and discovered everyone already paired. Once again, he was the odd man out. Clutching his paper so tight it crackled, he spotted Tessa. He had no choice but to ask her to act as his sounding board. "You're stuck again." He approached slowly. "I need a partner."

His words echoed in his head, and he heated from deep within his core. Massaging tight neck muscles, he squelched a grimace. Definitely, he didn't seek a companion in his personal life. Before Bree arrived on the scene, the one, long-term relationship he pursued soured over time.

He didn't need someone who spilled emotion like water and pried into personal spaces he didn't care to visit. Dropped into parenting duties, he soon found little time and less patience with any woman who competed with Bree for his attention. At this point in his life, dating caused too many headaches. A girlfriend, let alone a spouse, would give and demand far too much.

"I'd be happy to be your partner." Tessa flashed a bright smile.

Did he imagine a hue change, or did she tint pale pink under her freckles? Obviously, she referred to a role in class, but perhaps she, too, detected the double meaning in her words. Of course, he'd never pursue a relationship outside of work. He almost laughed at the ridiculous idea. Finding a quiet corner, he positioned two chairs facing each other. The swirly pattern of the aqua carpet almost dizzied him. Or was the cause something—maybe someone—else?

"Tell me about your role model." Tessa sat opposite, crossed her legs, and rested a water bottle on her knee.

She didn't waste any time. He cleared his throat and reviewed the key points he rehearsed. "I've learned from many people." The image of Dad's firm face appeared instantly, and he forced it away. He took a deep breath. "But I'll highlight what Liz taught me."

Tessa blinked and nodded.

Mark glanced away and then back. Her serious expression grabbed his attention, and his heart thumped an extra beat, surprising him with its intensity. Even frowning, she glowed as attractive as ever. Up close, he admired her smooth complexion and high cheekbones.

Dragging his attention back to the assignment, he fisted hands on thighs. "Liz promotes and supports excellence, plain and simple. She makes me a better engineer because she never settles for second best. She demands advanced techniques and top quality." He stopped and waited. "Done. What's next?"

She sipped water and examined his face. "Liz and you share a lot in common. You both expect and respect technical excellence."

Swallowing through a narrowed throat, he nodded and waited for the next questions. Her inquisitive eyes and parted lips announced she'd fling many more. The whole exercise sent him off balance like learning to ride a bike.

"How does Liz motivate you to do your best?"

He reflected on the question, shifted, and gathered a calm, patient tone he did not feel one bit. "She does the typical things I always appreciate from a good boss. Nothing over-the-top remarkable. She makes time to listen to ideas, lets me know when she expects more, and recognizes a job well done." Surely, his detailed explanation would satisfy Tessa's probing mind. The description was much more detailed than he typically offered anyone. Focusing on her wide-eyed, expectant expression, he clamped his lips.

"Good examples." She nodded and tilted her head. "Now…"

He traced the movement of her shiny hair spilling over her left shoulder, and then yanked back his attention. The drone of other voices faded to the background.

"Now, tell me more about Liz's approach. How does she deliver bad news without making you feel inadequate?"

"When I know she isn't happy, I feel plenty bad…and I should." He rubbed a thigh.

"I understand you want to always produce topnotch results." She leaned forward. "Does Liz ever share her own experiences?"

He folded and unfolded his arms before she could read too much into his body language. "Sometimes she describes mistakes and misjudgments she made early in her career. She mentioned the toll work took on family life." He drifted his thoughts over fond memories and valuable insights gleaned over the years.

"Did the personal revelations make you think more or less of Liz?"

"Definitely, more." He blurted the words and winced inside. He jumped right into the trap. Personal relationships did matter. The connections Liz nurtured spurred him to outstanding accomplishments. Giving a single, firm nod, he signaled he caught the point.

"Nice work." She flashed a solid thumbs-up. "I'll circulate to check on the others, and then we'll continue. In the meantime, think about other positive influences in your life..." She scooted away before he could protest.

Not again. Originally, she only asked him to name one person. Just when he hurdled a challenge, he encountered another. Secretly, he wanted to please her and see her smile, and he needed to ace the class, but he could only test himself so far. Discussing a work relationship was routine compared to sharing personal details.

Could he reveal enough to satisfy the teacher's demands yet guard his emotions? He rotated his achy shoulders and stared at a blank wall. The situation was so complicated. How could he conduct himself in a way that would have made Dad proud and still impress Tessa?

Chapter 12

Wednesday evening, midway through the week's class, Tessa called Julie to check on Ellie and Mom. Still processing the demanding day, she paced on the plush, taupe carpet in her hotel room. Even the warm tones of the décor didn't soothe her exhaustion. A certain participant still caused trouble.

"First things first. I'll let you talk to Ellie."

A rustle signaled Julie handing over the phone. In the background, kids' chattering voices and Ginger's muffled woof filled the air. Much as she enjoyed family, she appreciated an occasional break from the constant demands.

"Mommy," Ellie shouted. "I miss you."

Ellie's voice quivered. "I miss you, too, sweetie. But I'll see you soon." Familiar guilt nudged her stomach. She anticipated the uninterrupted nights still ahead. Demanding in a different way, a business trip was a welcome relief from daily life.

"Ginger grabbed my cookie and ate it."

"Aw, you sound sad, sweetie." Tessa swallowed. "What a silly, hungry dog. Did Auntie Julie give you another?" Ellie's dark, narrow eyes probably glistened with tears.

"Yeah, she did, and I'm better now. Quinn wants to play."

"Bye, sweetie." Silence told her Ellie already ran to

join her cousin.

"Don't worry. She's happy." Julie took over.

"Thanks for being such a great sister and auntie." Her throat ached. She'd never survive without Julie's support. "How's Mom?" Changing direction, she swished her feet on the carpet and headed for the opposite wall.

"She made fast friends with Rose. They dine and attend all the activities together. She relays glowing reports on everything they share in common." Julie chuckled.

"Good to hear. A nice companion will keep Mom busy."

"I should warn you, though. Rose decided you *must* meet her son, Champ." Julie laughed. "She figures you need a husband, and Ellie needs a father, which would give him a wife and a mother for his girl."

"She mentioned her matchmaking idea, but she didn't convince me. I said, 'Thanks, but no thanks.'" She sighed and laughed. Only a superstar would measure up, and after a few so-so dates, she resisted more. Her life was too full and interesting to waste time on the wrong guy. She forced away the image of her former fiancé Roger's sneering face. One terrible match was enough.

"I'm not surprised." Julie spoke over the shrieks of kids in the background. "Just wanted to give you a heads-up. Those two plot and plan. They also want to go on a shopping spree together, although an excursion could never happen without a driver and chaperone."

"Thanks for all the news. I won't call Mom and confuse her with details on why I'm away, but I'll visit her Saturday, for sure." She paused and weighed whether to broach another topic. "Um…"

"What else is on your mind?"

Julie sensed everything. "Remember the reluctant participant I mentioned? Mark." A flush raced to Tessa's face, and she placed a cool hand on her warm cheek.

"You anticipated some complications."

Tessa spun and retraced her steps. The room air conditioner clicked on, and she shivered. "I've experienced some unusual challenges…and interesting developments…" She couldn't get into the details on the phone. Why did she raise the topic?

"You like him."

Julie's hushed tone held a hint of amusement. "No, I…" Tessa flopped backward onto the bed and stared at the ceiling. She ran a hand over the mocha, sateen bedspread. Sometimes, her older sister's uncanny perceptiveness and honest assessments shook her to the core. She drew a shaky breath. "When I get home, I'll explain."

"Sure thing, little sis."

As Tessa ended the call, she could practically hear the smile in Julie's voice. She'd focus on the course for the next two days and sort out her jumbled emotions on the weekend. Glancing at the clock, she still had time to get some evening air to clear her head.

Normally, Leadership Camp flooded her with energy, but a reluctant participant, no matter how attractive, made every exercise a minor ordeal. She slipped on a windbreaker, gathered her hair into a ponytail, dropped the room key into a pocket, and ran down the stairs. As she crossed the lobby, decorated in calming, spa-themed shades of blues and greens, she spied Mark's back.

He sped out the door.

She followed at a safe distance. Outside, a gentle breeze tickled her cheeks. Should she turn left and catch up or veer right and avoid him? Her heart rate accelerated, and she pressed a hand on her chest. The dim lighting and fresh air might make conversation more relaxed than facing each other in the meeting room, so she dared follow. "Hey, Mark." She jogged a few steps. "Mind if I join you?"

He slowed, glanced over a shoulder, and stopped. Eyes glinting, he narrowed them for an instant.

Tessa shifted and flexed her ankles. Would he accept her offer? Did he curve the corners of his lips into something close to a smile?

"Sure, why not?" He accelerated toward Crescent Park. "You didn't want to hit the spa with everyone else?"

"Usually, I separate business and pleasure." She increased her pace to keep up with his long strides. "I leave the pool to participants. What about you?"

"I'd rather exercise than soak. I told Samir I'd join him later for a beer." He pointed and directed her toward the pathway.

Edging the park perimeter, she strode in silence for a few minutes. Birds twittered and flew to branches adorned with new leaves. Green overtook the brown in the grass and held the promise of spring. Breathing deeply the cool, fresh air, Tessa pondered a nagging topic. "Today, we didn't finish our conversation about role models. I sensed you held someone in mind aside from Liz." To learn more, she would probe but not pound.

Swinging his arms like pendulums, he jutted his chin. "My father."

"Oh, many in the group mentioned older family members." She folded her lips together and waited. If she stayed patient, he might elaborate and make progress.

He stared into the distance and increased his pace.

Puffing slightly, she matched his stride and absorbed the peaceful surroundings. A moth fluttered by. Finally, she couldn't contain her curiosity and persistence any longer. "Tell me about your dad."

"He is…was…the most important person in my life. I lost him when I was seventeen."

His lips stretched into a firm line. "Oh, I'm sorry." The orange and pink sunset gently lit his somber face.

Feet rustling the gravel along the pathway, he shook his head and stared ahead.

Instant sympathy and guilt strangled her. Maybe she shouldn't have prodded him for more. Clearly, she hit a tender spot. His father was the driving force behind this intelligent and measured man. She searched for a neutral topic. "I love springtime…"

Staring at the path, he strode at a steady pace. "He was brilliant and successful…and he taught me how he achieved his goals."

"You learned well." His dad's influence produced a son with grit and integrity, qualities that would make any father proud. He must ache with the loss of his beloved role model. Glancing over, she stumbled over a fallen branch and nearly lost her balance.

Without a pause, he clasped an elbow and steadied her.

Sudden heat rushed up her arm. "Thank you, kind

sir." She straightened and smiled. She didn't intend to interrupt his silence. Maybe he would finally examine how his family history impacted his inner self.

He hustled along the path. "My father taught me a strong man keeps his feelings in check. Dad maintained a stiff upper lip, no matter what. I can't get hung up on how I feel inside. Actions and results are what matter. Anything else just gets messy."

His taut voice matched the lines in his profile. The revelation explained everything. No wonder he carried an impenetrable shield. His idol taught him to prove his strength. The only place for emotions was buried deep inside.

"We finished our second loop." She lost track of time and couldn't believe the ground they had covered. Angled toward the hotel across the street, she searched his expression. "Mark, thank you for sharing. You showed a lot of courage."

"Yeah, sure." He checked for traffic before they crossed the street.

In the distance, a car horn broke the stillness. On the other side, she stopped at the corner and placed fingertips on his arm. "Don't reveal everything, but if you share a sliver with the class, you'll gain respect and understanding."

He nodded and swallowed.

His eyes glittered in the light. He must trust she always respected class ground rules and kept private all individual conversations. She would never let him down. Her integrity and respect of confidences were crucial to building trust with peers and students. "Think about it." She dropped her hand, and the intimate mood evaporated.

"A beer would taste good right about now." He hurried to the hotel door. "Want to join us?"

She drew in a quick breath. More than anything, she'd love to spend hours in his company and learn more about the complex man inside the rigid facade. But she couldn't. Not when he awakened foreign and unwelcome feelings. For the sake of her personal standards, a social relationship was off limits. She must finalize tomorrow's agenda and not venture to places her heart did not belong. "Thanks, but I'd better tackle some work. See you in the morning."

Heart pulsing, she paused and admired his muscular frame until he disappeared down the corridor toward the hum of the pub. Mark still didn't fully measure up in class, yet he opened, just a crack, the door to his soul. She'd pry it wider and help him grow as a leader. As always, she'd stand strong and maintain her professional reputation, but how could she convince her racing heart to remain firm and detached?

****

In the morning, Mark arrived alert and on edge. In the hotel classroom, bursting with colleagues' banter, he beat back tension so he didn't snap at someone for no reason. How would he manage his deep regret over last evening's revealing conversation?

Before the outing with Tessa, he had called home and talked with Bree.

"Tomorrow's the vote for the grad committee. I don't know if I'll win."

"Just do your best and think positive. No one knows you're nervous on the inside. Act confident, and people will believe it." If he was a real dad, he'd be there to support her the night before a challenging, new experience. But she was strong and would handle it the way he did—like a champ. Her grandpa would have expected nothing less.

"Okay."

Her near whisper brimmed with uncertainty. "Hey, chin up, Breezy. Good luck." He pictured her deep frown and downward gaze. "I'll call you tomorrow evening, and you can tell me the news." Unsettled, he ended the call and punched a pillow. Perhaps, he should have listened more than he talked.

Replaying the interaction with Tessa, he laid awake much of the night. Mark seldom mentioned his father, even though Dad loomed large in his psyche. Her gentle probing and empathetic manner lulled him into a weak moment. Now, he faced her in the cool meeting room, filled with buzzing classmates.

"Today's a fine day for leaders." She greeted him with a wide smile.

"Good morning." He paused and rubbed a temple. How could she act as though nothing happened? Her enthusiasm both boosted and drained his energy in a confusing seesaw. Exuding confidence and caring, she never let up. He nearly slid by and dodged further contact.

She brushed a hand on his arm. "Up too late in the pub?" She narrowed her eyes.

"Just worked late and had a lot on my mind." If she knew she topped the list, she might spin from surprise. Was the meeting room warm, or was it just him? Suddenly, the light walls squeezed close and smothered him with a force he needed to escape. Last evening, outside of class, he confided in Tessa, and now, he just wanted to pretend it didn't happen.

"Party guy, who I am, called it a night after one beer." Glancing over at the refreshment table, he shifted. He'd soon escape her quizzing. Tessa would keep confidential his revelations, but he hated the threat of unleashed emotions. Striding to fill his water bottle, he clenched the bottle so hard his fingers cramped. She knew more than most about what really made him tick. He hinted at his deep sorrow over the loss of his dad, but he still guarded the tragic story of why he assumed custody of Bree.

"Ready for another round of discovery?" Holly smiled and poured coffee. "I learn more every day."

"I'm here." Mark selected a muffin. A bitter scent and faint steam from coffee floated his way, but he wasn't tempted. "And prepared." He would never admit to lack of preparation for an engineering task, so he treated the class with similar dedication. Still, more than anything, he defended his feelings.

"Do you miss your usual busy days of plans and calculations?" She blinked and peered over the brim of a coffee mug.

Her dark eyes and wide smile radiated warmth. "I feel best in my usual world. Load me with large projects, short deadlines, and technical challenges." He guzzled water and shoved a hand into a pocket.

"What about the family you left at home? I miss my kids...and my husband, too. Do you find the out-of-town sessions difficult?" Holly tilted her head.

He avoided eye contact and focused on her black, frizzy hairstyle. "Yeah, I prefer not to travel." His classmates showed genuine interest and true sincerity but crossed frequently from business to personal topics.

He missed Bree, Mom, and Rufus, but the more he

shared, the more he'd get asked. "I keep busy at work and on the home front." He cooled his burning insides with another gulp of water. Shifting, he cleared his throat and glanced at Tessa to see if she might provide him a graceful way out by calling the class to order. She raised an arm and waved everyone to seats.

Did she read his mind? Gradually, the loud chatter tapered, and the clatter of dishes from the snack table faded.

"We've arrived at the half-way point of the week and the course." Tessa stretched to her full height and clapped together her palms.

"Time flies when you're having fun." Samir leaned over.

Mark acknowledged the murmur with a slight nod but kept his focus trained on Tessa. Today, she gave her curls free rein and brushed away the dancing strands. Glowing in a casual, aqua dress that matched the carpet and accentuated her gentle curves, she mapped plans for the session.

"Tomorrow, I'll meet to discuss your individual progress and plans for the final week." Making eye contact with every participant, she scanned the room.

He met her gaze and held it for an instant until a flush leapt to his cheeks. A rush of desire hummed in his limbs and propelled him to high alert. Lovely, yet tough as ever, she meant business. He lowered his head and tuned his attitude for the day. Already, he could feel his heart protest.

Throughout the morning, Mark listened to theory and discussed a variety of topics with his tablemates. "I see your point." He addressed a trio of classmates. "But I disagree." He then debated the merits of his position.

Dissecting ideas was okay. He didn't achieve success without speaking up.

"Are you staying open to others' perspectives?" Tessa swept by and continued to the next group.

Her light, sweet scent trailed, teasing his insides up and down. With her pointed question, she might as well have rapped him on the knuckles. He sealed his lips and retreated into a safe, silent space. Revitalized after lunch, he rotated around the perimeter of the room and exerted extra effort to post ideas at each flipchart station. He suspected they wouldn't gain popularity.

Back in a small group discussion, he scanned his classmates for nods of agreement with his opinions but detected few. "Motivation rises from within. You're on your own. No one else can build your commitment and energy." Uncertainty thudded in his veins, and he gripped his cool water bottle.

The segment mentally exhausted him. Tessa never quit. He glanced at his watch and noted the afternoon break would take place within minutes. Rearranging chairs for the next exercise, he spotted her speaking with a hotel employee at the door.

She nodded, scanned the room, and marched straight toward him. Extending a hand with a piece of paper, she crinkled her forehead. "Someone from your niece's school asked that you call right away." She paused and touched his arm. "I'll excuse you for a few minutes. I hope everything's okay."

His pulse jumped. A class rule to switch off phones meant urgent messages arrived by way of the hotel front desk. Heart thudding, he hurried to the hallway. The space was cooler and quieter than the meeting room, and he hugged elbows to his sides. Something bad happened to Bree. The only other time a teacher called during business hours was to report her sprained ankle in physical education class. Was she sick or injured? She would never cause trouble requiring discipline. She'd never missed an assignment. He consulted the paper and punched a number. "May I speak with Mrs. Franklin?" He pursed his lips.

"Good afternoon."

Her clipped tone sent a no-nonsense and efficient image. "My name is Mark Delaney, Bree's uncle." He steadied his breathing. Maybe she recruited supervisors for a school event. Perhaps, the reason for the call didn't even concern Bree.

"Thank you for responding quickly. Bree is fine now."

Her voice remained calm. If Bree was fine now, she wasn't seriously injured, but what about earlier? Bree needed him. She counted on his parental love, consistent strength, and daily guidance. He filled his lungs and stretched the suffocating hold on his chest. He should have stayed home and not abandoned her for so many days in a row. Work was important, but family was everything.

"She's right here. I'll hand over the phone."

"Uncle Mark?"

Her voice shook. "Yes, Breezy. What happened?" He breathed out in rush. At least, she was well enough to squeak out a greeting. He paced to a window and stared at the traffic.

She took a deep breath. "I lost...you know, the election..."

"Hey, I'm proud of you for trying. You were very brave." He massaged the back of his neck. She disliked failure as much as he did. To interrupt him at work, she must feel terrible about the loss.

"Desiree...she's one of the girls who won...said she knew I wouldn't get any votes..." She lowered her voice.

"Oh, Bree, I'm sorry. People sometimes say things without thinking."

"So I yelled something mean." She sniffed. "I said, 'I lost, but you're a loser.' Everybody laughed."

Her small voice wavered, and her breath trembled. Bree never struck out or sought confrontation. He waited in total silence. "And then what?" He could practically hear her squelch her pain and fight to stay strong.

"Then she slapped my cheek really hard. I bent my head and ran to my next class. My math teacher asked why my cheek was bright red, so I explained what happened. He told Mrs. Franklin, and she said I better call you."

Her shaky voice sounded thin and lonely. An insult was bad enough, but a slap—any type of physical violence—was unacceptable. In his online searches for parenting tips, he never anticipated he'd need advice on this kind of nasty situation.

"When will you come home?" She whooshed out a sigh.

Pacing back and forth, he dragged his feet over the thick carpet. He wanted to kick it. Anger and guilt pulsed in his limbs. How dare Desiree bully his sweet, gentle niece? He should be there. Bree counted on his steady presence. He always comforted and cheered her efforts. Mind racing, he tipped his head side to side to ease the tension in his neck and clear his muddled brain. After a brave attempt to weather a tough experience, Bree needed him. "Tell you what. This evening, I'll come visit for a short while and then return to Moose Jaw later."

"You don't have to..." Bree sighed.

"I want to. Hang in there, and I'll come as soon as I can. Now, please let me speak to Mrs. Franklin."

"Okay. Thanks, Uncle Mark."

He gripped the phone and stared across the street at the flashing casino sign. Inside the brick building, people gambled all the time for entertainment. Bree took a chance, and it didn't go well. Now, he dealt with a risk of his own. He would soon learn the impact of his impulsive decision. When he promised to visit Bree, he didn't contemplate Tessa's reaction. But her judgement paled next to his responsibility for Bree. She was all that mattered. He blocked the laughter of hotel patrons passing by.

"Hello, Mr. Delaney? We notified the other girl's parents. Tomorrow morning, we will convene a meeting for the girls so they can calmly talk out their differences and apologize to each other."

"Thank you, Mrs. Franklin. I appreciate your help." He ended the call. Poor Bree. She was made of tough stuff and would recover, but inside, she might sting for a while.

Now, he faced his own predicament. Maybe he should have made Bree wait until the course ended on Friday, but he couldn't let her suffer alone. In person, he could bolster her confidence and counsel her on how best to approach the meeting tomorrow. Nobody else could take his place. Nice as she was, Nicole couldn't possibly come close.

He called Bree and himself the dynamic duo for a reason. They were an inseparable pair. Through ups and downs, he soldiered on. Sometimes, he laughed, and sometimes, he barely coped, but he never encouraged tears. He taught her to ride a two-wheeler and learned to braid hair. She taught him to notice flowers and learned to pair socks. He wouldn't trade the demands of parenthood for a single minute, and he suspected she appreciated him more than she showed. Bree made him a better person, and he couldn't let her down.

Still, the image of Tessa's lovely, but firm, expression loomed. Weight bore down from his shoulders, through his middle, and to his knees. Right now, she held his career destiny in her hands, and he couldn't afford to seriously test her boundaries or tolerance. How ironic *she* could stretch his patience as much as she wanted.

Resolving to show her a glimpse of the sensitive core she probed to uncover, he jammed his hands in pockets and stomped to the meeting room. Tessa understood the importance of personal values, so she should support his responsibility to put family ahead of work. Or would she? He couldn't guess. She demanded absolute commitment.

He slipped in the door to the classroom and found the group milling during a break. His timing was ideal. The loud chatter and scattered laughter covered his entrance, and he paused and scanned for Tessa. Within seconds, he braced himself for the arrival of an aqua blur that sped his way.

"Is everything okay?" Tessa stopped and stared.

He nodded. "Fine, thanks." He would wait for the right moment to tell her the promise he made.

"Good to hear." She nodded and dashed away.

Loosening his collar, he checked the time. The room was uncomfortably warm, and for the rest of the session, he fought to concentrate. Between Tessa and Bree, he bounced from one uncomfortable situation to another.

Wrapping the afternoon's program, Tessa clapped together her hands and waved them apart. "Meet in the lobby at seven to head in a group to the bowling alley." She numbered the participants to create groups for the evening event.

Mark churned inside. He was well aware of class requirements. Tessa frequently emphasized everyone must participate in every session, including classroom activities and social functions. He waited for the last of the participants to straggle out the door before he approached her. Finally, the class chatter faded into the hallway. "Can I speak with you for a moment?" He chose a neutral tone.

"Of course. I hope you know how to throw a few strikes because you're on my team." She lifted an eyebrow and inched back.

Sure, she was in charge, but did he make her uncomfortable? Pressure like a bowling ball thundered in his chest. "About tonight's plans…"

"Don't worry, I won't hassle you about your score." She tossed her hair and laughed.

"I can't join you." He shifted and fisted his hands.

"Oh? You already know the social events count as mandatory. I expect everyone to participate and expand connections. Networking is a critical component of the whole experience." She frowned and searched his face.

"Bree, my niece, needs me." He inhaled strength.

"She encountered a tough situation at school and had an upsetting altercation with another girl. I'll eat dinner with everyone and then duck out before bowling." Rushing his words, he glanced at his watch. He could easily make the forty-five-minute drive back to Regina, console Bree, and return at a decent time.

"I understand family commitments. I really do...." She bit her lip. "But I also treat all participants equally and maintain program standards. Obviously, I can't dictate your decision, but your classmates will expect an explanation. I'll add the topic to your progress review."

He clenched his jaw and nodded. He would worry about Tessa's reaction later. His actions might prove he lived his belief in balancing work and family. He narrowed his eyes and quickened his breath at her mix of compassion and determination. She understood, but whether she accepted the hard fact or not, she couldn't control everything—least of all, him. Just let her try.

Chapter 13

At dinner with the group, Tessa sat beside Samir and across from Mark and Holly. She avoided the informal gatherings in the local pub, but she participated in the organized social events. Tonight was a chance to strengthen informal connections.

The burger joint next to the hotel whirred with noisy voices and clattering dishes. The red, black, and white color scheme suited a trendy diner. Surveying the group seated at one long table, she absorbed the animated voices and tinkle of laughter. Quick bonds grew deep among a group who spent concentrated time together. Even Mark joined in the banter.

Tessa chewed a salty fry. Although his interactions were slightly stilted, he made a concerted effort, which was all she asked. She flitted her gaze around the restaurant and landed it back in his direction. Her food nearly caught in her throat at the way his blue T-shirt displayed his firm biceps and carved torso. Hand quivering, she sipped sugary soda until she regained her composure.

"You cheered with impressive volume during the relay." Holly speared a bite of salad.

He flashed back to an afternoon exercise that demonstrated effective teamwork. "What can I say?" He grinned. "I like to win."

"We thought you were nothing but a quiet, studious

engineer." Samir thumped a hand on the table.

"You'd be surprised what's inside this brawny body." Mark shoved a thumb into his breastbone.

"Did you say brawny or brainy? Let's get it straight." Samir hooted and gulped soda.

"Confidence counts." Holly laughed and raised her water glass in a toast. "Here's to believing in yourself—inside and out."

"Amazing, the side benefits of the course." Tessa jumped in. "People learn to appreciate their physical, as well as leadership, strengths." She laughed at the jokes but admitted his body and brain sizzled in a dangerous way.

A choppy wave rippled through her. She'd never experienced such instant attraction. In his presence, she must proceed with extreme caution. Only at a safe distance, maybe she'd confide in Julie how hot she found him. Somehow, she needed to release the growing tension between her professional role and shocking desire.

Shifting in his red, wooden chair, Mark grimaced and swallowed a swig of milkshake.

She offended him. Tessa bounced forward, tapped a fork, and searched for a way to make amends. She didn't mean to embarrass him. Now, just when he made progress interacting with the others, he'd probably clam up. "Everyone's having fun." Maybe she could divert attention in another direction.

"Wait until you see us at the bowling alley." Samir let out a whoop. "Then the competition will heat up. Might get ugly." He chuckled and wrestled a large bite of burger into his mouth.

A few minutes later, hearing Mark laugh and rejoin

the banter, Tessa relaxed her breathing and tilted her head. He still worked to fit in with his peers. Thank goodness, she didn't create any lasting strain. She checked her watch. "Excuse me. I'll meet you in the lobby in fifteen minutes." She glanced at Mark, even though he likely wouldn't join the group.

He thrust back his chair and followed her from the restaurant to the street.

"Well, what did you decide?" She spun and waited. A brisk breeze swept her hair across her face.

"I can't attend." He zipped his jacket. "But I'll return as soon as possible."

She lifted her gaze from his broad shoulders to his rocky face. Heart hopscotching, she nodded. "Your classmates will comment, but I understand. Travel safely." She didn't linger and strode inside to the elevator. She had just enough time to make a call before she met the others. In the hush of her hotel room, she called her sister.

"Well, how is he today?" Julie giggled over the phone.

"Missing in action at the moment. A personal situation yanked him away from the evening session." She pictured his drawn face. He was as devoted to his niece as she was to Ellie.

"You just can't control the guy, can you?" Julie laughed.

"Hey, you told me I should stop." Tessa kicked off her shoes and grabbed jeans and a T-shirt. The second she ended the call, she would change clothes.

"How do you feel about giving him a longer leash?" Julie paused and shushed the kids in the background.

"Like one of us will trip and fall." She peered at her reflection in a mirror and relaxed her wrinkled brow and pursed lips.

"I think a sisterly chat is in order. But we'll save it for the weekend. Here's Ellie to say hello."

"Hi, Mommy. I miss you." She giggled. "Stop, Ginger, don't lick me."

Ellie's merry, little voice lilted, and Tessa blinked away sudden tears. She never forgot for an instant Ellie's adorable expression and black braids, and she ached to give her a giant hug. The knot of guilt over her ambivalent feelings about single parenthood loosened from a distance. "Pet that crazy, old dog. I'll see you tomorrow, sweetie. Have a good sleep tonight and fun at daycare."

"Bye, Mommy. Here, Auntie Julie." Ellie rustled the phone.

"Give the poor guy a break." Julie sighed. "If I told you Ellie needed you, you'd race home so fast you'd risk a speeding ticket."

"I know. Thanks for everything." Tessa overlooked Julie's comment, but as she hurried to dress for bowling, she couldn't quite erase it. Julie had a point, but she didn't run Leadership Camp or work with colleagues who monitored her actions. Tessa built a reputation for results, high standards, and personal integrity. An office romance would muddy everything.

Julie's role as stay-at-home mom demanded a whole different skill set. Still, Tessa didn't know anyone much wiser than her beloved sister. Before she grabbed a tote bag and dashed out the door, she splashed her burning cheeks with icy water.

Joining the group swarming and buzzing in the

wide lobby, she called directions to the bowling alley, in case any stragglers lost their way. The group's motion mirrored the swirly-patterned carpet, colored like tropical water.

Leading the way, she set a brisk pace down the street and breathed cool, refreshing air. The clean scent of springtime floated close. Moose Jaw's Main Street held an eclectic mix of businesses—gift shops, a florist, theatre, and quaint restaurants—to attract residents and tourists. Drinking in the local flavor, she hurried along.

Striding beside her, Yvonne, an intense woman from the Legal Department, glanced over her shoulder. "I don't see Mark. Did we forget him?"

"He can't join us this evening." A quick rush of defensiveness travelled up Tessa's spine, and she stiffened. Yvonne meant well but forced her into an awkward position. How could she respond without betraying Mark's confidence? Silence hung for a few rapid steps. "He needed to attend to a family situation." She sputtered the explanation.

"Oh, nobody ever misses a session. The big boss doesn't allow it." Yvonne quirked an eyebrow and laughed. "I hope the issue isn't anything too serious."

"He promised to return when he can." Tessa pressed together her lips. She ran the show and didn't justify his behavior to anyone, but the innocent question of Mark's whereabouts tore her in two. She understood family commitments but disliked outward rebellion. Speeding along Main Street, she wished he could connect with others and let loose over a game. He would definitely benefit from more supporters. Back at the office, he'd only succeed if he established and repaired relationships. If he truly aspired to a top role, he needed to ramp up his people skills. In the attract-Tessa category, he already excelled.

She led the group around a corner to an ancient building with a neon sign flashing *Bowl City* in red and yellow. Mark chose family over her stiff expectations. She resented his resistance but couldn't fault him for following his heart. She would do the same for Ellie.

All week, the class delved into their innermost feelings, so how could she complain when she taught him to listen to the call? Their park conversation confirmed he was a complex guy. The firm lines of his face pointed to pain deep inside. Widening her eyes to contain sudden moisture, she swung open the door of the bowling alley.

Followed by the chattering group, she trooped downstairs to the lower level. Dim lighting, musty air, and clunking balls greeted her. After checking in, she laced up well-worn, red shoes and headed for the lanes. During the game, she handled three participants' inquiries about Mark. Each time, she tensed and gave a brief reply. With great effort, she forced herself not to overreact to raised eyebrows.

Focusing on the cluster of pins, she threw the weight of guilt and frustration into every shot. In his position, she would make the same choice. Still, she read surprise in his classmates' expressions that he dared to skip an organized activity.

"I'm happy to declare Holly's team winners of the class bowl-off." Tessa doled treats from her tote bag of prizes. "Congratulations on bragging rights."

"You won't hear the end of our performance." Holly grinned and pumped her fists. "I say we hit the pub and toast our big win. C'mon, you runners-up, fall behind."

The short trip back to the hotel included lots of joking and jostling, creating precisely the upbeat mood Tessa intended. The breeze hustled at their backs and whisked dust along the curbs. A tangerine and pink sunset peeked between buildings.

A few minutes later, in the hotel lobby, Holly pointed the way to the pub.

"Have fun." Tessa lifted a hand in a single wave. A faint guitar tune meandered down the hallway. "Don't stay up too late tonight." As usual, she'd avoid the complications of the bar and alcohol and get a good rest for the demanding day ahead. She covered a yawn yet tingled oddly alert.

Back in her plush room, she wouldn't relax until Mark rejoined the group. Surely, his minor emergency wouldn't interfere with tomorrow's plans. Should she trust he returned as planned or call his room to check? Phone contact might overstep her bounds as group leader, and Julie might protest.

She should leave the poor guy alone and wait until morning, but she couldn't resist. Heart hopping like Ellie in a candy store, she inched toward a place she should not tread. She cared but wasn't a pushover. How would the wayward student feel about some special attention from the teacher?

****

After dinner, Mark made a quick exit and avoided classmates' probing questions and raised eyebrows about why he bowed out of bowling. The activity wasn't nearly as important as his current mission. In the car, he switched on mellow music, gripped the steering wheel, and scanned endless prairie. The flat terrain stretched black, brown, and gold with a light spray of green. The monotonous scenery did nothing to erase the image of Tessa's downturned lips at his news. Yet beneath her dominant, don't-resist manner, he detected a deep and warm pool of compassion. She understood family commitments and left him to make the decision.

He rotated his shoulders. No doubt tomorrow he'd get reprimanded and ribbed for missing the social segment, but he accepted the inevitable. He compromised on some things but never on a promise. He'd do his best to comfort Bree.

Forty minutes later, he parked in the driveway at home and grinned at Rufus's panting muzzle in the window. The dog's greeting always cheered him. He jumped out of the car, hurried up the sidewalk, and swung open the front door. "Hey, Rufus-boy." He bent, ran his hands along the dog's soft sides, and received a sloppy lick on the forehead. The air inside was a little stuffy compared to the fresh evening breeze.

"Bree said you'd come to see her. She's in her room." Clutching a pen and notebook, Nicole met him at the front door. She wrinkled her brow. "She lost the vote, and something bad happened at school today, but she wouldn't give me any details." She shifted.

He nodded. "She doesn't open up easily. I'll talk with her."

"I'll continue my homework at the kitchen table. If I can help, let me know." Wearing moccasin slippers, Nicole shuffled away.

"Come, Rufus." A little canine moral support wouldn't hurt. He headed down the hallway and tapped on Bree's bedroom door.

"I want to be alone."

Bree's clipped tone mimicked the one he couldn't contain when he was under stress. "It's Uncle Mark. Can I come in?" He twisted the knob and let Rufus burst into the room and onto the bed. The exuberant dog might entice a smile.

"I guess so." Cross-legged on the bed, she leaned and hugged Rufus.

Mark sat on the edge and touched her back. "Rough day, huh?" A teenage girl's room was still foreign territory with piles of clothes on the floor, colorful posters on the walls, and the fruity scent of body spray in the air.

She petted Rufus and stared at the quilt.

Her face was stiff and pale, except for a faint reddish streak on one cheek, and her eyes reflected pink and watery. "I see where Desiree slapped you. How does it feel?" He placed a hand on her arm.

"It doesn't hurt anymore." She jerked away. "I hate her."

"I don't blame you for feeling angry." He searched his brain for soothing words and advice to guide her. His own fury boiled like lava and fired the tension that hid inside when he disappointed Tessa. "I'm mad, too."

"Rufus is on my side."

Her flat voice was glum, but she managed a small laugh at his lolling tongue and swishing tail.

For a few minutes, she sat in silence and stroked the dog's smooth head and furry sides. "I don't want to meet tomorrow." She fisted a hand and pounded the bed. "They can't force me. I'll sit there and not say a word." She huffed and bowed her head.

"Mrs. Franklin probably won't give you a choice. Maybe you'll feel better after you air your differences."

The interaction wouldn't be easy, and he ached to help her in some small way. "You're strong, and you can handle the situation. Show her..."

Mark took a breath and regrouped. He was about to advise Bree to show her strength and contain her bad feelings. He nearly delivered an updated version of Dad's counsel to keep a stiff upper lip, but just in time, he swallowed his words. Tessa's advice reverberating through his head, he formulated a new tactic. "Maybe we should talk more about how you feel and might approach the meeting."

"I don't want to say anything." She scowled and shook her head.

"Could you explain your hurt? Not the slap on your cheek but the pain you feel inside?" He swallowed and rubbed her stiff back.

She covered her quivering bottom lip and shook her head.

In a torrent, memories flooded back. After the tragic crash, he had distracted Bree with toys and candy. She fell off her bike, and he cleaned her scraped knee, stuck on a bandage, and urged her to get right back on. She lost her best friend to another city, and he told her not to worry and go make a new friend.

Now, he massaged his forehead and cringed at the unintentional damage he caused. He meant well, but in the same way Dad coached him, he taught Bree to suppress emotions. When he witnessed her closet her pain and protect her heart, he might as well peer into an unforgiving mirror. Tessa was right. Feelings mattered.

Bree slouched, stared at the floor, and drew her lips into a seal.

He waited and let her mull over his suggestion. She

needed gentle support and quiet space.

"How would I tell Desiree?" she murmured in a voice so low she nearly whispered.

"Tell me what you wish she would understand." He waited, dropped a hand to Rufus's head, and petted in smooth, soothing motions.

"I know I was wrong to call her a loser, but she made me *feel* like a loser. When I heard her say I'd never win, my insides balled into a big cramp." Tears filled her eyes. "I didn't want her to see me cry, so I bit my cheek so hard I tasted blood."

He winced. "I bet you felt awful."

Through glassy eyes, she glanced up and away out the window.

Her pain clawed its way into his skin and became his own.

She sighed. "I wanted to run fast all the way home without stopping." She threw herself down and buried her head in the pillow.

She didn't want him to see her weep. "Don't worry, Breezy. Crying is okay. Seriously, we all get hurt sometimes, and a strong person is never afraid to admit mistakes, or sadness, or tough things." Mark's advice jolted him straight. Clearing sudden confusion, he raised both hands and massaged his temples. Who said these words? Had Tessa infiltrated his voice track? He—the guy who guarded his privacy and feelings in an iron vault—just advised the complete opposite.

He shook his head, leaned sideways, and grabbed a tissue from a box on the nightstand. He cleared his throat and blew his nose. Apparently, he took to heart more of the class than he realized. Tessa would be shocked and pleased. He hated to be prompted to reveal more than he wanted, so he treaded gently with Bree. "I'm very impressed you own your part of the incident. Accepting responsibility for a mistake shows you're a leader."

"I'm not a leader. I didn't get elected." With her mouth buried deep in a pillow, she shouted.

"Trust me. You are more of a leader than you know." He stretched and stared out the bedroom window. The front lawn grew greener every day. Soon, he'd need to cut it twice a week. Nature was a welcome antidote to the tough parts of life.

"Do you really think so?" She heaved to an upright position and wiped her eyes.

"I *know* so." Mark faced her and patted a hand. "Let's get ready for tomorrow." He rubbed the back of his neck. Dealing with emotions zapped his energy.

"Do you think if I tell her how she hurt me, she'll tease me more?" Bree blinked.

The idea brightened her expression. "I can't say for sure." He shrugged. "But she might learn something and act a little nicer. She might even respect you more for daring to share."

Bree sighed and took several deep breaths. "Okay, I'll do it."

"I'm proud of you, Breezy." He squeezed her shoulder.

"Now, can we go to Cool Cones before you leave?" She smiled and widened her eyes.

With his backing, she must feel huge relief. If he hadn't already witnessed her teenage mood swings, he might have been more surprised at her swift change in attitude. "Oh, why not?" He swung to his feet, laughed, and motioned to follow him. Sweets helped everything, and Bree knew how to charm him into buying ice cream. "We'll take Nicole's order and buy her a treat, too."

A few minutes later, on a bench outside the ice cream shop, he devoured a chocolate sundae, and the rich taste overshadowed his troubles. Drips from Bree's giant cone splatted on the pavement. "Feel any better?"

"A bit." She licked around the edges of the cone. "I'll order a strawberry sundae for Nicole."

Feelings were okay. She would work through them. His stomach felt more settled than when he arrived. Driving toward home, he sang along with a current hit and laughed at Bree's groan. "Good luck. Dig deep and show Desiree how you felt." He parked, swung out of the car, and hugged her with one arm along the back of her shoulders. "See you tomorrow. You can tell me all the details."

"Thanks, Uncle Mark." She raised her chin and scooted to the door.

Her hint of a smile gave him hope that tomorrow would be okay. All the way back to Moose Jaw, he reprimanded and then encouraged himself. All these years, he did his best, but he wasn't perfect. Far from it. When he taught Bree to repress her sorrow and pain, he did her a grave disservice. This evening was a small step, but maybe he could model a new way. The process exhausted him but wasn't impossible. He would demonstrate how to learn and practice. Maybe he could even help her resolve any grief that lingered over the loss of her parents.

Alternating speeds, he stomped on the gas and then braked so he wouldn't get a ticket. He would convince Tessa he could make up for lost time with the group. He pictured Bree as she mustered courage to confront her foe and reveal her pain. Then he visualized himself as a vulnerable and open person who formed stronger connections with others. Tomorrow, he would demonstrate he followed his own advice. Tessa was one wise woman.

Arriving back at the hotel at ten o'clock, he gathered the shreds of his energy and scooted through the lobby before he encountered any classmates. He dragged himself into his room and peeled off his jeans and T-shirt. Sprawling on the bed, he caught part of the provincial evening news on TV. In contrast, the beige surroundings and gentle hum of a fan rested his senses.

Then the phone jangled, and he jumped and rolled off the bed to answer. Did Bree need him again? They were an inseparable duo. He grabbed a sleeve of a shirt strewn on a chair and whipped it against the bed. He abandoned her without his support. "Hello." Swinging the shirt, he hit another satisfying lash.

"How are things at home?"

Mark froze. Thank goodness, the call wasn't from Bree, but he didn't expect to hear from Tessa. An odd nervousness rippled through his torso. "Fine, thanks. Everything's under control." As though she saw his partial nakedness, he raised the shirt and covered his bare midriff. "Did I miss a good time?"

"Good and valuable." She paused. "At our meeting tomorrow, I'll say more."

Bree wasn't the only one with a meeting to dread. He'd remember his own advice and let Tessa know how he felt. "Sure thing." He wanted to swallow his discomfort and shield it from scrutiny. "I had no choice. My niece needed my support." He heaved a breath.

"She doesn't have a mom or dad, and I do my best to fill both roles. I wish I had backup, but I don't."

"I respect your dedication. Thanks for sharing."

Tessa sounded warmer, as if she'd curved a smile around her words, and he sank onto the bed. "Thanks for calling." He leaned forward and examined in the mirror his reddish cheekbones. He didn't relish at all a reprimand, but he anticipated more special time in her charming company. "Maybe we can take a walk again next week." If he felt discomfort after their last private outing, so what? Her influence might pay dividends, after all. Silence hung in the air.

"I don't usually meet alone with students after class, but...maybe. Well, good night."

Ending the call, he imagined her reclining on a bed with her lush curls strewn on a pillow and shapely legs exposed below pajama shorts. The heat in his face intensified as though he leaned near a gas flame. Shaking his head, he forced away the image. She was right. He should stick to the group social events and not seek individual time with the teacher. Still, even a cool shower didn't douse the burning in his chest.

He opened a window to allow in springtime air and dilute the faint smell of cleaning products. Settled in bed, he flipped through work messages on his phone. Then he tilted back, tossed aside the phone, and rested his head on clasped hands. No possible way could he concentrate on work right now. Tessa loomed large. She was a determined teacher and an attractive woman. Would the changes she demanded really make him a stronger leader? Did she notice progress? How could he convince her to overlook the missed bowling event and praise him for living his family priorities? Considering everything, did he really want to connect with her after class?

He snapped off the light, and the phone rang. Bolting upright, he grabbed it. His heart rate jumped. The call must be from Bree. "Hello." He braced himself for his niece's voice in distress. She'd never call this late unless she was distraught.

"I can't sleep. Please, don't quote me, but I might bend a rule."

At Tessa's teasing lilt, he leapt out of bed. The rule to avoid personal contact with students was hers and not his. He shared her reluctance to date a colleague, but at the moment, he'd do anything she asked. "Oh? What do you mean?" He paced beside the edge of the bed.

"Care to join me for some late-evening exercise?"

Chapter 14

Pacing around Crescent Park in moonlight trimmed with stars, Mark breathed fresh air and slowed his erratic heartbeats from the shock of Tessa's invitation. Apparently, the woman who directed the class with the precision of an air-traffic controller could flex...at least, a little. She wanted to spend extra time with him, and he couldn't refuse.

"I didn't think we'd bump into other participants at this late hour." She hugged tighter her windbreaker against the cool breeze. "We won't mix business and pleasure. I'm strictly off duty, and so are you."

"Okay, Tessa, whatever you say." Zipping higher his jacket, he strode and sniffed moisture riding the wind. Guilt tiptoed around his collar, and he couldn't escape the feeling this outing was a bad idea. He should avoid her, except in class, yet he accepted her invitation. But why did she break her own rule and contact him? "If I can't discuss work, can I ask you a personal question?" He admired her profile with pert nose tipped to the sky, breathing the fresh night air.

"I guess so since I'm the woman who persuades everyone else to dish." She laughed and brushed a curl from her cheek.

Streetlights alternated with a full moon to light the pathway. Their footsteps crunched on gravel, and their murmured voices broke the peaceful silence.

"Ready." She tucked her hands in jacket pockets.

"Is *Mr.* Shore waiting at home?" He winced at his forward question. No sense beating around the bush. He shouldn't pine for someone else's wife.

"You weren't kidding. Your question *is* fairly personal." She laughed and twisted toward him. "No, I don't have a mister. But, as you know, I'm the mom of a beautiful daughter."

"So you're divorced." His heart jumped. She was available, too. A relationship was not impossible.

She shook her head. "I was engaged once, but my strong personality got in the way." She accelerated and lengthened her strides.

"Oh?" He swallowed and fought the overwhelming urge to sweep her into his arms. She always took charge, but was her willpower really such a bad thing?

"I totally bought into a future together and wanted more than anything to have a baby. I sacrificed a lot to make our relationship work. He delayed the wedding and finally informed me he couldn't stand being with a dominant woman. He said he could never co-parent with someone who made all the decisions." She tipped forward her head and shook it. "After many sparring matches, I realized I couldn't live with a weak man, and I ended our engagement. We haven't spoken since we parted."

"He's not the father of your daughter?" He'd ask questions until she refused to answer. The more he learned, the more he craved. Sure, he'd been determined to remain independent and free of a woman in his life. But why? His concerns blew away in the breeze.

"Definitely not. Ellie was one year old when I

adopted her from China. With the perfect man nowhere in sight, I couldn't count on a partner to make me a mom." Her voice wavered. "I showed my former fiancé—and everyone—I didn't need a man to help me raise a child. My mother was horrified, and my sister was concerned, but I ignored their advice."

"And?" He urged Tessa to continue. She juggled a lot with work and family. Her gumption would stagger anyone without her strength and assertiveness.

"Ellie's four years old and a bundle of energy and joy. I miss her. Being away is the only part of my job I don't like."

He strolled in silence and rounded the far end of the park.

"But…"

"Yes?" Deeper meaning hid behind her hesitation, and he glanced at her unsmiling profile. She must trust him if she intended to share something serious. The hoot of an owl drifted from the black sky.

"I have a confession…I'm so…ashamed. No one else…knows. Should I…continue?"

Her soft voice whispered uncertainty and pain. He didn't expect to see this side of Tessa, a dramatic contrast from her bubbly, confident image. "Go ahead." He'd never betray her trust.

"My mom and sister were right." She slowed her pace. "I completely underestimated the life-consuming responsibility of single motherhood. After I adopted Ellie, reality hit within weeks. She cried, and I couldn't make her stop. She spit out food, and I couldn't make her swallow. As she grew older, she threw tantrums, and I wanted to scream, too. The day she arrived, my personal life spun out of control. How did I make such a terrible mistake?" Staring into the distance, she breathed in spurts. "I love Ellie with all my heart. But I fight every day to regain the order I crave."

Subdued night-time sounds of insects in nearby bushes rustled and chirped. The calm setting hugged her sagging shoulders. What could he say to reassure a woman who lived every single day with the worst mistake of her life? "If you ever want to talk, I will listen. No matter what, believe you're an amazing mom. Take solace from the fact." Energy fell from his limbs. At times, he, too, was an unwilling parent. He lived her pain. In her tone, he recognized exhaustion and shame. When everything she did followed a structured plan, she agonized over her life-changing choice.

"Tell me about your niece." She picked up speed and swung her arms.

The moment of quiet revelation ended. He breathed out a cross between a sigh and a huff. She brimmed with her own personal questions, too. "Bree is smart, determined, and reserved. She works hard and always excels." He smiled. She was the most important person in his life, and sometimes, he burst with pride at her scholastic accomplishments.

"A totally amazing girl," said Tessa.

"I think so. But then I might be biased." He chuckled. Stepping on a twig, he snapped it with a crack. "Of course, the teen years promise a bit of a challenge. She's a loner and, lately, more withdrawn. Recently, her best friend moved away."

"She's lucky she has you for a role model."

"You give me too much credit, but she resembles me enough to fool people into assuming she's my natural daughter."

"Her appearance might not be the only thing similar to her uncle." She glanced over and smiled.

Mark groaned. He couldn't deny she was a self-portrait in actions as well as appearance. Sometimes, she was too much like him and more so than he admitted before Leadership Camp.

"I meant the comparison as a compliment." She touched his forearm without changing her brisk pace. "I don't mean to pry, but I'd be interested to know how you became Bree's substitute parent..."

The moon shone a spotlight and drew his gaze to her shimmering emerald eyes. "The topic is tough." His throat strangled his words. "Even worse than when I described my relationship with my dad." He sucked in a mouthful of cooling air. Pain flared and burned deep inside. If he spoke now, his voice would waver and crack.

She strode beside him along dark shrubs and trees fringing the path.

The hotel lights peeked through the trees, and he mustered his inner strength and whooshed out a rush of air. He could just tell her he wasn't comfortable and couldn't share. Recounting a tragedy wasn't crucial to his success. But this conversation was personal. Taking her lead, he shelved business for the evening and crossed into uncharted territory. By inquiring about her personal life, he set the tone. In return, she assumed his family situation was fair game.

He clamped his mouth and then let it fall open. He squeezed hard fists and then uncurled stiff fingers and stretched them wide. The recent weeks were the tensest situation he'd experienced in years. Liz's sudden resignation was an open wound. The demanding sessions, layered with Bree's issue, exhausted him. "Seven years ago, I became Bree's legal guardian." Rubbing a hand across his chest, he plunged in. "Her mother was my older sister. A drunk driver crossed the ditch and hit her vehicle on Ring Road. The crash happened at such high speed..." He paused and steadied his voice. "My sister and brother-in-law were both..." He swallowed and steadied a catch that squashed his voice. "They both...died." He crept his gaze to her face.

"I'm so sorry." A tear slipped down her cheek.

"The pain has dulled, but it'll never disappear." He blinked rapidly and cleared his throat. Bree must feel the same. Why did he think he could sweep away pain in a little girl? Bree deserved the chance to deal with her feelings and not act as if they didn't exist. He'd broach the topic and see where it led. He breathed in jagged spurts.

"How terrible." She bowed her head and ran a finger under her eyes. "I understand why you find the situation so difficult to share. Thank you for opening up."

"I always promised my sister that if anything ever happened, I would take care of Bree. I never imagined a tragedy would strike." He shook his head. "At the time, my mother showed early signs of dementia, so raising a grandchild was out of the question. I was the only option."

"You've dealt with your share of challenges." She grasped a hand, slowed, and tugged until he stopped. "Can I hug you?"

"Uh..." Her warm tone and natural compassion

caught him off guard. She meant well, but she was the session leader and a demanding business associate. She could turn into a dangerous distraction from his stable lifestyle, focused on work, Bree, and his ailing mother. "I…" No matter how tempting, a relationship might only lead to more heartache. Could he handle more ups and downs and possible loss? His heartbeats thumped in his temples. She attracted him like no one else.

Tessa didn't wait for confirmation and inched forward. When her toes touched his, she nestled close, slid her arms around his waist, and squeezed.

He stiffened, paused, and then encircled her shoulders. He stared at the dark sky, and a flashing light broke the black curtain. Was it an airplane crossing overhead or a falling star? Normally, he scoffed at those who believed in the magic of wishes, but with her warm curves snuggled against him, he reconsidered the possibility.

She burrowed the length of his body.

He drew in shaky breaths and inhaled the summery scent of her hair. She belonged right here in his arms. A jolt of surprise didn't stop his desire. He savored her delicious mix of soft and firm. Her curves felt new, yet somehow familiar. Relaxing a little, he dodged a rush of guilt.

She dropped her arms and backed away. "Sorry, I hugged you without your permission." She lowered her head, pivoted, and strolled forward. "I wanted to make you feel better."

"Don't worry." Uncertainty smothered him, but he meant his reassuring words. She showed the courage to share her empathy and initiate a deeper connection. "I didn't mind." He cleared his throat. "Actually, I enjoyed it…a lot." In two strides, he caught up, and sizzling heat burned his face. Clasping her hand, he swung it for a few seconds, raised, and brushed it against his lips before he relaxed his hold.

Gasping, she slowed and swiveled. "I wish things were different…" She swept her gaze from his face to the path.

"Me, too." He resumed a slow pace. What had he done? He followed her down a dangerous path with no Stop sign. How could he turn back now? Swallowing to moisten his dry mouth, he waited for the breeze to cool him and help him regain his usual, unfailing composure.

The demanding course wasn't a strong fit, but the intriguing instructor was a totally different story. Her irrepressible determination and overflowing enthusiasm wrangled him into new territory. Her energy and magnetism kept him awake at night and revved his senses into overdrive. A foreign combination of anticipation and elation slid the length of his body. But was he ready for this complication in his life, no matter how appealing?

Nearing the hotel, he sucked in deep breaths to tame his racing heart and growing desire. He must revert to a strictly professional relationship. Inside, the lobby lights beamed bright, but the area rested silent. Next to the teacher, he rode the elevator like a stowaway and chuckled at the clandestine mission.

The doors opened on the second floor, and Samir appeared, wearing a robe and carrying a towel. He snapped his head from Mark to Tessa and smirked before he stepped on. "I'm heading to the pool. Fancy meeting you two together so late this fine evening."

Instant embarrassment and regret dropped Mark's stomach to his knees. Reflected in the mirrored wall, the color drained from Tessa's face. An innocent stroll transformed into a terrible mistake. He never should have accepted her invitation. He knew better, and now, he'd pay. Clearly, the situation mortified her, and he shared the blame. He grimaced, punched the Close button, and held his breath until the elevator reached the pool level. Samir loved to tease. Now, would damaging rumors swirl?

****

The next morning, back in the hotel classroom, Tessa kicked off an assignment. Murmured discussion signaled strong engagement, and colorful notes and sketched diagrams decorated the plain walls. Clasping her hands, she strolled by Mark's group and offered a cautious smile. Was a normal day possible?

He flicked up the corners of his mouth, nodded, and glanced away.

She pressed a hand to her middle to still her churning stomach, and she inhaled but couldn't fill her lungs. Last evening, she lost her mind and made a huge mistake. Attraction was a dangerous thing, and she should not have called Mark a second time. When she got caught by Samir, she forced a smile over clenched teeth and wished she could snap her fingers to become invisible. Now, what had she done? Guilt aside, she savored the spontaneous hug and sensual kiss, but she needed to cool the lingering warmth.

Teasing her heart and testing her willpower, the memories kept her awake much too late. As she worked through the entire list of participants and led individual meetings, she tingled in Mark's sizzling presence, and the uneasy lump inside her expanded. His stiff body language echoed her own discomfort.

Late in the afternoon, she braced herself and called Mark to his individual progress conference at a table in a back corner of the room. She saved the toughest discussion for last. "Have a seat." She motioned to the chair opposite.

He dropped into place and opened a notebook.

"The purpose of this session is to evaluate your participation and set goals for the final week and beyond. Do you want to add anything to the agenda?" She bit her lip. Their sudden personal bond hovered like an unwelcome guest.

He shifted and shook his head. "I have nothing to add." He stared at his hands.

"How do you feel about your progress?" After last evening, how could she conduct a normal review? She admired the man behind the façade but risked her reputation over a silly attraction.

He cleared his throat and braced forearms on the table. "This experience—and you, as the leader—live up to your reputation as strong and demanding."

"Thank you for the positive feedback...I think." She nodded and scratched a note. The ebb and flow of conversations around the room offered them privacy. "At least, I'll take it as positive."

"I can't criticize the program. It might be excellent for most but is definitely not for everyone. I still reserve judgment." Mark leaned back. "What do you think?"

"First, give me your assessment." She wouldn't allow him to jump in and reorganize her usual flow. She straightened and crossed her legs.

"Showing people and explaining my personal side

is still difficult." He shifted and guzzled water. "The theories bear consideration. The group is inclusive and supportive. I've expanded my professional network. I learned no one judges my feelings." He leaned forward and narrowed his eyes. "Madame Leader, what have you observed?"

Heart racing, she moistened her lips. Through intense, navy-blue eyes, he drilled right through her. How could their icy depth spur such a hot reaction? She wanted to leap over the table and onto his lap. He'd improved some skills and, in private, unveiled the pain beneath his crusty surface, but she couldn't favor him over other participants and lower her expectations to meet his personal challenges.

"I recognize the efforts you've made to participate in exercises and group discussions. Last evening was an exception, of course, when you skipped bowling." She ran fingers through a tangle of curls. "However…if you truly want to be successful, you must make more changes." She drew in a long, deep breath. Admonishing him was as painful as a bruise. How could she uphold the program's strict standards yet show compassion and support?

"After two evenings together, I understand so much more about why you deadbolt lock inside your emotions." Riding a wave of tenderness, she raised and lowered a hand before she dared to touch him. Last evening was a mistake that lingered like smoke from a fire. She wanted to let attraction take over, but from now on, she couldn't forget her professional demeanor for an instant.

"Offer specific examples of how you've applied your learnings and how you intend to use them back at the office." She twisted a corkscrew of hair around a finger. "As well, show the other participants a hint of the experiences that shaped you. You need to open up within class."

"More effort? You expect *more* effort?" He widened his eyes and glared.

Steeling herself at his raised tone, she clenched her hands around her water bottle. "I can't evaluate your performance in the program by what you shared after hours." In the background, other participants conferred in low voices. "You need to exhibit more open dialogue, vulnerability, and humility. Remember, build relationships. People don't care how much you know until they know how much you care." She allowed him a moment to calm his outburst. "I only ask you to meet the same standards as the others."

"I'll think about your demands." He frowned and shook his head. "I'll let you know if I can comply."

"Take the weekend, and let me know Monday." A knot looped tight around her waist. What would he decide? Did she just scare him away? "I hope you persevere."

"I never quit." He forced back his chair. "I also *never* compromise my values." He leapt to his feet and swung in the opposite direction. Stiffening, he stormed across the room to rejoin the group activity.

She rose and stared at his back. He could rebel all he wanted. Challenging mediocrity was her job. Her reputation rode on the success of each and every participant. Circulating around the room and addressing questions, she wrung her hands and replayed their discussion. Mark reacted with wide, fiery eyes. He fully believed he demonstrated the required effort. Outside the classroom, he revealed his wounded inner life, but in front of all his classmates, he still held back honest emotion.

"Tessa." Holly tapped her shoulder.

"Oh, I'm sorry, I didn't hear you." She dragged back her full attention. She had better practice what she demanded of the group—concentrated focus at all times. She bustled to address the latest question and sidestepped Mark's personal challenges and heavy baggage. Still, the image of his glassy eyes and firm jaw haunted her, no matter how hard she fought to erase it.

To wrap the week, she played upbeat music and urged participants to share their key takeaways. She pointed in rapid-fire succession and singled out random observations. After her debriefing session with Mark, she hesitated to invite his contribution to the discussion. But equity considerations forced her to give him a turn.

"Let's hear your highlight, Mark."

"This weekend, I'll digest and analyze things." He thrust out his chin. "But I see how the learnings apply at home as well as work."

"Thank you for sharing, Mark." She nodded encouragement. Had he actually listened to her advice? She'd explore further and test him. "Would you care to give specifics?"

"Not right now, thanks." He shook his head, stared, and blinked. "Maybe next week."

"Sure. I'll hold you to your word." *If* he attended next week. Addressing the larger group, she threw wide her arms and smiled. "Congratulations, everyone. Your list of accomplishments impresses me." She scanned the room.

Mark studied his fingernails.

"Now, return home, apply your learnings, and recharge for next week. Safe travels." She dropped her arms to her sides.

The group stood, stretched, and gathered their belongings.

As a buzz of casual conversation spread, Tessa removed notes and charts from the walls and tossed colored markers with a clack into a plastic container.

"Thanks for another great week." Holly followed and disassembled learning tools that dotted the room. "When I debut my new listening skills at home, I bet my husband and staff won't recognize me." She laughed and swept building blocks into a box.

"They'll appreciate the new you." Tessa bathed in a familiar rush of accomplishment. Clearly, participants recognized the value they gained each week. She was proud of their results. "Have a good weekend." Slipping into a cluster, she dared glance at Mark, and sparks flew throughout her body. Did he have any idea she wanted to chase him out the door and kiss him goodbye?

"We shared bowling highlights with the teacher's pet." Samir gave Mark a playful punch on the shoulder and hooted.

Shaking his head, Mark inhaled a sharp breath and glanced from Samir to Tessa.

"Don't be too sure. He still might get detention." Forcing a smile, she raised her eyebrows. "See you next week." She spun and hurried to gather the rest of the supplies. From a distance, the banter faded, but she shuddered at the accusation. A black, heavy cloak fell on her shoulders. A perception of favoritism, no matter how unfounded, could be a red flag for current and future program participants. Nobody respected an instructor who overshadowed the class with a personal relationship. No one tolerated favorites. Did Samir refer to Mark's pass on bowling, the elevator encounter, or something else?

As she lifted the container, she couldn't stop her hands from quivering. She definitely needed to halt Samir's innuendo before it escalated into a full-fledged rumor. Attraction was a powerful force. She allowed her desire to know the complex inner Mark and his overwhelming allure to cause a momentary slip in her judgment. She couldn't protect her sterling reputation amidst allegations of impropriety or favoritism.

Whenever she observed Mark's lean, muscular physique and carved, handsome face, she wanted to explore his mind and body. When she learned of his buried grief, she wanted to comfort him and soothe his pain. She revealed her awful secret about motherhood and sank into a safe net.

But the consequences of a work romance were not worth the risk. Still, he teased her imagination in a shocking way. Did Samir detect the truth? She'd make sure she provided not a shred of evidence he might be right. From now on, before, during, and after class, she'd keep her distance and treat Mark the same as every other participant. She might offend him, but what else could she do?

Chapter 15

The next morning at home, Tessa prepared a special breakfast for Ellie. The sweet scent of pancakes, butter, and syrup filled the cheery, yellow kitchen. A special breakfast kicked off a relaxing weekend.

"Did you have fun at Auntie Julie's?" She flipped a pancake and then hugged Ellie so tight she squished her daughter's full cheeks.

"Yup. She let Ginger sleep on my bed." Ellie wriggled away and held out a hand for the dog to lick.

"Oh, what a lucky girl and spoiled dog." She smiled at the cute pair. "What else did you do?"

"We went to see Grandma." Ellie furrowed her eyebrows.

"What's wrong? You like to visit Grandma." She squatted to eye level. "Tell Mommy."

"Grandma's friend says I need a daddy, and I don't have one." Ellie blinked and rubbed her eyes.

"Aw, sweetie." Encircling Ellie in her arms, Tessa stroked her sleek, black hair, so different from her own. "I'm sorry Grandma's friend made you feel sad. I will always take care of you. Some boys and girls live with a mommy and a daddy."

"Like Zach and Quinn."

"Right." She rubbed Ellie's back. "But some kids live with only a mommy, and some boys and girls live with only a daddy. Every family is different."

"I know. My birth daddy lives in China." She backed away and nodded. "I won't see him." She hopped onto a chair at the table. "I'm hungry."

"Good because breakfast is ready." Tessa adjusted the chair to discourage Ginger from resting her furry head on Ellie's lap. "See the slices of orange and banana beside your pancake."

She slid onto a chair opposite her daughter, sighed, and cradled a coffee mug. She arrived home from Leadership Camp more drained than usual. Last evening, she switched on a movie to amuse Ellie and flopped on the couch.

Overall, participants showed great progress, but the revealing, personal conversations with Mark unsettled and stirred her sensitive core. Then Samir labeled Mark teacher's pet and raised a teasing accusation she couldn't ignore. Her face burned at the memory. She prided herself on fairness and consistency. Workplace romances inevitably caused complications, so she had no choice but to retreat. Sipping coffee, she tugged back her attention to Ellie's running dialogue.

"At daycare, we built a house out of boxes, and I painted it pink." Ellie gobbled a mouthful of pancake.

Syrup dribbled down her chin, and Tessa unfolded a napkin and wiped the sticky streak. "I bet it was beautiful. Eat another bite." A ring interrupted, and she jumped and grabbed the phone. "Hello."

"May I speak with Tessa Shore?"

The voice on the other end of the line clipped her words. "This is Tessa. Who's calling?" She stiffened.

"Irina from Heritage Haven. Your sister isn't home to tell her what happened."

Unease sprinted through her stomach. Something

must be wrong with Mom.

"I'm sorry to report I can't locate your mother." Irina cleared her throat. "After breakfast, she and Rose left the dining room. I assumed they went to sit in the lounge, as usual. But when I checked, I discovered they weren't there. Adele is not in her room or anywhere in the home. Neither is Rose. They must be together. Do you have *any* idea where they went?"

"I don't." Not another disappearance. Was Mom's wandering a trend? Alarm whirled through her mind and made her slightly dizzy. "She's not with my sister. Julie travelled with her family to a ball tournament." She bit her lip. Mom could converse well enough, but she muddled details, soon forgot conversations, and became easily confused. Alone, without a responsible companion, she could easily get lost, robbed, or led astray.

Heart quickening, Tessa paced across the kitchen and flashed a thumbs up at Ellie. Her daughter's mouth bulged with far-too-much food. "I'll come and see you in a few minutes. Maybe Mom and Rose just wandered off to explore the neighborhood." She smoothed her tone into a calm she didn't feel.

"I'm so sorry."

Irina raised her voice to a distraught pitch. She must know the dangers a person with dementia could encounter. No doubt, she feared the consequences if anything awful happened. "We'll find her," she reassured Irina with quiet control. Placing blame or getting angry would only escalate the situation. Still, Tessa shuddered. A care home should provide constant supervision and give families confidence their loved ones were safe. She expected more from Irina and her staff.

Glancing at Ellie, she swallowed and spread her quivering lips into a weak smile. She ended the call and abandoned food, dishes, and utensils. Her breakfast could wait.

"Don't you want to eat, Mommy?" Ellie dangled a slice of orange from her mouth.

"Maybe later." Appetite gone, she squeezed Ellie's shoulder. "You can help me with an important job."

"Okay." She swiped a finger through the syrup covering her plate and licked it. "What?"

"We need to find Grandma. She left home and didn't tell anyone where she went. So you and I will be detectives and find her."

"Okay, I can help." Ellie grinned and bounced off her chair.

Tessa wiped Ellie's sticky face, grabbed her purse and water bottle, and hustled to the car. Dementia was a horrible disease, but in some ways, nothing had changed. All Tessa's life, she managed frequent issues with her demanding mother and did backflips to keep her happy. Now, serious illness handed Mom a legitimate reason for outbursts and erratic behavior.

Any sense of control jerked away and contorted her insides into a painful lump. She tapped her fingers on the steering wheel, and minutes later, after a speedy ride through light, Saturday traffic, she arrived at Heritage Haven.

Wringing her hands, Irina met them at the door of the single-storey, brick building. "I'm so sorry. Adele and Rose haven't returned. Rose's son didn't answer his phone, and I feel terrible. Where did they go?"

Irina's pink blouse was crisp, but her demeanor and

posture sagged. Holding Ellie's hand, Tessa stepped inside. Lingering scents of toast and oatmeal greeted her. Usually, the aroma of meals wafting throughout the building made it feel comfortable and homey, but today, the odor nearly sickened her. The place didn't at all live up to its image as a safe refuge.

A balding gentleman occupied a chair near the entrance in a floral armchair. He nodded and smiled.

Why wasn't Mom here, too? Tessa barely smiled back. "On the way over in the car, I wracked my brain." She squeezed Ellie's hand. "Recently, Mom and Rose mentioned a shopping trip."

"Maybe I should call the police." Irina sighed and clutched her hands to her chin.

"Wait." Tessa raised a hand. "We'll figure out a plan."

Irina's face alternated between pale and flushed. She shifted and covered her cheeks.

"Did they hop a bus to a mall or downtown?" Tessa shuddered at the plight of two disoriented seniors as they navigated an unfamiliar transportation system.

Irina drew a sharp breath. "You might be right. Adele asked me what buses stop at the corner. I explained that one travels north, and one heads south. At the time, I didn't pay much attention."

"With any luck, I'll find them at one of the shopping malls. Before you call police, let's contact the bus dispatch center. Maybe they can reach drivers who pass here." Tessa fumbled in her purse and retrieved her phone. Tapping a foot, she searched and punched in the number. Fortunately, the representative who answered reacted with kindness and concern. He must hear the fear in her voice.

"I'll check with the drivers and call back as soon as possible."

After the call, Tessa shifted her gaze to Irina. "Stay near the front door and listen for the phone. I'll drive around the neighborhood and check the south mall." She couldn't hit a panic button too soon. "Try to call Rose's son. I'll update you soon."

Heart racing, she buckled Ellie into the car and crept up and down the nearby streets. Usually, she admired the varied homes and overhanging trees in the neighborhood, but today, she concentrated only on finding her missing mother. She clenched her fingers into fists around the steering wheel. "Watch for Grandma, sweetie."

"I don't see her, Mommy." Ellie swung her legs and bumped the front seat.

"Don't give up. Remember, you're a detective." Tessa scanned left, right, and behind. Blinking away tears, she swirled through the mishaps that might befall her mother, unescorted and away from supervision. Mom helped herself to items from former neighbors, and if she pulled the same stunt in a store, she could face shoplifting charges. For the second time in two weeks, Mom vanished and threw Tessa into a state of alarm.

She toured the area and spotted no sign. What a nightmare to start her weekend. Trust impatient Mom to forge ahead with an excursion. She always wanted things arranged her way. A pinch of anger stirred with concern and heated Tessa's neck.

"Hey, Ellie, jelly belly..." She slipped a free hand over a shoulder and wiggled fingers in an encouraging wave. "You're a good helper." Glancing in the mirror, she caught sight of her daughter's dark eyes, glossed with moisture.

"What if we never see her ever again?" Ellie wiped a fat tear from her cheek.

"Don't worry, sweetie." She kept her tone more upbeat than her dread inside. "We'll find her."

Back at Heritage Haven, Tessa lowered a window, and warm air tickled her cheeks.

Irina raced to the car. "I feel terrible. No one has ever wandered farther than the front sidewalk." She shook her head and frowned.

Normally neatly styled, her short hair fanned in scrambled strands. Clearly, she recognized the severity of the awful situation. Definitely, she wasn't her usual, composed self.

"I want Grandma." Ellie stuck out her bottom lip.

"I do, too." Tessa swiveled and rubbed Ellie's restless legs.

"My hunch is Mom headed to City North Mall. She liked its fabric store. I'll drive there now and check. If you hear anything, call me. I'll stop and answer."

Irina nodded and swept her gaze up and down the street.

Driving north on Albert Street, Tessa willed her phone to ring. She lowered the radio volume, so she wouldn't miss the sound. She ran a light and checked the rearview mirror for flashing lights. Distracted, she half listened to Ellie's commentary on what she spotted out the window.

"I see a bus," Ellie shouted and pointed. "Maybe Grandma's riding on it."

"Maybe, but I think it's traveling the wrong way." Just in case, she squinted through the bus windows to discern the riders. None of the people who whizzed by in a blur were her mother. She chewed her bottom lip and tapped on the steering wheel.

Fifteen minutes later, as she approached the mall, her phone rang. Turning onto a side street, she braked and picked up the call.

"I received a clue. A driver stopped downtown, and two older women asked for directions."

Tessa winced at Irina's shouted report. "Did he remember which bus they caught?" She groped for her water bottle to moisten her throat. Confused by a fleet of buses lined up, the pair could easily end up anywhere in the city.

"You were exactly right. They transferred to the northbound bus." Irina sighed and moaned. "Should I call the police?"

"If I don't locate them at the mall, I'll let you know." Tessa stared ahead and swallowed. "Then we'll file a missing person report."

"Okay. Oh, I hope you find them."

She ended the call, wrestled an arm between the seats, and squeezed Ellie's knees. "Here we go, detective. Let's find Grandma."

"I run fast." Ellie bounced in her booster seat.

At the shopping centre, Tessa leapt out of the car, held Ellie's hand, and jogged to the door. The sooner she combed the place, the better. Inside, she paused and then veered left. This early, few shoppers clogged the common area, and cheery but annoying music tapped a beat. Her mission was anything but happy. "Let's see how fast you run." She held tight to Ellie's warm, little hand and scurried in and out of the stores Mom might visit. At the fabric shop, she wove between large bolts of patterned fabric.

"I don't see her." Ellie stopped and stomped a foot. "Where is she?"

"I wish I knew, sweetie." Tessa's throat dried. She scanned rows of buttons and ribbons. Approaching the cashier to quiz her, she paused. Murmurs and giggles floated from the notions corner. Her heart rate leapt, and she changed direction. The voices sounded familiar. "I think they're at the back of the store." She tugged Ellie down the far aisle.

"What a coincidence." Mom squealed and nearly dropped a pin cushion.

She wore a lime, gauzy blouse and yellow, billowy skirt. If Tessa didn't know better, she'd assume Mom was a healthy, flamboyant senior and fully capable of managing an unchaperoned outing. The lump in her stomach shrunk and crept to her throat. Appearances deceived. Although not obvious on the outside, Mom was no longer a strong, independent woman. Her faculties diminished by the month. Tessa blinked and swallowed.

"Who are they?" Rose peered at Tessa and Ellie.

"My daughter and granddaughter." Mom kissed Tessa's cheek and smothered Ellie in a tight hug. "Tessa isn't married."

"Hmmm. Now I remember." Rose creased her forehead, nodded, and smiled.

Wearing a white, tailored shirt and crisp, black pants, Rose contrasted with Mom's colorful ensemble. Was the instigator Rose or Mom? Either way, Tessa couldn't trust them to stay out of trouble.

"You should meet my son, Champ. He would make an excellent husband and father."

"We found you, Grandma." Ellie wriggled out of her grip.

Tessa tensed her shoulders. Rose wouldn't ease pressure to find a man. She forced a polite smile and slipped a hand around Mom's left elbow. "I was worried. Irina didn't know where you went."

"Don't be silly. I'm a grown woman." She huffed and plopped a hand on a hip. "I can shop if I want. I won't ask anybody's permission."

"Your mother is right, dear. What is your name?" Rose adjusted her glasses.

Speechless, Tessa threw down her hands. When Mom ventured out on her own, she had no idea of the concern she caused or the danger she risked. Her friend was no different. Store sounds of a clerk snipping and tearing fabric drifted from another aisle. How lucky other shoppers were to enjoy an ordinary day. "My name is Tessa, and her name is Ellie." She tipped her head toward her daughter.

"She doesn't resemble you." Rose scrutinized Ellie and frowned.

"Excuse me while I make a call." Tessa dug in her purse for her phone. "Ellie, stand right beside Grandma, and don't wander." She strode up the aisle out of earshot, shielded the phone, and called Heritage Haven. "I found them." She blurted the news before Irina could ask.

"Oh, thank the Lord." Irina squealed and sighed. "I just talked to Rose's son, and he's on his way here. Will you drive the ladies home?"

"As soon as I can tear them away from the fabric store. They have no idea they were lost." Tessa giggled and tucked a wayward curl behind an ear. "Why did we worry?" Now that she'd found Mom, she appreciated a glimmer of humor in the situation. Sometimes, despite sadness, she needed a release to keep her sanity. After the call, she rejoined the women and Ellie. "Tell you what, gals. Your lunch is ready, so I'll drive you home."

"A nice bus driver said he'd give us a ride…" Rose hugged her purse.

"Maybe another time." She spoke firmly. "Besides, Irina just told me your son wants to see you."

"Oh, you mean Champ." Rose grinned and stood straighter. "He's such a good son."

After a little more cajoling, Tessa coaxed the women outside and into the car.

Rose settled in the front passenger seat.

Mom squeezed in the back with Ellie. "Where are you taking us?" She tapped Tessa's shoulder.

"Back home." Straining to concentrate on the traffic, she blinked to contain her tears and not alarm her passengers. She could train a group of leaders to improve their skills, but she couldn't do a thing to fix Mom's memory.

Before long, she steered off Albert Street toward Heritage Haven. As she slowed in front of the care home, a tall man paced on the front sidewalk. With a jolt, she recognized the striking figure, and a swirl of heat and confusion collided in her middle.

"I see Champ." Rose pointed and waved.

Tessa nearly choked. Mark Delaney was Champ? Should she laugh or cry? Apparently, despite her best intentions, she couldn't avoid another encounter.

Chapter 16

A white car braked in front of Heritage Haven, and Mark squinted and froze. Trees and traffic faded to the background. His mother rode in the front seat beside Tessa. Why were they together? Irina reported his mother and another resident disappeared, but she didn't specify a name. He clenched his jaw. Adele was Mom's partner in crime, and now, Tessa returned the favor and rescued *his* mom. He wanted to see his charming teacher, but not in this situation.

Pulse quickening, he widened his eyes. The alarming news his mother disappeared ruined a relaxing start to the day. Mom never wandered. Maybe her dementia worsened, or maybe Adele was a bad influence. A flicker of anger at the whole mess burned in his chest. Either way, the situation didn't bode well for the future.

Earlier this morning, he had clicked off his phone for a run around Wascana Lake with a cousin. He and Paul connected a few times a month to catch up on family news. Rounding the end of the lake near Broad Street, he glanced over at Paul. "The constant soul-searching at Leadership Camp drives me nuts." In the mild air and bright sunshine, he inhaled air scented with new growth and enjoyed a welcome reprieve from intense training sessions.

"You've always been your father's son." Paul

laughed through quick breaths. With heavy strides, he pounded the pavement.

He was one of Mark's few trusted confidantes. Familiar with family history, he avoided too many questions. "You should see the course leader." Mark stared ahead at a clump of evergreen trees. "She's gorgeous. Somehow, she convinced me to share details of my personal life I never tell anyone."

"Grab the opportunity." Paul veered and slapped Mark's back. "You could smooth your bristly edges and add a little romance in one package. Why hold back?"

Mark laughed. "Thanks for the generous vote of confidence." He matched Paul's pace and curved along a path past the park bandstand and toward Albert Street. The quacks of ducks and honks of geese echoed across the lake. Close to nature, he relaxed his stiff shoulders and cleared his mind for possibilities.

"Tell her how you feel. You've nothing to lose." Paul checked his fitness tracker.

His candid cousin made a good point. Mark had everything to gain. Maybe he could dull the persistent ache and loneliness inside. "I'll stick with the program and see what develops." He clamped shut his mouth and concentrated on his speed as he passed the Legislative Building and headed for the final stretch. For awhile, he ran in silence. "Thanks for the advice."

"No problem. Have a good week." Paul dashed toward the parking lot across from one of the park lookout spots.

Near a totem pole, Mark eased right and crossed behind the art gallery toward home. Beating his runners on the path, he visualized an intimate conversation with Tessa. An electric current jolted to his limbs. Could he express his strong, affectionate feelings? He'd arrange a quiet, private setting to set the stage. The idea both excited and daunted him.

After the run, he showered and embarked on errands with Bree. He left off his phone, so he relaxed and chatted without interruption. Strolling through a grocery store parking lot, he glanced at her serious expression. "Feeling okay about the Desiree thing?" He already heard her mumbled report of the discussion and apologies, but a casual check-in couldn't hurt.

"Better, but I still don't like her." She scrunched her face.

"I don't blame you." He patted her back. "Good job handling a tough situation. I'm proud of you."

"Thanks." Bree smirked and tipped up her chin.

When he arrived home after a pleasant outing, his land line and personal phone had lit with panicked messages. Now, he faced Mom, Adele, Tessa, and her daughter, all spilling out of the compact car.

A soft wind swept by and tousled Tessa's curls. In an instant, his temperature jumped to uncomfortably warm. He should have worn a cooler T-shirt. His heart thumped as hard as during exercise, and overwhelming affection filled his entire body. At the same time, a threatening mix of anger, relief, and sorrow squeezed his throat, and he swallowed. Clearly, Mom's dementia continued to worsen, and she required more supervision, especially around her spunky, new friend. At least, she arrived unharmed.

His mom dove and hugged him.

"Hi, Mom. Where were you?" He raised his eyebrows. If only he could commiserate with Tessa and laugh in private.

"Hi...Champ?" She tilted her head and clapped a hand over her mouth.

"Tell me your name again." Rose quirked an eyebrow and pointed. "Wait, do you know Champ?"

"I'm Tessa, and I know your son through work." She dropped her hands and smiled. "But I usually call him Mark." Shifting her gaze, she crinkled her eyes and sucked in her cheeks.

With humor written all over her impish expression, she probably stifled a giggle. Clearly, she enjoyed the surprise meeting but didn't know how to react. "Dad nicknamed me Champ." Mark shrugged. "No matter what challenge hit, he expected me to tackle it like a winner. In our family, the name stuck." He chuckled and rested an arm along his mom's shoulders.

"I wanted you and..." Rose paused and stared at the sky. "You and this woman to meet, and here you are."

"Mark, meet my daughter, Ellie." Tessa rested her hands on the child's shoulders.

"Your mom told me you're a special girl." He smiled down. Obviously, despite Tessa's misgivings, she shone as a mother like she excelled at work.

Ellie grinned and jiggled her tiny body.

"How wonderful, ladies. You came home," Irina shouted and hurried out the door. She hugged Rose and Adele. "I missed you. Let's all go inside."

"Why don't you stay for lunch?" Adele led the way and called over her shoulder.

In the lobby, Bree lounged and read a book on a floral sofa near the door. She surveyed the group and narrowed her eyes.

Her ripped jeans and red T-shirt stuck out in the

tranquil atmosphere inhabited by seniors. Contrasting with the fresh air outside, a stifling warmth smothered Mark.

"Breezy's here, too." Grandma Rose rushed over, kissed her cheek, and then rubbed off a red lipstick smear. "Oh, what a perfect day." She clapped her hands.

"This young lady is my niece, Bree." Mark swept an arm in her direction. Surely, she would raise her chin and acknowledge everyone. She'd rather burrow her nose in a book than meet new people.

Flipping a page, she scanned the group and smiled at Ellie. "Hi."

Ellie batted her eyelashes and squiggled close to Bree. "Want to play?"

"She discovered the shuffleboard game in the lounge," said Tessa. "You can play until lunch is ready."

Ellie giggled and tugged Bree's hand.

Bree shrugged, flipped a glance at Mark, and, swinging Ellie's hand, scooted away.

"When I met your mom the night of the storm, I found her pretty distraught." Mark sauntered behind Adele and Mom to the dining room. "But not today. Look at the way they chat like long-time friends." He sucked in a sharp breath at Tessa's full lips spread into a grin. She understood what he dealt with as a single parent and caregiver, and she stirred new yearnings.

"I need to thank you, again. You rescued Mom *and* Ginger."

"Your golden retriever is the same breed as my dog, Rufus." She must love dogs as much as he did. He ticked another box. She captivated him in every way, and for the first time, he considered the possibility of life with an ideal partner.

"Ginger is my beloved, canine child." She laughed and glanced up. "Sometimes, she listens better than my darling, girl child."

Joking about Ellie, Tessa radiated love and pride. She showed no hint of the ambivalence that haunted her and the secret she confided in an intimate moment. Whatever strain and guilt tested her, she never faltered as a dedicated mom. A hot rush surged from Mark's torso to his limbs. Every time he shared her company, she grew more beautiful. He couldn't soak up enough of her natural complexion, interested eyes, and self-deprecating humor. He flashed back to the classroom and the structure she demanded. At the moment, he didn't even mind her persistent grip on the balance of power.

The aroma of oregano, thyme, and fresh-baked bread wafted out the dining room door. Mark's mouth watered at the prospect of minestrone soup and homemade buns, and the growl in his stomach signaled a healthy appetite. Neck tingling, he anticipated lunch with Tessa, even if surrounded by others. Maybe someday they'd dine together on a private date.

The hostess seated them at a table by a large window. "Lunch will be ready in about fifteen minutes." The room was homey with upholstered chairs and round tables covered with pastel tablecloths. Although not his taste, the colors probably appealed to many of the female residents.

"What is your name?" Mom squinted and pointed.

"She's my daughter, Tessa," said Adele.

"Oh, I see." Mom furrowed her brow.

Mark rubbed a temple. Dementia transformed his mother from organized and intellectual to scattered and forgetful. But Tessa would understand. So far, Mom could converse well but might not remember the exchange minutes later. She always recognized Bree and him, although she often forgot others. She still smiled and laughed, but her faculties would continue to diminish. The sad facts sandpapered his core, and, for the first time, he admitted and didn't squelch his pain.

"She's the one, Champ." Mom nodded and tapped a coral fingernail on the table. "She will make a perfect wife for you and a good mother for Breezy."

"Oh, what a wonderful idea." Adele giggled and clapped. "Ellie needs a father."

"Mom, please…" He sighed and shook his head. His mom never played aggressive matchmaker, but these days, she often surprised him. She didn't intend to embarrass him.

Tessa covered her cheeks. "We couldn't possibly date because we work together. I don't think an office romance is a very good idea." She laughed and shook her head. "He's a busy guy, and I don't want to distract him."

"Champ is pretty stubborn." Rose squeezed her son's arm. "He might change your mind."

"I'm sure he would make a very suitable husband for someone." Tessa tilted her head.

Tensing his jaw, Mark forced a laugh. She ruled out herself as a candidate for his wife.

Just then, the server appeared with pen poised over an order pad.

"Excuse me, I'll call the girls." Exhaling with a whoosh, he slid back the chair and escaped. By the time he returned, Mom and Adele might converse about a less-personal topic. Cooling his hot face, he strolled to the lounge. Tessa could fend off their matchmaking efforts for a few minutes.

She made clear she could picture him as husband material for someone but not her. Sure, she shunned office romances, and he always avoided them, too. She would never allow a relationship to disrupt her career and other plans unless...he could possibly change her mind. At the wild idea, his heartbeat jumped. He rounded the corner into the mellow surroundings of the lounge and stopped to absorb the surprising scene with standoffish, reserved Bree and cute, bubbly Ellie.

Off to one side, past groupings of muted, floral chairs, Bree hoisted Ellie so she could reach over the edge of the chunky shuffleboard table and better grip and slide a puck.

Ellie skidded a shot past the target, and it clunked over the edge of the playing surface into the gutter. Laughing, Bree set down Ellie and tweaked her ponytail.

"I want to try again." Ellie squealed and bounced on her toes. She spun and mirrored Bree's wide smile.

"Hi, Bree and Ellie." He hated to interrupt. Seeing Bree interact confidently and hearing her tinkly giggle were a rare experience these days. Little Ellie was quite a charmer. "Time for lunch, girls."

"I'm not hungry." Ellie stood on tiptoe to snag a rock.

"I am." Bree glanced over Ellie's head to Uncle Mark. She smirked and touched the tip of Ellie's nose. "Hey, let's race to the dining room. But you aren't allowed to run. You can only speed walk."

Ellie dropped a rock and waddled away, ponytail swishing.

"Hey, no fair. I saw you got a head start." Bree accelerated but allowed Ellie to lead.

Behind the happy pair, Mark strolled the wide hallway framed by soft blue walls. He breathed the spicy air and expanded his chest where a pang of regret settled. He massaged the ache, but it refused to dissipate. Then instead of fighting, he absorbed and nursed the pain until it eased. Bree had no idea of everything she missed by not having a mother or a sibling. He did, though. He understood all too well. Smiling, he sauntered behind the girls to the table.

Still laughing and puffing, Ellie chose a chair beside Bree.

Sliding into place, Mark scanned the group. He was busy enough already, and marriage was unlikely. Or was it? Tessa forced him to rethink everything. Clearly, while he was away, the topic stayed the same. He doubted any of the quiet conversations that floated from other tables was quite as sensitive.

"Your son is a nice man." Tessa broke a bun. "I'm sure he'll make a woman very happy. Oh, this soup is delicious."

"Yes, minestrone's my favorite." He smiled at the patient way Bree showed Ellie how to stir the soup to cool it.

Across the table, Tessa fixed her gaze on her bowl.

Mark cut a warm, crusty bun and slathered on butter. Her comment was a compliment any mother would appreciate. Inhaling steam, he sipped a mouthful of hot, savory soup, laden with the flavors of sweet tomatoes intermingled with hearty vegetables. Her assessment and the comforting meal should soothe him. After all, he didn't seek a bride. But why did a mysterious force grip his heart whenever she appeared, and why did he feel so rejected?

Chapter 17

On Sunday, Tessa strolled with Ellie and Ginger to Julie's place. She couldn't wait to fill in her sister on the latest developments. The delicious fragrance of chocolate-chip cookies enticed them inside the welcoming, colorful surroundings.

"Good timing." Owen scooped Ellie into a hug. "Come with your cousins and me to the park. We'll take Ginger, too." Grinning, he led the kids and dog outside.

"Have fun, sweetie," Tessa called out the door but failed to catch Ellie's attention in the excitement of seeing her cousins. Alone with Julie, in a rush of emotion, Tessa clutched a clump of hair on either side of her head. "You won't believe what happened yesterday." She followed her sister through the cool hallway to the kitchen.

"Grab a chair, and I'll make tea." Julie filled the kettle and plunked down across the table from Tessa. "Okay, shoot. We have a lot to discuss."

Tessa swept her gaze from Julie's crinkled forehead to a giant, framed picture of orange, green, and yellow peppers. The décor shouted happy energy and always made her feel at home. "Can you believe Mom actually disappeared again?" Curls bouncing, she grimaced and shook her head. "After a very tense hour, I found Mom and Rose. Then I drove to the care home, and when I realized Mark is Champ, I nearly crashed the car."

"Mom concerns me. But let's talk about fun things." Julie laughed. "I can picture your shock at Champ's identity." She bustled to the counter, poured tea, and served a plate of warm cookies.

"I rejected matchmaking services from Mom and Rose, but I understand their point. If I wanted a guy in my life, I might choose Mark." A tingle raced from her stomach to her chest and down both arms.

"Let me correct you, little sis." Sitting opposite, Julie pulled forward her chair, smiled, and raised her eyebrows. "You're attracted, big time. Why fight it? You just have to get your head around the idea a man could make your life even better."

"But..." She daydreamed about tracing with a fingertip the symmetrical lines of his face. In her imagination, she ran her hands through his thick hair, nuzzled a hint of stubble, and slipped an arm around his trim waist. Another, longer hug tempted her more than the most decadent ice cream. Her sister was right.

"Even though he stays cautious and reserved around others, he shared enough to show me what's beneath his crusty surface." Barely smiling, Tessa sipped her tea. "The extra time I spent after class came back to bite me, though. One of the other participants called him teacher's pet. The perception could seriously tarnish my reputation."

"Hmmm, the person might be right." Julie widened her eyes.

"Maybe, but I thought I covered it well." Tessa flew the palms of her hands to her flushed cheeks.

"Apparently not." Julie laughed.

Tessa dropped her hands to her lap. "I didn't lower my standards to accommodate him. I insisted he open up more in class, and he reacted with shock. Deep down, I hated to demand so much."

"Oh?" Julie tilted her head and twisted a curl.

"He's an introvert. He'll never be the most popular guy at the office, but no one could show more intelligence, integrity, and inner strength." Tessa straightened and thrust forward her palms, laying his positive qualities on the table. "If he buffs his edges, he'll prove he's more sensitive than he appears."

"Does he listen to your advice?" Julie ran a finger around the rim of her cup.

"If he wants to graduate from the class, he has no choice." Tessa rolled her lips into a tight seal. Her heart squeezed at the way his expression softened and flickered into amusement at the sight of Bree's and Ellie's antics. "I'm in charge."

"But will you let go and allow him to achieve his goals his own way and not exactly your way?" Julie blinked and sampled a cookie.

Tessa couldn't stop her hand from shaking, and it vibrated the tea in her cup until the scent of lemon wafted. She set it down with a clink and spilled a few drops. Julie's question poked like a stick. If anyone but her sister challenged her approach, she resisted or refused to listen. But Julie knew her better than anyone, and Tessa respected her perspective.

"You could change your mind." Julie narrowed her eyes and propped her elbows on the table. "Don't shun all men because of one bad experience. Why not loosen your grip on a few things?"

A disastrous relationship filled with conflict and

tension sent her running from her fiancé and propelled her into adopting Ellie. She never forgot Roger's bitter words. His scathing assessment of her controlling nature cut to the core. She didn't take to heart his feedback, but she listened to Julie. Could she release her firm grip on every aspect of her life? Did she deceive herself to think she should or could control every situation? Tessa sighed and slumped in her chair.

She couldn't force Mark to bowl with the group and shouldn't have questioned his decision. He mirrored her belief family belonged first. She guided her family but couldn't control them, either. Despite expert medical advice, she couldn't heal her mother and restore her memory. Even when silence was more appropriate, she couldn't contain Ellie's effervescent personality.

"Maybe I could relax...a little." Tessa stared out the open kitchen window at the lush leaves and blue sky. Twittering, a sparrow flew by. The peaceful setting hugged her. "I hate to admit I'm wrong...but maybe I'm not right."

"I love you, warts and all." Julie smirked and crunched the last bite of a cookie. "But your future husband might not agree."

Tessa giggled and uttered a mock huff. "Now you sound like Mom and Rose. Mark is just a co-worker and student. I can't marry the guy, but he possesses the most magical combination of dark hair and blue eyes I've ever seen."

"You're smitten." Julie laughed. "Make sure you choose me as matron of honor."

"One thing at a time." Tessa giggled. The conversation drifted in a ludicrous direction. Another thing she didn't control. "First, I'll make sure he graduates. My role is to produce good leaders. I don't groom husbands."

"I'll try not to gloat when I say, 'I told you so.' " Julie clattered dishes and cleared the table.

"When I see your promise in action, I'll believe it." Tessa jumped to help. She set down plates and hugged her sister. An ache filled her throat at the way she loved Julie and the tragedy of the sister Mark lost.

As soon as the park group returned, Tessa hurried home with Ellie and Ginger to prepare for the week. She shoved Mark from her mind and achieved success for about six seconds. Knowing her expectations, would he return for the final session? If he didn't, how would she feel?

On Monday morning, at the office, Tessa's phone rang at precisely eight o'clock. Shelves tidied and sticky notes arranged on the desk, she plunged into the day. On the second ring, without checking Call Display, she grabbed the receiver. "Hello, this is Tessa Shore speaking."

"Count me in. I'll complete the program."

She would know Mark's voice anywhere. She clapped a hand to her heart. Her instant smile reflected from the window. His tone held a hint of warmth, but he didn't waste words.

"I thought so." She relaxed her shoulders. "I'm so glad to hear the news. I'll see you tomorrow at the Prairie Retreat Center just outside Lumsden." Her throat squeezed, and she paused. "But Mark, please, will you drop by before then? I need to talk about…well, us."

"My day is pretty booked, but if you're free now, I

can spare five minutes."

His all-business tone gave away nothing and masked whether her request pleased or bothered him. Waiting for his arrival, she straightened a picture and brushed away a wrinkle on her skirt.

A few minutes later, he strode into her office.

She swung closed the door to give them privacy from Karen or anyone else within earshot. This meeting was private and difficult. "Please, sit for a moment." She gestured to the table by the window. She needed to connect with his softer side. Inner tenderness didn't stand a chance against his business bristle.

"I can't take long." He leaned forward.

"I know. Take a moment to listen." She moistened her lips and clasped her hands.

He set a fist on the table, clenched, and released it.

"No one has ever accused me of favoritism, so when I heard Samir label you teacher's pet, I felt sick. The personal time we shared was very special, and I wish it could continue." She swept her gaze out the window, bit her lip, and blinked. She wouldn't crack her professional image and cry now, here at the office. "You haven't told me how you feel about our relationship, but I sense you might care the way I do."

He shifted and searched her expression. "I expected you to lay down the law about class." He lifted one eyebrow and squeezed a fist so hard the knuckles faded to white. "Not toss me out like litter."

"Stop." She squeezed his hand. "I loved our walks, talks, and even our lunch date at the care home." She stroked upward to his wrist. "You're one of the most attractive and strong people I've ever met. You defend your principles." How could she continue? Her pulse pounded in her ears.

"You challenged me to get in touch with my inner self. Here it is." He placed his other hand on hers, so they intertwined. He whooshed a giant sigh. "I've never believed in love at first sight, but you changed my mind."

Lips quivering, she inhaled a shaky breath. "Oh, Mark." Rising from the chair, she tipped forward, threw her arms around his shoulders, and rested a hot cheek against his warm face.

He eased to a standing position, drew her close, and kissed her forehead, cheeks, neck, and mouth.

Stirred by his warm and gentle touch, she parted her lips and ran her hands along his shoulders and under his arms to his hips. For a glorious moment, she melted into his soul and a world she never dreamed she'd inhabit. Nothing else mattered, and she relinquished any semblance of control. Pure joy and intense desire danced in her heart and spun until she was breathless. Overwhelming emotion swooped and weakened her knees. Finally, breathing in ragged bursts, she raised firm palms to his chest, stepped back, and sank into a chair.

"I'm nearly late for my meeting." Mark smiled, adjusted his jacket, and cleared his throat. "Where do we go from here?"

"I'm sorry." Still shaken by her intense reaction to Mark and her shocking behavior at work, she lowered her gaze and stared at the floor. "We go to Leadership Camp tomorrow but only as friendly, professional business associates. I can't see you outside of class, except in a group. An office romance is too risky. I made a huge mistake. I'd love to explore where our attraction leads us, but I can't." Regret crushed her spirit, and his expression fell like night.

"You won't take a chance?" He studied his watch and then glared into Tessa's eyes. "Your decision doesn't align with the lessons you teach." He pulled back his shoulders and shook his head. "I need to leave, but I'm not through with this discussion." He strode to the door and yanked the knob. "Listen to your own advice."

He tossed a pained dart of a look over his shoulder. It lodged in her heart and intensified her anguish. "Mark, please, don't be angry. Try to understand." She wrung her hands. Rejecting him tore her to shreds. He was right. She told others to explore their feelings and listen to their inner voices. How could she refuse to do the same?

Without a second glance, he flung open the door and disappeared down the hallway.

She bowed her head, and her heart contracted into a hard lump of clay. Now what had she done? She should have quashed temptation from the beginning and avoided any social contact with Mark, but she didn't. Breaking her own rule awakened something fierce neither Mark nor she wanted to tame. How could she live with her choice to send him away?

****

On Tuesday morning, Mark drove and lectured himself all the way to Leadership Camp. Brilliant sunshine and mild temperatures outside didn't cheer him, and the rich scent of the car's leather interior did nothing to lift his mood. He would fulfill Tessa's request to demonstrate more compassion and reveal learnings from the experiences that shaped him. He'd throw himself into discussions and exercises and force a smile. In short, he would do his best to transform into a model student.

Yesterday afternoon, he had returned to her serene and orderly office to convince her to give their relationship a chance. She flushed, stammered, and cut short the conversation. "Tempted as I am, I can't risk the gossip or stress of an office romance. My reputation is too important."

"You're all talk, Tessa Shore. You demand your students step out of our comfort zones, and yet, you stay entrenched in yours. I didn't think you were that kind of person. I expected more from a leader." Mark had stormed away before he unleashed more emotion, already verging on saying too much.

Snapping back to the present, he surveyed the road and watched for the turnoff. This week's location nestled in the scenic Lumsden Valley, just fifteen minutes north of Regina. Rolling hills interrupted the flat prairie and as leaves filled tree branches would soon be a lush oasis. Although the venue was close to the city, class rules stayed the same. Stay and interact with the group to build and learn from the network of budding leaders. He rolled his eyes. The experience was better than expected, but aspects still contradicted his definition of a good time.

He tramped from the parking lot to the sprawling retreat center, covered in weathered cedar siding, and breathed the clear air, scented with sweet blossoms. A robin flitted and trilled nearby. If only he was so happy and carefree. Shoulders tensing, he reviewed Tessa's high expectations. After the daily sessions ended, he wouldn't seek her company for private time. Barring a catastrophe, he wouldn't return home in the middle of the week. But he refused to release his end of the invisible rope that tugged.

"Hey, TP, wait up," Samir hollered across the parking lot.

"What's with the new nickname?" The teacher's pet reference stung. Mark gritted his teeth and paused on the wooden steps.

"Just razzing you. How was your weekend?" Grinning, Samir caught up and held the door.

"Do me a favor. Drop the TP label, especially around Tessa." The nickname would only make things worse. Pausing, Mark barely forced a chuckle. If Samir persisted, he would embarrass and anger her. "Don't want to get on the teacher's bad side."

"Yeah, right. She might fail us." He elbowed Mark and laughed. "At least, she might fail me."

Mark shot a warning glare and headed for the refreshment table.

"Ready for another round?" Zipping by, Tessa greeted them in her usual flurry.

"Yep." He nodded, but she was already gone. The aroma of baked biscuits made his mouth water, and he loaded his plate with baked products and fruit before he settled into a spot. He surveyed the rustic surroundings dotted with wooden tables and worn chairs. The place was basic but comfortable. No doubt, she chose the upbeat, country music that twanged in the background. Although not his favorite sound, it suited the place and boosted the energy in the room.

Sitting next to Holly, Mark tracked Tessa's enormous presence around the room. Her animated overview of the week drained his enormous attitude until he reverted to a child who'd had his candy snatched. She initiated a personal relationship yet, just as quickly, backed away. She expected one thing and did another. He leaned back and breathed to relieve pressure in his head. Catching her pointed scrutiny of his pose, he adjusted forward and braced his forearms on the table. Responding to a question, he kept his tone even and interested, but every ounce of his body hollered resistance.

Tessa lured him into sharing, and now, where did his vulnerability lead? Nowhere. She uncovered his personal struggles and nasty demons, then she fled. His secrets and hurts laid exposed for her to consider and evaluate. Stilling his vibrating arms and legs, he mustered all his will to remain in place. His worst fears were realized. Keeping feelings bottled was much safer.

Tuesday dragged. Mark participated in the daytime sessions and meal conversations, but nothing eased the pain of losing Tessa. None of the exercises prompted a natural smile, and he forced himself to go through the motions. Even though the light, paneled walls were broken by ample windows, he still felt trapped in a place he'd rather escape.

"Anything bothering you?" During the evening activities, Holly plunked beside him on a lumpy sofa. "You've reverted to the Mark of week one."

"Maybe a little tired." He flicked a glance at her crinkled expression and stared at his hands. "I find the back-to-back weeks a little draining." No way would he share the real reason for his apathy. He had confided personal details and didn't like the results. He scanned the room, transformed from daytime classroom to evening lounge, an arrangement designed to encourage informal interaction and casual networking among the group. Shabby velour sofas and matching gold chairs framed the room, and participants shifted them into small groupings. Soft music strummed from a speaker in a corner. The effect was warm and relaxed, but even the cozy atmosphere did little to boost his spirits.

"Okay, I'm here if you want to talk." She sipped her drink. "Not that I'm an expert in solving my own problems, let alone anybody else's."

"Hey, I'll challenge you in table tennis." Mark jumped off the sofa and grabbed a paddle. "Let's see who's champ." He winced. In Dad's eyes, he was always a winner. Every time Mom used the pet name, she reminded him. Would his dad be proud now? He would never condone efforts to relax a stiff upper lip and reveal private inner weaknesses.

Clenching a fist around the handle, Mark wanted to bat away a tangle of conflicted feelings. The business world had changed. Employees expected openness and empathy. Maybe Dad's advice wasn't always the best anymore. "You're on." Grinning over her shoulder, Holly headed to the table-tennis table. "You don't know what you asked. I've played a game or two. Watch out, mister."

Mark couldn't help but glance at Tessa. She played a board game with a small group, laughed, and rolled dice. How could she ignore him and enjoy herself so much? Could he convince her to change her mind? Probably not. She wouldn't let anybody else choose her direction. Even when she could let go, she held on to control. She trusted him with her secret burden yet still withheld her heart. He whacked the ball as hard as he could until Holly set down her paddle and stilled a bouncing ball.

"Okay, I give." Shaking her head, she raised both hands. "Let's see how Samir handles your wicked serve."

Samir took his position on the opposite side of the table and rallied well but was no match for the torrent of disappointment Mark unleashed on every shot. The aggressive clack of the ball on the wooden table spurred him on.

"I'm done." Samir laughed and tossed his paddle on the table. "Who else wants to take his punishment?"

"Nah, time for a cold drink." Mark forced a chuckle, but inside, he burned. "You take on Holly." A game couldn't distract him from the stab of Tessa's rejection. Maybe his dad's approach was right. Tightly wound feelings couldn't unravel into a messy tangle. His efforts to open up sent him nowhere except to a place of confusion and disappointment. Drawing in long, slow breaths, he diluted the pain.

Mark scanned the lounge. Spotting everyone else engrossed in games or conversation, he slipped away unnoticed. He tortured himself long enough. Back in his compact room, he breathed woodsy air, scented by the knotty pine furniture and wall paneling. He paced until the motion dizzied him.

Flopping on the bed, he emailed a few work messages and called Bree. Wide awake, he flipped TV channels and obsessed about Tessa. Staring at the yellowed ceiling tile, he replayed the state of their relationship. She might not realize the undeniable fact now, but she needed him as much as he needed her.

The next morning, he had little appetite but still joined the group and ate breakfast across from Holly and Samir. Pans clattered from a connecting kitchen, and the scent of burnt toast thickened the air. Bright sunshine beamed outside picture windows that lined the room, but a cloud still shadowed his personal space.

"Why so glum, chum?" Samir gestured with a glass of orange juice. "Sad this session is nearly over?"

"Maybe I'm tired." Mark concentrated on the mound of hearty food on his plate. He couldn't possibly explain the real reason.

Tessa sped by. "Morning, everyone. We'll start in fifteen minutes."

The momentary distraction took the attention off Mark, and he filled his mouth with creamy, scrambled eggs. The scent of bacon, usually a favorite, floated from his plate but didn't tempt him. Did he imagine something, or did she avoid eye contact and smile only at his classmates? Did she believe she made a terrible mistake? Or had her feelings already mellowed into pure friendship? Did his heavy internal baggage frighten away any chance at love?

Maybe the excuses she gave concealed deeper concerns. He stabbed a fried potato and wracked his brain for insights. A painful twinge of frustration and uncertainty pinched his temples. If only he analyzed people well enough to quit the guesswork and read Tessa's mind.

"I can't believe Leadership Camp ends so soon." Holly dragged a bite of toast through egg yolk. "After this week, I'll graduate. Think you'll pass, guys?"

"No doubt, *he* will." Samir laughed and pointed a fork.

Mark glared at his plate and chewed. Brain freezing, he couldn't muster a witty retort.

"Since you're so darn popular with the instructor, maybe you should represent the class at the closing ceremony." Samir tipped his fork and banged the table.

"Maybe I should." A flicker of an idea nudged Mark, and he sat taller. "Guess the class will decide. If everyone agrees, sure." Instantly, his breakfast became a lot more appetizing.

"Done. When the topic comes up, I'll nominate you." Samir grinned.

Mark flashed a thumbs-up, devoured his last bites of toast and eggs, and carried his plate to the bin for used dishes.

"Let's get started." Tessa raised a hand and motioned toward the workspace. She skipped her gaze like a pebble over Mark. Dressed in a cream sweater and matching jeans, she exuded style, professionalism, and a captivating quality he couldn't name. Frustration and tension stabbed between his shoulder blades. Rigid in a chair, he stared out the window at a bumblebee that circled an apple blossom. A bee sting paled next to the smart of romantic rejection. He could swat away an insect but not his melancholy.

"Mark, what do you think?"

Tessa's firm voice interrupted his reverie, and he swallowed.

"Let's hear you share a highlight from yesterday's session." She tossed and caught a marker.

The question prickled like a burr, and he wanted to refuse. But he was a leader, and nothing—no one— could block his way. He'd travelled the rocky, Leadership Camp road this far, and he wasn't about to turn back now. He'd rise above his wounded psyche and show her how wrong she was. "The discussion about how to manage change was helpful." Heat expanded in Mark's cheekbones. "I appreciate the tools to work through all kinds of situations." He believed his comment, but a vein pulsed in his temple. Adjusting to everyday, business changes was one thing. Adapting to unwanted, personal changes was quite another.

One thing was certain. He couldn't let her go. Did she still care? Could he convince her to reverse her big mistake?

Chapter 18

"Thanks for sharing, Mark." Tessa hurt all over, but she remained determined to deliver a positive session. The center's warm, woodsy surroundings should provide a relaxing backdrop, and the scent of fresh-baked buns should soothe anyone's cares but didn't have the desired effect on Mark. His body language screamed he wanted out, but to his credit, he persisted.

Throughout the morning, his strained, drooping expression blended with the room's shadowy walls. His haunting sorrow was all her fault. She gave in to temptation and built his hopes. Selfishly, she confided something she never dared share with anyone and initiated physical contact. Then she threw up a barrier.

Even though she was the one who quashed their relationship, she ached just as much. If she changed her mind, she wouldn't break a company policy, but she would test her own beliefs.

At lunchtime, the aroma of garlic drifted from a buffet of salad and pasta, and she felt slightly ill. She avoided a spare seat next to Mark and zigzagged to a table on the other side of the room. If she sat close, his clean, masculine scent would only stir her regret. Fortunately, other participants' animated conversations, punctuated by laughter, helped divert her attention. Until she fulfilled her mission to build success for every leader in the group, she wouldn't lose focus or relax her energy level.

Just as she called the group to start the afternoon exercises, she glimpsed the back of Mark's tall, lean frame as he disappeared out the door. Casually dressed like the rest of the participants, he wore jeans that hugged him in all the right places. Sighing, she ran fingers through the sides of her hair and forgave a late break.

The retreat center didn't staff an attendant to screen calls, so maybe he stole a peek at his phone and needed to handle an important message. If he didn't soon rejoin the group, he'd suffer the latecomer's penalty. After she established ground rules on day one, she found no one tested her. Nobody wanted the embarrassment of explaining to the entire group the reason for tardiness. The ploy worked every time, except now, with Mark.

"Break into clusters of three or four, and practice constructive feedback." Tessa swept an arm across the group. "Make yourselves comfortable anywhere in the room. We'll debrief in thirty minutes. Any questions?" She scanned for the sight of furrowed brows. "No? Then let's go."

She padded across the room to the hallway. Even though Mark was very special, he still didn't earn extra privileges. When the door clicked shut, the hum of lively chatter inside faded. She headed in the direction of his murmur and then stopped a few meters away to watch him pace. His crinkled forehead signaled the depth of his concern. Did Bree's teacher alert him to another issue? Maybe he dealt with too much on the home front to remain fully immersed in the program. She stared until he finally concluded the call.

Mark strode the narrow space toward her.

His eyes glinted determination, and not a trace of remorse darkened his face.

"Major problem in the field. Liz called. I need to leave right now." Frowning, he jammed his hands on his hips.

"What's up?" Tessa hunched her shoulders. She couldn't argue with an urgent request. If Liz demanded Mark's presence for a business emergency, she would get her way. When a pipeline ruptured, natural gas was a dangerous substance. A major leak sometimes produced deadly consequences.

"A gas line exploded a few kilometers north. I designed the pipeline installation project, and Liz needs my input...immediately." Mark thrust back his shoulders. "Will you explain to the group? I'll gather my things and head out." He spun and sped toward the room where his laptop and notepad waited. "As soon as I can, I'll return."

As he tossed the promise over his shoulder, he revealed the firm set of his profile. Her heart clutched at his confident aura and the scary situation ahead. Was anyone injured? Would Mark return to the class? How would the group react when she announced he would be absent again? When she gathered everyone to debrief their breakout session, she'd explain.

A few minutes later, she positioned herself at the front of the room. "Liz Nelson called for Mark's help." Gauging reactions, Tessa scanned the group.

"What happened?" Samir narrowed his eyes.

"I don't know any details to share except a pipeline exploded in a field, and Liz assigned Mark to lead the Emergency Action Center." She stiffened at frowning expressions and widened eyes. Concern about the accident was legitimate, but they shouldn't dare to question Mark's unavoidable absence. "We can check messages on breaks. I'm sure the Communications Department will send everyone updates."

That evening, in the quiet of her cramped room, she checked the company website and local news. No one was injured, but the explosion in a farmer's field sent a fireball so high that people for miles around witnessed it. Only good fortune averted a human tragedy.

She pictured Mark, testing his new and improved leadership skills, at the helm of the emergency operation. He would deliver instructions, oversee the team, and solve the problem, but would he perform in his former or new way? Uncertainty spread a wavy, out-of-control sensation to her core, but she refused to own the responsibility that belonged to Mark. Only he could connect with the team in a positive way and prove himself.

Near midnight, her phone pinged, and she opened a text message.

—*Still at the office. Will return if and when I can.*—

Unable to calm her jumpy heart, she tapped a quick reply to his curt message.

—*I hope you're okay. Take care. Assuming all goes well, see you soon.*—

The next day, she received an even briefer update.

—*No change.*—

The weight of his absence cramped her shoulders, but she shouldn't hold her breath awaiting his return. Still, anticipation sent a delicious tickle up her spine.

The time in class passed quickly, but Tessa never forgot something—someone—was absent and changed the dynamic of the group. She stole frequent glances at the door, as though Mark might appear at any moment.

"Any word from our classmate?" Samir furrowed his forehead.

"He's still too occupied to join us." She shook her head and shrugged.

"What happens if he can't finish?"

She narrowed her eyes and inhaled a deep, calming breath. Mark's status in the class wasn't Samir's business, and she fought the urge to snap a reply. "He and I will cross that bridge later." Mark would never know the fierce, protective instinct she smothered.

"I hope he shows up before we finish." Frowning, Samir rubbed the back of his neck.

"Me, too." She excused herself to get a cooling drink of water. Samir had no idea how much she wanted to see Mark, not only to learn he was okay after the stressful incident but to seek reassurance they remained friends.

By Friday at lunchtime, Tessa resigned herself to the situation. Mark might not rejoin the class, and she probably wouldn't see him until she returned to the office. The murky mix of anticipation and apprehension sent her stomach into uneven waves like she sailed in a boat. She wasn't tempted by the aroma of melted cheese and tomato sauce. While participants chatted in the buffet line, she rotated around the room and examined flipchart notes, stuck in colorful groupings on the wood paneling.

"Here I am." Mark plunked his leather briefcase on an empty chair.

Pulse racing, Tessa whirled and faced him. Faint lines radiated from his eyes, and his hair spiked in several directions. She'd never seen him even slightly disheveled. Usually so crisp and put together, no doubt he ran short of sleep the past two nights. "I'm glad you're back."

She wanted to throw her arms around his strong midriff, tip back her head, and soften her lips for his delicious kiss. Instead, she rocked heel to toe and raised her arms in a mini-cheer, the same enthusiastic greeting she would give any participant. She pretended she didn't favor anyone. Nobody here needed to know she contained her quivering hands around a bundle of colored markers.

"*Are* you?" He stared down.

Flushing, she nodded. "I value your contributions to the group, and I want you to gain the full benefit of the program." She twisted her hands around the pens like she wrung out a damp cloth.

At four o'clock today, the class would end, and the frequent encounters would stop, too. She'd see him in two weeks at the celebration luncheon and, maybe occasionally, in an elevator at work. Of course, she might also encounter him at Heritage Haven. She both anticipated and dreaded the chance to see him again. Attractive as he was, he would only complicate her life.

Studying his tired but handsome face, she lifted and then dropped a hand to stop herself from touching his arm. "Your timing worked well." She smiled. "You arrived just in time for lunch." She pointed a moist hand toward the end of the buffet line.

"After you." He motioned the same direction.

"Uh…I should organize for this afternoon, but why

not?" She tossed the bundle of markers with a clack onto a table. Leading the way to the buffet, she placed a palm on her jittery stomach. He was everything she wanted in a man, if only she let go and allowed their relationship to blossom. Why, oh, why did she let her feelings spiral out of control and force her into this mess?

****

Mark dove in and chomped rich, spicy lasagna for lunch. Seated at one of the round dining tables near the kitchen, he settled into the laughter and chatter of classmates. Smiling, he surveyed the group, and energy surged through his limbs. He fit in. Glad to return and resume the final stretch, he would do his best to make amends for his sudden absence.

"Welcome back, TP. Is everything under control?" Samir smirked and stabbed a bite of salad.

"Yeah, the job took a while, but we got the pipeline repaired and gas flowing again." He ignored the jab and glanced at Tessa in time to see her grimace.

"Good work." Holly grinned and pumped a fist.

At the end of the meal, Mark faced Tessa, seated across the table. "I should apologize for my absence and ask for the group's support."

"Yes, please do." She nodded and swept a hand through her hair. "I'm sure they'd appreciate an update, and so would I." She swallowed.

"Thank you." He shifted and digested her reaction. Did he imagine her tone, or did she sound slightly flirtatious? Anything was possible. She had surprised him more than once. "Good to hear." Raising an eyebrow, he cracked half a smile.

"Your attention, please." Striding to the front of the

room, Tessa clapped together her hands. "Before we start, Mark wants to speak." She stepped aside.

The murmurs hushed.

"Duty called. Everything's okay now." He jammed his hands in pockets and rocked from side to side. "Sorry for the impact on the group. I didn't want to miss the sessions, and I hope you'll give me a crash course on everything you learned while I was gone." He scanned the room and, at the supportive nods, his pulse settled. To his surprise, he actually missed something these last two days.

During the emergency, he had applied some of his new-found skills, interacted with multiple team members, and enlisted their support, and the results astounded him. In the long, imposing boardroom that served as the Emergency Action Center, he mapped plans.

Technical experts swiveled in leather chairs and scoured notes and formulas scribbled on the whiteboard at the front of the room.

He sniffed the smell of strong coffee and marker ink. The walls were papered with maps and diagrams. The information and tools to launch the meeting hung ready. Instead of leaping directly into instructions, he remembered Tessa's advice. "You caught me fresh from Leadership Camp. Apparently, someone figured I needed hands-on practice." He raised his eyebrows and chuckled, and the tension in the room loosened a smidgeon. Still, his arms tingled with a burst of adrenaline.

"I want to thank each of you for jumping in here." Mark tipped back a water bottle and wet his throat. "You were invited because of your strong skills, and I encourage you to speak up and contribute whenever you can. Dealing with this type of incident doesn't happen often, so everyone has a voice." He looped his gaze around the table to show each person he valued his or her contribution. "I'll give an overview of the situation, and then we'll brainstorm solutions."

The team nodded and tilted forward in their chairs.

He had hinted at his own inexperience in the situation, hooked them with respect, and readied them for the challenge.

Now, he delivered a message in front of his classmates, and the same principles applied. He demonstrated commitment and humility. Swallowing, he shrugged and glanced from the group to Tessa and back. "I won't delay the afternoon's agenda any longer." He rubbed the side of his jaw.

"Thanks, Mark." She dashed to the center of the room. "Feel free to talk to any of your classmates for details. We won't hold a major explosion against you."

"Not this time. But enough's enough. Don't dare play hooky for the rest of the afternoon." Samir slapped a palm on a table.

His crack sent a ripple of laughter through the room. The class joker, he probably meant no harm with the teacher's pet comment, but underneath the humor flowed a vein of truth.

She paced until the group settled. "Is everyone ready to limbo?"

The group chuckled and widened their eyes.

Scanning their expressions, she raised both hands. "I mean it. True leaders accept every opportunity to stretch themselves beyond their comfort zones. Mark just demonstrated a real-life example." With a flourish, she retrieved a broomstick from under the table, switched on Caribbean music, and peered at the group.

Catchy drumbeats and tambourines filled the room. Mark liked the reggae sound but not the activity it accompanied.

"Who volunteers to go first?" She twirled the pole like a baton. "You can take turns holding the bar." Grinning, she handed it to Yvonne and Samir.

Mark flexed back his shoulders. Her words about his recent experience contained a direct compliment. She acknowledged he applied his leadership approach in a new way. Still, he used his natural restraint to contain an eye roll.

The next activity leapt far beyond his limits. He stiffened and waited for another volunteer. He'd far rather practice skills in the Emergency Action Center than shimmy in a rustic retreat lodge, but he had no choice. He returned for the final afternoon, and he'd participate in whatever Tessa deemed mandatory.

She grinned, waved her arms, and clapped.

Her sense of fun was almost contagious, and he gave her credit. She engaged a group and taught lessons in an entertaining, memorable way. "I returned too soon." With trepidation, he stepped forward for a turn.

"Nice moves." Holly cheered and beat a fist in the air.

"Well done." Tessa applauded and tapped a foot in time to the music.

Her face colored pink as a delicate rose, but maybe her reaction bloomed from exertion and not his dance style. Finished with the silly exercise, he bowed and smirked. The back of his neck dampened. He tolerated the activity but still didn't seek attention for anything other than engineering work.

Over the balance of the afternoon, Tessa reviewed learnings over the multi-week program. "Grab a chair and form a circle." She waved her arms toward the center of the room.

He rearranged chairs with the others and dropped into the nearest spot. Tracing a sunbeam across the scuffed floor, he felt a light inside. If chosen first to speak, he no longer minded. Listening to classmates debrief and share their biggest takeaways, he swallowed twice to rid a lump that clogged his throat. He belonged. The stiff, reserved guy who started the program just a few weeks ago had disappeared. He was a new, improved person, both at work and home.

Tessa set the transformation in motion, and he'd be forever grateful. But his gratitude dodged shards of pain and regret. Dedication to work made her powerful and successful, but the same qualities stole her away. Waiting for his turn, he squeezed and released a fist. Tessa's efforts made a difference, and he wanted to grow closer and absorb everything she offered. Sure, she hated to relinquish control, but he'd find a way to touch her heart.

"Your turn, Mark." She tossed a fake ball in his direction. Then she settled into a spare chair and waited.

"By now, you all know I'm not the most expressive guy in the room." He fought the urge to shake the lingering tension out of his thighs. "So I notice a bigger difference than most." He tipped back a water bottle and swigged to moisten his throat. "My biggest takeaway is you—Tessa and everyone in this room— have shown me I can become a better me. Not perfect, but better." He slid his gaze over his classmates and landed it on Tessa. "I'm up for the journey, day by day." He breathed and waited for a reaction.

In the pause, Bree's pinched expression floated through his mind. Blinking, he brushed away the image. He could become a better father figure, too, and help her unpack the emotions she tucked away. "I also learned Samir delivers a mean table-tennis slice." He joined his classmates' laughter and leaned back. His new comfort level felt great.

"Rubber match in the lunchroom on Monday." Samir grinned. "You're all welcome to come and cheer for yours truly." He stuck a thumb in the center of his chest.

"Watch out." Mark flashed a thumbs-up. A little fun at work couldn't hurt.

"Let's all take a moment to reflect on what we've shared." Tessa waved wide her arms and swooped together her palms.

The emotion in the room flowed like a stream. More than a few sniffs punctuated the silence. He'd never spill feelings the way some did, but he no longer labeled a sensitive person as weak. Leadership Camp unearthed honest vulnerabilities, long hidden right beside inner strengths.

"Thank you, all." Palms together, Tessa tipped forward in a semi-bow, swiveling to acknowledge each person in the circle. "Every time I lead a class, I learn something from each participant. This session, I learned to combine structure with a bit of flexibility to let go and trust other people will make the best choices. Thank you for teaching me as much as I've taught you."

Mark riveted his gaze and expanded his chest. Her expression transformed from somber to bright. Dressed in jeans, shirt, and jacket in shades of beige and white, she shone as fit and fresh as spring. Topped off with her subtle freckles and unruly hairstyle, she could pass for a university student, ready for an end-of-term party. If only she'd agree to a dinner date. He'd prove she belonged in his arms.

"In two weeks, we'll celebrate your progress at a luncheon with executives and managers." Tessa bobbed her head.

Her curls swung into their own celebratory dance. In his mind, Mark traced the outline of her tipped nose and breathed her summertime scent. He craved more, and the unfolding scene was his opportunity. He shrank from public attention for completing an internal course, no matter how prestigious. He still believed hard work produced its own reward, but he'd do anything she asked.

"For the event, I would like a volunteer from the class to speak about highlights of the Leadership Camp experience…someone who would make you proud to represent this group."

For an instant, Tessa's gaze burrowed deep into his soul. A burn plunged inside him and fueled his simmering desire. Did she feel the intense connection, too? She must. It was too real to ignore.

A chorus of voices rose, dipped, and swirled.

He rubbed the back of his neck. Did his name warrant classmates' support?

"Well?" She clasped her hands and lowered them. Tipping from heel to toe, she waited.

"Mark will do it." Planting a hand on each knee,

Samir leaned forward. He winked across the circle.

"You'd do a great job." Holly scanned the group.

Hope jumped in his chest, and he scanned the circle for objections. His pulse quickened. Given a chance, he'd show everyone he was the right guy for the job.

"You're the man, buddy." Samir grinned. "You get the star on the HeatNow Hall of Fame."

"Mark? How do you feel about the honor Samir bestowed upon you?" Tessa smiled and tilted her head.

He gripped his water bottle. Of course, he'd accept. In front of everyone at the lunch celebration, he could show her the depth of his feelings. Glancing around, he sensed agreement from other classmates' nods and smiles. He straightened and jutted his chin. "Sure, I'll do it." To his surprise, the group applauded, and he guzzled water, but it didn't cool his heated core.

In two weeks, he'd rise to center stage and express his heartfelt appreciation to Tessa. He'd even throw in a dash of creative flair. In front of a roomful of people, he'd display his soft spot, but she was more than worth the risk.

Now, he'd bide his time. The next two weeks until the windup event would drag. She was a hunger he couldn't satisfy, and he craved relief. Would she open her heart to love? She expected everyone else to change, but would she let go and apply the same teachings to her own life?

Chapter 19

On Saturday morning, a persistent ringing jolted Tessa out of a deep sleep. Rolling over and squinting, she fumbled for the phone on the nightstand. Strips of sunlight peeked through the blinds and streaked the gold quilt and cream walls. At eight o'clock on a weekend morning, the caller could only be her mother. No doubt, Mom wondered when she would bring Ellie to visit.

Over the last few months, Mom had grown less aware of time and social conventions. Early morning and late-night calls were not uncommon. This weekend, Tessa needed to rest, regroup, and cleanse her heart of Mark. Annoyance twinged in her forehead. She cleared her throat and gathered patience. "Good morning, Mom."

"Good morning, but I'm not your mother."

"Mark?" A tingle raced from Tessa's toes to her heart, urging it into rapid beats. Mark's rich, slightly-hesitant voice was the last sound she expected to greet her. Did he call about another incident with their mothers? "Is anything wrong?"

"Everything's fine. Sorry to wake you. Irina at the care home gave me your number."

She waited to hear the reason for his unexpected call and savored the memory of his broad shoulders and trim torso. She relived the warmth and excitement of his body hugged close. A delicious sensation crept from her core to her lips, and she smothered a shaky breath. So far, she wasn't nearly as effective as she expected at cooling her unsettling attraction. He was an irresistible temptation she couldn't ignore.

"I invited Mom for breakfast, and she insisted Adele join us," said Mark. "After the runaway incident, Irina won't let her disappear out of sight without your permission."

His call was nothing personal. She maintained she wanted only a professional relationship, but deep down, she hardly believed her own words. Her dreamy reverie disrupted, she rolled and swung her legs over the edge of the bed. Did Mark sense her regret? Did he picture her fresh from sleep? She rubbed her free hand over a thigh draped in lilac, silky pajamas. Maybe he imagined her in something more revealing than work attire. Hand quivering, she lifted it to soothe her wavery middle.

"Okay, Tessa?"

"What a thoughtful invitation." Sudden jealousy jumped behind her words. She should be the lucky one to enjoy breakfast with Mark. "I'm happy you'll include her."

"Great, and one more thing…just a moment…"

His muffled voice rumbled in the background. What else was on his mind?

"Ladies, I'll just finish this call, and we'll go." He rustled the phone. "I'm back."

"They must be pretty excited." Mark would keep busy with the eager pair. When Mom set her mind on something, her patience soon snapped. Rose must be anxious, too. A lump of sorrow lodged in her throat. Dementia was unpredictable. It lurked ready to burst through a person's natural filters and crush a normal life. "You wanted to say something else?"

"Bree asked if Ellie could come along. You might enjoy a free hour or two."

He lived the tug-of-war of a single parent, too. The role encompassed abundant joy and tough challenges. She wasn't alone in her ambivalent feelings. For a second, she dared imagine how the right partner could both ease her burden and enrich her life. She loved her weeks at Leadership Camp, but they demanded buckets of energy she should conserve for her rambunctious daughter.

Just then Ellie bounced into the room and onto the bed. "What will we do today, Mama Bear?" Ellie giggled and hugged Tessa's shoulders. "Hey, Ginger, stop." She wiped the dog's sloppy lick off her cheek.

Tessa shushed Ellie and rubbed the dog's thick, golden coat. She dearly loved her energetic daughter and couldn't imagine life without her, but daily Tessa hauled the weight of motherhood. Challenging as her work days were, single parenting topped the charts. "I'm sure she'd like to go." She swept her gaze over Ellie's black, straight hair and dark, flashing eyes. The sparkles on her unicorn-patterned pajamas glimmered every time she squirmed.

"Can I pick her up in fifteen minutes?"

"I'll get her ready." Tessa nudged away a sliver of guilt over her quick response. She'd make the most of the precious free time. "Thank you very much." Maybe even though they couldn't become lovers, they could remain friends and support each other. She ended the call and hugged Ellie. "Want a surprise?"

"What?" Ellie widened her eyes, jumped off the

bed, and jiggled.

"You can go to a restaurant for breakfast with Grandma and her friend, Rose." Tessa swung her legs over the edge of the bed, stood, and clasped Ellie's hands. "Remember Bree and Mark? They invited you."

"And you, too, Mommy?"

"Not today." What if Mark had invited her, too? Her heartbeats skittered. Even just seeing him would be like a taste of forbidden fruit. "I'll take Ginger for a long walk and big play. You're the lucky ducky. You get a special treat and can tell me all the details." She hustled Ellie toward her own room. "Let's hurry. They'll come soon."

Ten minutes later, Tessa was dressed, presentable, and perched on the front step next to Ellie and Ginger. Remembering an important detail, she leapt and retrieved Ellie's booster seat from the car and positioned it near the driveway.

"Look, a squirrel!" Ellie jumped and pointed.

Ginger rumbled a growl and woofed.

Immersed in Ellie's excited chatter, Tessa drank in the fresh scent of new leaves and the sweet perfume of apple blossoms. She belonged in her tidy home and treed yard on this quiet street draped in elm leaves. Even though family life overwhelmed at times, she handled it. She had much for which to be thankful.

"Here they are." Ellie ran next to Ginger to the edge of the grass and stopped.

Her equilibrium riding a sailboat, Tessa strolled behind. Through the silver SUV's windows, she spotted Mom, Rose, and Bree, all waving at Ellie. She raised a hand but honed in on the driver. Through the car windshield, his relaxed body language confirmed he relished his chauffeur role to four females.

Grinning, he leapt out of the car. "Good morning, ladies. You look happy, Ellie."

She nodded and bounced on her toes.

"Hi, Mark." Could he read on her face how much she appreciated his gesture? Although his sunglasses obscured his eyes, they couldn't entirely mask his intense expression. Suddenly warm, she swayed to create a slight, cooling breeze. She'd love to join him for a meal—or anything else. Swinging open the back door, she bent to greet her mom and Rose. "I'm glad to see you. Have a nice time."

"I'll take good care of Ellie and Adele. Enjoy your free morning." He nodded and slid into the car.

"I will." Definitely, she would savor every minute. Waving, she trusted her daughter and mother rode safely in his care. Only her heart was at risk anywhere in his vicinity. For a fleeting instant, she imagined how she would feel if Mark was her partner—even her husband—and helped with the demanding logistics of her life. His moral support could help relax the grip of a responsible job, ailing mother, and effervescent child.

She patted Ginger, spun, and meandered to the house. With a few precious minutes alone, she stopped to pull a weed and drink in the grassy scent. A sparrow twittered from a bush. Peaceful on the outside, she dipped and swayed in a wild dance on the inside. Her reaction was ridiculous. He couldn't possibly belong in her overflowing life. But what if she dared consider the possibility?

****

Back at the office on Monday morning, Mark plunked a box of donuts on the counter in the coffee area, where several of his engineering teammates congregated. "Good morning. Help yourselves." The cramped space was stuffy, and he didn't stick around for their thanks or questions. The hardworking group deserved a treat and, according to Tessa, a little recognition and fun mattered. He twitched a hint of a smile at the enthusiastic comments that followed him down the hallway.

Surfing a weekend high, he sped to his office and assessed the mountain of work that covered his wide desk. He prioritized piles but couldn't focus. Staring out the window at the treetops below, he congratulated himself on the way he concocted a perfectly valid reason to see Tessa. As soon as possible, he would repeat the feat.

The whole experience had filled him with a pleasant fizz. On Saturday morning, he swooped in, gave her a little time off, and helped her in a meaningful way. A few hours later, he returned Ellie, full of waffles and happy stories.

Tessa strolled from a flowerbed toward the car. "Did you have fun?"

"I played shuffleboard with Bree." Grinning, Ellie hopped out and waved.

"In the last three hours, I bet I laughed more than you." Mark's heart thundered so loud Tessa might hear it. He couldn't help but notice her gentle curves, accentuated by faded jeans and a white T-shirt. In no rush, she appeared more relaxed than usual.

"I can't thank you enough." Tessa smiled and opened her arms to Ellie.

Her gratitude warmed his core, and he searched her face for any hint she regretted her decision to cut personal ties. Sadly, he had found none.

Lugging the disappointing memory, he arrived early at the gym, and the first person he encountered was Liz. The workout area was cool and quiet with only a sprinkle of coworkers who concentrated on their own workouts. Exercise equipment and weights clanged in the background. Maybe the exertion would ease his distress.

"Congratulations on your crisis management." Liz stopped him on his way from the locker room to the treadmill.

"I appreciated the challenge." Lowering his head, he shrugged. He thrived on attacking the toughest engineering problems anyone threw his way. No one wanted to deal with the aftermath of a gas explosion, but the experience tested and broadened his technical skills. His expertise wrestled the alarming situation under control.

"Mark, I don't just mean you dealt well with more complexities and risk than usual." Liz glanced sideways. "You led the emergency meetings in a different way—like you cared about others. I was very impressed you asked for the team's input and showed appreciation for their efforts. Leadership Camp has already made you a stronger leader. Keep up the good work."

"Thank you, Liz." He would miss his wise mentor but remember her counsel. He straightened and allowed his quiet confidence to rise like the sun. Liz noticed changes. Definitely, Tessa built leaders. He relaxed his shoulders, inhaled the gym scent of sweaty bodies and cleaning products, and allowed a rush of gratefulness to fill his core. "I learned a thing or two in the sessions."

After his morning workout, Mark hurried to his desk to attack a pile of new requests and follow-up details from the explosion. A few minutes later, he thrust away from the stack of work and stared out the window. He gazed past the edge of the city to the wide, flat prairie beyond. Usually, nothing distracted him, but today, his concentration jumped around like a pesky grasshopper. He craved contact with Tessa, the music of her laughter, and the glimmer in her eyes.

Pacing the length of the office, he squeezed and released his hands. In his mind, he shoved away pipeline details and replaced them with her animated expressions and lively gestures. At the moment, her inspiring presence, novel ideas, and inside jokes interested him more than anything else.

Her secret hid in his inner vault. He guarded the truth of her private, conflicted feelings about single motherhood—a momentous challenge taken on by her own deliberate choice and not circumstance. He acknowledged her admission without judgment or alarm. Like Bree, Ellie impacted everything, and Tessa trusted him enough to admit she struggled.

With great effort, he tore himself away from the window, swung shut the office door to block the hum of coworkers, and yanked his attention back to his desk. Dropping into a chair, he ran a hand over the top of his hair and flicked the lingering dampness from his post-workout shower. His goals for the day included a Tessa encounter. His heart pumped an extra beat. Short of riding the elevator and hoping for a chance meeting, he didn't have a brilliant idea. He also must complete a lot of serious work. Shaking his head free of the enticing sweetness of Tessa's pink lips, he dove into pipeline analysis, and the morning flew by.

Near noon, a rumble in Mark's stomach lured him away from work to replenish his energy. He'd dash down the street and grab a takeout sandwich from the deli a block away. The thick, spicy sandwiches with meat piled an inch high on fresh, fragrant bread were a local specialty. On a whim, he swung by Tessa's office. "Care to join me for lunch?" His chest filled with anticipation.

Clicking on her computer with her back to the door, she jerked up her head.

He caught his breath and dared to enter and plant himself in front of her desk. Her personalized space provided the perfect backdrop for her natural beauty. Unlike his desk, hers was organized into neat piles of papers labeled with colored notes. A picture of Ellie's mischievous, round face and flashing, black eyes stared over her shoulder from its spot above her workstation. Ellie kept her mom tuned for action. For an instant, a pinch tweaked his temple. Thanks to dear Bree, he well understood the challenges of raising a precocious child.

Tessa spun and stared.

A couple of russet curls sprang to her forehead. He used all his willpower not to dive over her desk and twist them around a finger. A flash of light danced across her face and then darkened to dusk.

"Mark, I'm starved, but you know we can't see each other at work." She tossed the strands off her forehead and planted her hands flat on the desk.

Her eyes, as green as budding leaves, flashed determination and then softened into a wistful pool. How could he change her mind? For sure, they belonged together.

"We shouldn't see each other at all." She rose, straightened, and shook her head. "Nice as you were to treat Mom and Ellie to breakfast and give me a break, you can't rescue me from my life." Tears welled in her eyes. "I'm strong and independent, and I intend to stay that way."

He raised a hand to stop her protest. If only she'd allow him the opportunity, he could love, support, and enrich her life. In one smart, stubborn, and alluring package, she summed up everything he missed. He yearned to draw her close, inhale her sweet scent, and succumb to her magical touch. His desire fought so hard his body ached from the battle. Breathing deeply, he forced a flash of anger to dissipate. "Tell you what." Maybe a little levity would work. "Don't marry me today. Just take a short break and join me at the deli."

She smiled but stayed planted. "Tell *you* what. If I planned to wed, I might consider you." She tilted her head. "But I can hardly imagine marrying anyone, let alone a co-worker and student."

"*Former* student."

"Hey, until the celebration in two weeks, you haven't officially graduated. I could still award you a big, fat F." She scrunched her nose. "But if you insist, you can deliver a sandwich. I appreciate the service."

"Deal." Her offer was better than nothing. If he returned with lunch, he'd gain a few more minutes in her charming company. He nodded, turned, and as he approached the doorway, he focused on a blurred motion outside the office.

"You two at it again?" Samir stuck his head in the door. "You can't fool me." He chuckled. "I dropped by to thank you for a great learning experience, Tessa, but

I see you're busy. Have a good day."

Grinning like a detective who just scooped key evidence, Samir whistled down the hallway.

"Samir's a joker. Don't let him bother you." Mark would do anything to ease her discomfort. Her face shaded the color of pink lemonade.

"See what you've—we've—done." She clapped her hands over her cheeks. "If Samir notices our attraction, he isn't the only one."

"Don't worry." He studied her pained expression and tensed his shoulders. "Samir should mind his own business."

Dropping her hands, she shook her head and sank onto her chair.

"Get back to work." He mustered a mock stern tone. "I'll return soon with a delicious lunch, and you'll forget Samir uttered a word." At a furious pace, Mark strode to the deli and back. Sure, Samir razzed Tessa and him about their personal life. So what? He didn't care how anybody judged their romance. When he wanted something, he chased it, and nothing stood in his way. Dad would be proud.

"Your lunch, Miss Shore." Fifteen minutes later, he plunked a brown bag on her desk and gulped extra breaths to calm his skittering heart. Should he push his luck and linger? The deli meat wafted a rich, spicy aroma, but his appetite faded. He wasn't welcome here.

"Thank you, Mr. Delaney." She blinked and shifted her gaze to the window. "I'll work while I eat."

"See you again soon…I hope." He backed toward the door.

"I wish…but no…" She shook her head, opened the bag, and stared inside. "I'm so sorry."

Mark clenched his jaw and bolted. He didn't want anything—anyone—more than Tessa. If he could unlock his inner vault in front of his peers, he could convince her to consider a new life together. Or could he? His presentation at the graduation event might chase her even farther away to safety. Then again, nothing ventured; nothing gained.

She taught him leaders take risks with their own stories and feelings. His approach might surprise her, but he'd risk anything to win her back. He wasn't afraid to share the truth in front of students and colleagues, but how would she react? Would a heartfelt speech make things better or worse?

Chapter 20

The next Sunday afternoon, in the tranquility of Wascana Park, Tessa clung to Ginger's leash, the leather stretched to the limit. Her mixed emotions twisted just as taut. She needed to stomp out her recent obsession with a certain handsome force in her life.

Owen took Ellie, Zach, and Quinn for a swim and freed Tessa and Julie for a brisk circuit of the lake.

Ginger romped and lunged at Canada geese.

The sprawling park sheltered enough birds and squirrels to keep a dog on high alert for the entire, hour-long adventure. Tessa breathed the mild, earthy air and filled with such buoyant optimism she could float above like a hot-air balloon. Spring was her favorite season. For a precious sixty minutes, she could process the highlights and challenges of the past week.

In Tessa's office last Monday morning, Liz Nelson had extended a handshake. "I see how you earned your reputation for building leaders." She smiled wide, nodded, and signaled a thumbs-up. "You made a world of difference in Mark. I saw the way he led the Emergency Action Center last week. You smoothed his rough edges."

"Mark did the hard work." Tessa was as proud as the day Ellie learned to tie her shoelaces. She handed him the tools, but he applied them. Like a student striving for a grade of A-plus, he listened well and practiced hard. Difficult as he found the change, he took to heart her advice.

Later, in the elevator, Tessa met Holly and grinned at her wide, beaming expression.

"The experience really changed my life. Thank you." Holly sidled over and hugged her.

"I'm so glad I could help." Tessa's heart swelled. Did Mark appreciate her efforts as much as others did?

"You made a difference to us all, but the changes in Mark amaze me."

"I'm proud of the whole class." Tessa bowed her head to conceal the flush that crept along her cheekbones. Did Holly suspect he held a special place in her heart? The way it thumped, she might hear the sound.

During the next few days, she accepted more compliments on participants' results, especially Mark's transformation. Each time someone shared positive feedback, pleasure tiptoed up her spine. She achieved her goal and helped transform Mark into a stronger, relatable leader. She believed he could meet the challenge, even before he resolved to succeed himself. Several nights, she dreamed she congratulated him with a sensual hug and tender kiss.

Tessa tugged her attention back to the beautiful day in the park.

"Tell me the latest on your love life. How are you and Mark?" Turquoise windbreaker rustling in the breeze, Julie glanced over.

"Mark and I are not an item." Tessa jostled Ginger's leash and accelerated. A sister should listen and support. Julie meant well but shouldn't pester and prod.

"What holds you back?" Julie glanced from the scenery to Tessa and giggled. "Ellie adores him. Mom's ready to escort you down the aisle. Rose pegged you as the perfect daughter-in-law. Not to mention, you glow at the sound of his name."

"Julie." Tessa sputtered with frustration. "Please, stop. You don't understand." She rubbed a hand over her knotted middle. Mom and Rose's matchmaking added pressure, and Julie's comments only made it worse. When she had forced away the man of her dreams, she couldn't laugh.

"No, I guess maybe I don't." Julie pointed ahead. "Enlighten me."

A gaggle of yellow, fluffy goslings toddled toward the lapping water. Everything was so predictable and uncomplicated for wildlife. "People at work tease us." The embarrassment and invasion of privacy followed her like a shadow. She sniffed and filled her nose with the swampy odor of the lake.

"So what? You're not in high school." Julie threw wide her hands.

Tessa flinched. Maybe she had a point. Beside Julie, she rounded the curve near the Albert Street Bridge. The powder-blue sky stretched high and cloud free. "I hate the innuendo." Drawing comfort from Ginger, Tessa tilted sideways and ran a hand along her thick, wavy coat.

"I can't stand gossip, either. But let people talk." Julie sidestepped a puddle. "You and Mark work in different departments. The class ended. You fell in love at the office. People do it all the time."

Years ago, lucky Julie had met nice, eligible Owen through mutual friends, which was a natural, innocent way to connect. Was Julie right that an office romance was far from unacceptable? HeatNow didn't prohibit the idea. Could she loosen her own standards? A storm inside battered Tessa's heart. She was not like everyone else. She worked harder, strived higher, and always succeeded. Widening her eyes, she focused her attention over the water to the path ahead.

In the distance, a man with a golden retriever jogged at a steady pace.

She'd recognize his long, lean shape anywhere. Her breath caught in her throat.

Already, Ginger wagged hard enough to wiggle her hind end.

Tessa's mouth dried, and her pulse jumped. "Mark is headed our way."

"Great." Julie almost shouted. "Finally, I'll meet your future husband."

Tessa tossed a glare intended to shush her. "Now, behave. I mean it." Sometimes, her older sister teased too much, but then again, sometimes, she knew best. Julie's pronouncement exaggerated the possibility, but it also prompted a glimmer of anticipation. "I'll introduce you, but don't say anything to embarrass me."

"Would I ever do anything to make you feel awkward?" Julie laughed and bumped Tessa's arm.

Next to Julie, Tessa hustled toward Mark. Her pulse picked up speed to a crazy pace. His gray exercise shorts and coordinating T-shirt exposed strong, muscular legs and arms, and he looked fit and attractive as a model for athletic wear. Even if she tried, she couldn't tear away her gaze.

Steadily pacing, he raised a hand and shaded his eyes.

Ginger whined and yanked against the leash.

Acutely aware of her look-alike sister's presence, Tessa smothered a giggle at the idea Mark might think he saw double. Julie's casual appearance and energetic stride matched her own.

He approached and slowed. "Good afternoon, ladies." He ground to a halt and smiled.

Maybe the sun and breeze camouflaged Tessa's burning face. She didn't want either Mark or Julie to notice.

He extended a hand. "You must be Julie. I see the family resemblance."

Mark's dog wagged his tail and bumped his nose against Ginger.

"You're the superhero who rescued our mother in the storm and who charms Mom and Ellie every time they see you." Julie grinned and shook his hand. "I heard you starred in the last leadership class."

Tessa gritted her teeth. Julie already said too much. He would know he was a topic of family discussions, and she couldn't give him false hope.

"Thanks, but you give me way too much credit." He shook his head. "On all accounts."

"Thank *you* for the way you treat Mom. We share support duties, but Tessa, on her own, juggles a daughter and a mother who both demand oodles of attention."

"Julie…" Tessa nearly melted at the empathy in Mark's intense eyes. Julie's chatter echoed the burden Tessa confided in Mark. But Julie shouldn't elaborate. Just then a persistent buzz in Tessa's pocket grabbed her attention. "Excuse me." Tessa grabbed her phone. "In case the message concerns Ellie, I'll check it."

Glancing down, she scrolled to Owen's name.

—*Hey, Tessa, meet you back at our place. Ellie slipped on pool deck. Might need stitches on knee. She'll be fine but wants her mom!*—

Tessa groaned and slumped. She tapped a quick reply.

—*On my way.*—

She stuffed the phone into a pocket and shook her head. "Minor crisis to deal with. Ellie cut a knee and requires a trip to a medical clinic." The demands of single parenthood smothered the lightness of the day. On-call duty, day and night, exhausted her.

"Good luck. Rufus and I better let you go. I hope Ellie is okay." Mark raised a hand in a small wave. "Pleased to meet you, Julie."

"Good to meet you, Mark." Julie flashed a smile.

Maybe Tessa imagined a slight inflection on the word *you*. Surely, Julie would drop the subject for now.

"C'mon, Julie, let's hurry." Barely aware of the soft breeze and rustling leaves, Tessa dashed along the path toward the edge of the park. Ellie needed her. At a brisk pace, she would arrive and rescue her poor daughter in about fifteen minutes. The accident was minor, but it was still an unsettling interruption to a peaceful, refreshing afternoon. She shuddered. A distraught daughter and long wait for medical attention loomed.

"Don't worry. Owen will take good care of Ellie until you get there." Julie matched Tessa's speed.

"I know. He's a calm, caring dad. You're lucky." Tessa's chest prickled. Sometimes, she couldn't help but envy the support Owen gave Julie.

"I am." Julie breathed in quick bursts. "Mark's

nice. The full meal deal...brains...looks...personality. He's even a fan of dogs."

"Yeah, he's perfect—for some lucky woman." Tessa's heart skittered, and she sidestepped a hissing goose. In the distance, a canoe bobbed over the rippling lake and mirrored the waves unsettling her insides. Julie's observations hit close to home. If she could share the reins of life with anyone, she'd choose Mark.

"How can you resist? I saw the way he admired you. He practically drooled." Julie tossed her hair, and the breeze caught it. "*Why* don't you give the poor guy a chance? What scares you so much?"

"I..." Images of Mark swirled out of control like a tumbleweed. His furrowed brow and halting speech as he shared a personal feeling in class...his gentle teasing of his mother and Bree...his broad grin at Rufus's canine antics...his confident, yet reserved, demeanor at work...his understanding nod about her secret...his warm and enveloping arms. Her imagination swept her to a place she shouldn't venture.

"I'm not afraid. I just know what's best." Mark's strong, yet vulnerable, masculinity attracted her more than she dreamed possible. Weighted by guilt, she shoved away the unsettling memories of the intimate time they shared and quickened her strides. He weakened her resolve and complicated her life, but right now, her attention belonged with little Ellie, waiting and bleeding.

"I know genuine fear when I see it. You feel safe and secure in your own structured world, where you write the rule book and enforce it."

Tessa winced, but her sister's gentle tone soothed the sting. Could Julie possibly sense the truth?

"Hey, you're so stuck on rules, you could be a referee." Julie laughed and tapped Tessa's back. "Remember, you convinced me Owen was the right choice. Now, it's my turn to persuade you. Take a chance. A good man can make life better. You deserve a guy like Mark."

Julie had needed a nudge and couldn't have found a better partner. Was Tessa's own situation possibly similar? Reaching the street at the edge of the park, Tessa paused and pressed the Walk light. While cars whirred by, she jiggled her knees and petted Ginger. Only five blocks until she swept Ellie into a comforting hug. Just a few more minutes, and she could break free of Julie's persistent counsel.

The instant the light changed, she glanced both ways and charged off the curb. Soon, she could wipe Ellie's tear-streaked cheeks.

"Admit you're scared." Julie poked a finger at Tessa's side.

Julie was right, and the truth stung like a sunburn. Tessa threw out all kinds of reasons she couldn't get involved with Mark, but none touched the heart of the matter. Coworkers' unwelcome opinions didn't matter. Her independent streak could stay. She already proved she could parent alone. None of her excuses counted. She was afraid, plain and simple. How could she flex her rigid style enough to please a partner?

Tessa slapped a hand to her pounding heart. A relationship might only complicate things. Still, if she followed Julie's advice, she opened the possibility Mark might balance her overextended life. He was rooted in Regina with similar challenges. He already harbored her deepest secret, yet, he empathized and encouraged. In fact, he understood better than anyone because he parented alone, too. How wonderful Bree and Ellie even bonded like sisters. Overlooking Tessa's flaws, Mark believed in the strength a relationship promised. Of course, he also kissed her in the most stirring, tender, and sensual way she'd ever experienced. Reliving the moments, she tingled deep inside. If she returned for more, she'd never again resist.

"Strong relationships are like finger paints. Colorful, messy, surprising, and so much fun. Don't be afraid, little sis."

Julie spoke in a light, but measured, way, without any hint of her earlier teasing. "Thanks, *big* sis." A growing sense of peace smothered Tessa's anxiety. Bounding up the front steps of Julie's home, she took a deep breath and braced herself for the onslaught of Ellie's tears.

Tessa followed Julie in the door and swung it shut with a click. Inside, the light scents of lemon and flowers greeted her, and she held out her arms. "I'm here, Ellie."

"Mommy, my knee hurts." Sniffling and favoring her left leg, Ellie hobbled down the hallway to the front entrance and flung herself at Tessa. A wad of gauze covered the cut.

Bending, Tessa hugged Ellie close and stroked her hair. "Let me see, sweetie." Legs shaking, she squatted on the bright, flecked rug in the foyer, eased away the bandage, and examined the wound. A wide, raw scrape and small, gaping cut oozed drops of bright red blood. She winced, but thank goodness, the injury wasn't more serious. "Ooh, ouch. Don't worry, a doctor will fix it."

Tessa boasted broad shoulders and could handle a little mishap. At the same time, she rode a hilly path of emotions. She wouldn't act on Julie's advice today but very soon. Meanwhile, Mark waited and wondered about the state of her heart. How would he respond to her momentous decision?

****

Two weeks later, Mark dressed for the Leadership Camp windup celebration and selected a cobalt-blue tie to match his eyes. Mom once told him he should wear more of that color. When he stood at the podium and expressed appreciation on behalf of the group, he wanted to impress Tessa. Slowing his breathing, he checked his appearance a final time in a mirror on the wall above the dresser. The vivid color contrasted with the subdued, brown and taupe shades of the bedroom surroundings. With any luck, he'd stand out in her eyes, too.

In the past two weeks, he passed Tessa only twice in a hallway at the office. She smiled and asked polite questions about his latest project and Bree but gave no indication she wanted to see him outside of work. He hoped to overlap visits at the care home but didn't even spot her from a distance.

On that sunny day in the park, he had known right away her companion was her sister. With similar unruly hair and lively features, the women might confuse a total stranger, but he would never mistake anyone for lovely Tessa. She exuded a special glow that sparked him deep inside.

At the news of Ellie's accident, he wanted to hug Tessa and accompany her to the doctor. She likely dreaded another solitary, parenting challenge, but he stepped aside and traced the flurry of her rapid footsteps and bouncing hair until she bolted out of sight. At least, her sister accompanied her, but the responsibility still rested solely on her shoulders. If only she allowed, he could ease her burdens. In the same way, he'd welcome Tessa's moral support with Bree, Mom, and other life bumps. Maybe someday…

On Monday, he called her at work. "How's Ellie's knee?"

"Three stitches and a chocolate bar later, just fine." Tessa sighed. "Thank you for asking."

His throat squashed the words he wanted to say. He yearned to suggest a lunch date, but her businesslike tone suggested he would dislike her answer. "Have a good day." He had then concluded the call, dived into work, and forced daydreams of Tessa to the edges of his mind.

Now, satisfied with his appearance for the celebration luncheon, he tucked a prop into a brown paper bag, paced from his bedroom to the living room, and rehearsed his remarks. Ready for the big event, he petted Rufus, fist-bumped Bree, and headed to work. The morning at the office dragged, but lunchtime arrived too soon. Chest heaving, he gathered courage, exited into a hot breeze, and strode down the sunny street to the hotel that hosted the event.

Sandwiched between Holly and Samir at a table for eight, Mark extended a hand to greet Holly's husband and mother and Samir's wife and son. The banquet room was cool and ornate with royal blue, velvet draperies tied with gold cords. The formal atmosphere signified the importance of the gathering but tightened the knot in the back of Mark's neck. He stretched back his shoulders, straightened his tie, and clasped a thick, white napkin.

A week earlier, he had offered Bree the chance to join him.

She flicked up her gaze from a textbook. "I don't think so. Sounds sort of boring." She wrinkled her nose.

"You might be right." Without a spouse or significant other, he lacked anyone else to invite. He certainly couldn't include his mother. She was far too unpredictable to attend a business function, and she'd call him Champ. The pet name would prompt more ribbing by Samir, guaranteed. He had concluded he'd attend solo.

Scanning the plush surroundings and landing his gaze on his tablemates, he acknowledged a pang in his chest at his lack of a guest. The buzz of conversation from HeatNow leaders, Mark's classmates, and family members filled the room yet left an empty space inside his heart. He no longer wanted to navigate life alone.

"Hello, everyone." At the last moment, Tessa slipped into the remaining vacant chair, swept her gaze around the table, and flashed a wide smile.

Jolted by her beauty, poise, and energy, Mark contained an overwhelming urge to circle the table, envelop her in his arms, and kiss her smooth lips. She looked as delicious as candy in a caramel-colored dress that skimmed her gentle curves. His temperature rose, and he sipped water. Of course, he welcomed her presence, even if it tipped him way off balance.

"This guy's our spokesperson." Samir tilted his head toward Mark. "Teacher's pet." He chuckled.

"Hardly." Tessa flapped her napkin at Samir. "*You* nominated him to speak." She raised her eyebrows and nodded.

"She's right. You practically forced me into the job, but now, maybe you wish you volunteered." Mark quirked an eyebrow. "You were the class clown. Care to entertain us with a little stand-up comedy?" He jabbed right back at Samir and darted his gaze to Tessa. The corners of her mouth tipped up. Did she suspect he'd do anything to protect her?

"Don't quit your day job, Samir." She tilted her head and laughed.

Just then, a server, dressed in black pants and white shirt, arrived with plates of steaming chicken and wild rice.

Fortunately, Mark escaped further scrutiny. The savory scent of sage and thyme brushed his nose and should tempt him, but he had little appetite. He gulped deep breaths and ate enough of the baked entrée that nobody asked what was wrong. Surely, his rehearsed message would strike the right chord.

After the meal, Tessa checked her watch. "Excuse me. I always start events right on time." She stood and wove through the tables to the podium at the front of the room. "Good afternoon, everyone." Behind a lectern, she scanned the room. "Today is a very special occasion. We honor the latest graduates of Leadership Camp."

Mark studied her vibrant eyes, dewy lips, and tailored dress. Her appearance flawless, she must have tamed her usual curls for the occasion. Heat surging to his core, he drank in every word she shared about the program highlights. A rush of memories jostled to the foreground until she swept an arm in his direction. "Now, we'll hear from one of the participants, Mark

Delaney, with some reflections on behalf of the class."

"Here I go." Brown bag rattling, he swung off his chair and strode to the podium. Facing the crowd, he pulled notes from the inside pocket of his suit jacket. The soft clink of tableware faded to the background. Heart rate speeding, he nodded at Tessa, cleared his throat, and filled his lungs.

"I knew a little about the course, and, frankly, I didn't need it." He paused. "Boy, was I wrong." Laughter rippled across the room, and he stretched his tight lips into a half smile. His self-deprecating humor won over the crowd. "Designing pipelines, I spend my days managing risk." He made eye contact with Liz. "Leadership Camp forced me to take risks I never expected. I learned that unpacking my feelings and being authentic with other people feels far scarier than dealing with an explosive gas."

He rotated left to the side of the stage where Tessa waited. Her eyes glistened, and for an instant, he nearly forgot his next line. Sipping water, he regained his composure. His classmates expected him to make them proud. "While blindfolded, Samir built the tallest tower out of plastic blocks. But his best skill was the way he entertained the class. He earned the award for most-talkative participant."

Samir jumped from his chair and bowed.

Mark laughed along with the audience. Samir might be a thorn in his side, but he was popular with the class.

"Tessa, please, come and join me on stage." Now was the pivotal moment of the ceremony, and he barely contained his leaping heart.

The crowd fell silent.

She raised her eyebrows but crossed the stage, shrugged, and tilted her head.

Tessa stood so close he inhaled her sweet scent. A vein pulsed in his right temple, and he drew in a deep breath.

He had anticipated this moment for days, ever since his classmates nominated him for the honor. Demonstrating he truly had unlocked his emotions, he would express admiration for her dedication and results. Perceptive members of the audience might detect his affection simmered much deeper than a business relationship. But, right now, only Tessa's reaction mattered.

Sparks shooting to his limbs, he cleared his throat and set aside his notes. His message launched straight from his heart. Could his honesty and courage possibly change her mind and the path of his life?

Chapter 21

Returning to the center of the stage next to Mark, Tessa waded through a confusing mix of anticipation, dismay, and pleasure. She couldn't imagine what he intended to do next, but for the instant she waited, she savored his subtle, spicy scent. His eyes and tie matched the rich, blue surroundings. In his presence, her entire body tingled. Oh, how she wanted to rush into his world.

"Tessa, the group and I are indebted for everything you taught us. The simple words *thank you* are inadequate. I considered flowers or chocolate, but they are standard, run-of-the-mill gifts." He straightened and gave her a sidelong glance. "You deserve something different to show you're extra special."

"Aw…"

A teasing chorus interrupted him. Tessa slid her gaze to Mark. Did she detect a slight tremor in his hands, and what did he hold?

He paused until the crowd hushed.

She shook her head, and a curl bounced free and tickled her warm cheek. She scanned the crowd and, eyes misting, locked on his profile.

"You love dogs…" He rustled a paper bag and dipped inside.

"You got me a puppy?" Gasping, she covered her mouth with both hands and widened her eyes.

The audience laughed and leaned forward.

Mark raised high a stuffed toy, so everyone could see. "It's a golden retriever...to thank you for helping us *retrieve* our inner strengths, *dig* into new approaches, and *chew* on new ideas."

She giggled and clapped together her hands. He took a chance and displayed a sense of humor. The new Mark showed.

From the audience, Samir groaned.

Mark's exaggerated delivery of corny puns earned the good-natured, teasing reaction.

"Seriously, thanks to your expertise and guidance, you transformed a motley crew into stronger leaders." He swept a hand across the crowd. "I want to say a personal thank you...for the way..." He cleared his throat. "You changed my life." Then he presented her with the plush dog, shook her hand, and leaned in for a brief hug.

The crowd chuckled and applauded.

"You chose the perfect gift." She clutched the dog and rested a cheek on its side. Her voice faltered, and she blinked and wiped a tear. "Thank you, Mark." She poured her gaze deep into his soul and then scanned the audience. "I'm proud of all the graduates." Tucking the stuffed toy close to her side with one hand, she gripped the dark, wooden lectern with the other. Her pulse sped and pounded right to the tip of each finger. She was proudest of one participant, in particular, and Mark's relaxed posture shouted accomplishment and relief.

Grinning on the way back to his seat, he high-fived participants along the path.

Steadying her voice, Tessa shuffled papers to find her closing remarks. "Remember to share the real you, take risks—even if they're scary—and always stretch to become a stronger leader." She glanced over the crowd, and everyone but Mark faded to a blur. Could she follow through and take her own advice? Normally, a relationship frightened her, but everything about him was safe. He was the guy who belonged in her life.

Hands and knees quivering, she swallowed. Mark just proved he took to heart his learnings and revealed, in front of their business associates, the positive impact she made. His intense gaze whispered the depth of his feelings, and she savored the touching moment. Julie would love it. "When I witness the transformation and send off another class, I always feel a little emotional." She dabbed her eyes. "Thank you, friends, family, and colleagues for joining in our celebration."

Across the room, she caught Mark's wide grin and vigorous applause. He had taken a giant leap, and now, she would do the same. In the rush of hugs and congratulations amongst class participants and guests, she threaded through the milling crowd to thank him in person. Surely, her reaction showed how proud, touched, and grateful she was for his heartfelt words. Pausing to shake hands and chat, she wound in his direction, but when she reached the other side of the room, she couldn't find him. His disappearance and her longing to see him merged into a wrenching ache in her throat.

On this happy day, she should help fill the room with stories and laughter. But all she wanted right now was to grab a tissue and let tears flow. She blinked several times in quick succession, and the smiling faces and elaborate wallpaper sharpened back into focus. With the class and festivities over, she allowed exhaustion and emotion to overtake her. She would catch her breath and follow her heart the final, short distance to Mark.

Only her wait for the paperwork for Ellie's adoption preoccupied her in the same all-consuming way. In the days following graduation, images of Mark tapped her on the shoulder during the day and tiptoed into her sleep. One night, she woke shivering. In a dream, she heard someone pound on the front door of her house, but instead of hurrying, she approached in slow motion. By the time she answered, she spotted only Mark's back. Then he disappeared in the distance and was gone forever. She snapped open her eyes and bathed in a heavy wash of relief. Mark still waited. Or did he?

The next evening, she dropped by Julie's for a visit. Seated on a shady deck in the backyard, she smiled at little Ellie and her cousins, laughing and zigzagging in a game of tag. She'd love to feel even half as carefree. Overhead, leaves rustled and squirrels scuttled up and down branches. The peaceful scene didn't soothe her lingering apprehension over her unsettling dream.

"Make your move, Tessa." Julie snapped a finger. "Seriously, little sis, you don't want your nightmare to come true." She leaned forward, rested her elbows on a white patio table, and stared across at Tessa.

"I need to be sure I want him for the right reasons." Tessa sipped lemonade and puckered her mouth at the tart flavor. She avoided Julie's scrutiny and gazed at the patches of sky peeking through the greenery. Even the mention of Mark expanded her middle so full it might burst. She set down the cool glass and nearly tipped it.

"Oops." She steadied it and glanced at Julie.

"When you've met your perfect match, you have plenty of reasons to act." Julie stretched an arm across the table and patted Tessa's shaky hand. "Go home, get a good sleep, and don't procrastinate any longer."

Tessa nodded and leapt out of her chair. Julie never steered her wrong. "Thanks, sis." She hugged her goodbye and rounded up Ellie and Ginger for the short walk home.

Elm trees and multi-colored flowers in yards decorated the route, and a sprinkler spritzed droplets onto the sidewalk. Maybe, someday, she and Mark would stroll these streets and admire the eclectic mix of homes and landscaping.

Ellie giggled under the light shower. "Mommy." She tugged her arm. "Please, listen to my story."

Ellie caught her in another orbit, spinning next to Mark. "Sorry, sweetie, tell me again." She wrestled to focus on Ellie's monologue and shook off guilt for daydreaming. Tomorrow, her life might change forever. When Mark received her invitation, would he fall over from shock?

****

Riding on the high of the Leadership Camp celebration, Mark invited Bree out to dinner for a little fun together. Her choice was The Giant Sombrero. It wasn't fancy but beat fast food.

"I learned a lot more than I expected." He wedged a large bite of a spicy burrito into his mouth and caught a drip with a napkin. His mouth tingled with a hint of jalapeno pepper. "I'm glad the class is over. Now I can stay home." The air hung heavy, seasoned with chili and cumin, and Mexican music nearly drowned out their voices. The relaxed atmosphere worked for his taste.

"I didn't mind your trips." Bree shrugged and loaded a nacho chip with salsa.

Her orange T-shirt matched the bright, colorful décor. She was brave. During the last few weeks, she accepted a new caregiver, ran for the grad committee, and confronted a school bully. Considering everything, she had dealt with a lot. Squinting, he scanned her serious expression and forced a mouthful of food past a lump in his throat. She so resembled him that the reality hurt. Beneath her invisible bubble wrap, she encased emotions she couldn't express. Maybe, with his encouragement, she could set them free.

"I'm proud of you." Mark wiped his fingers. Young and vulnerable, she depended on him for everything. Perhaps, now he could grow into a better role model. "Not just for the way you handled the trouble at school, but for being a strong, smart, and kind person."

"Thanks." Bree shrugged again and barely smiled. "At least, Desiree doesn't say anything mean anymore."

Chewing, he nodded his approval. "Hey, I want to ask you something." He groped for the right words. How could he broach something without scaring her into total silence? Whatever he did, he needed to proceed with caution and pop one protective bubble at a time.

"Yeah?" Bree crunched a tortilla chip.

"Back when your mom and dad... passed away, I didn't...encourage you to talk about your sadness." He cleared his throat. Regret and sorrow spun like a tornado in his core.

Across the table, Bree blinked and focused on a piñata swaying from the ceiling. Her eyes glossed.

"I should have let you cry more." He followed her gaze to the pink-and-yellow decoration. He didn't know what else to say or how to explain. He couldn't change the past, but he could lead her along a new path. Grabbing his napkin, he swiped his upper lip and then his left eye. "I'm sorry." She must wonder what was wrong. He never acted this way.

Bree narrowed her eyes. Then she bowed her head and studied her plate. After a long time, she shifted, and a single tear landed on her taco. "Way to ruin dinner, Uncle Mark." She sniffed and shoved away her plate.

"It's okay to cry, Breezy." Was it? She might always imitate him and prefer to grieve in private. But she shouldn't feel ashamed. "Need a tissue?" He rustled in a pocket and handed one across the table.

She accepted it, blinked, and blew her nose.

Mariachi music filled the cracks in the touchy conversation. "I learned at Leadership Camp we shouldn't hide bad feelings. If we let them out, we feel better and stronger." Tessa taught him so much. Without her guidance, he wouldn't know his blind spot. "Then other people understand us…same as when you explained your side to Desiree."

She furrowed her forehead and stared at her hands. Tearing ragged strips, she shredded a napkin and brushed the pieces into a pile.

"You can decide later, but sometime, maybe you'd like to visit the place your mom and dad are buried." So what if his voice trembled a little? She should learn he dealt with emotions, too. "I could tell you stories about your mom. Think about it."

"Maybe." Bree sniffed, wiped her nose, and bowed her head.

Bombarded by loud conversation, clattering dishes, and brassy music, he chewed and waited for her to regain her composure. Maybe the rest of her meal would remain uneaten. Dragging away his attention, he soaked up the restaurant atmosphere. Too bad he wasn't as relaxed and amused as the other diners.

Servers, decked out in red shorts and yellow tops, whisked by with steaming, fragrant meals.

A few minutes later, Bree glanced up and slid her plate closer. Surveying it, she stabbed a chip with the tip of a finger. "I can't waste food, or I might get a boring lecture." She quirked her eyebrows and filled her mouth.

Her gentle jab signaled she forgave him for raising a painful topic. He chuckled and squeezed her forearm. Did he imagine a change, or did she relax her shoulders? Her eyes still glistened, but he caught a bare hint of a smile behind her taco, and the tropical storm inside him subsided. He could teach her what he learned from Tessa. The change wouldn't be easy, but it would be worth the struggle.

"Can I take group tennis lessons?" Bree licked the corners of her mouth. "A girl at school asked me."

"Sure. Sounds fun." He grinned and loosened his tight jaw. Online parenting tips stressed teens could be unpredictable, and Bree was no exception. After a few sorrowful minutes, she jumped to a fun topic. A new friend would brighten her days and ease some of his concerns. Her happiness mattered. He'd made progress, and he would continue to draw out her true reactions and model the way. For the rest of the meal, he chewed in time to the music and savored the festive mood.

That evening, as always, his thoughts drifted to Tessa. Every day for the past week, he hoped to meet her either at work or Heritage Haven but wasn't so fortunate. Either she avoided him, or chance was not in his favor.

During an evening visit to the care home, Mom had grabbed his hand. "You just missed a nice girl you should marry." She squeezed his wrist and glared over her glasses. "Choose a wife, young man."

"Darn." Frowning, Bree sighed and drooped her shoulders. "I wanted to play shuffleboard with Ellie."

Heart expanding, Mark felt the corners of his mouth tug upward. By now, Bree well knew Tessa was the woman her grandma pegged as his potential wife, and Ellie was a sweet part of the package. Bree thrived on the special connection with her little friend. Even better, Bree's bright expression around both Tessa and Ellie shouted she fully accepted them into Mark's life and her own world. Why couldn't Tessa see they all belonged together?

"Rose is right, you know. My dear girl lacks a husband." Adele huffed and tapped a red fingernail, the same color as her frilly blouse, on the arm of her chair.

Mark's longing and frustration crammed into his chest until it ached. He fully agreed with Mom's and Adele's assessments. Encircled by pastel, floral surroundings, the pair might be confused about a lot of things but not clever matchmaking. Tessa truly offered everything he desired. In return, he would strive to be her ideal partner. "Ladies, can I interest you in a cup of tea?" He gave both women plenty of attention to keep them content. They were such close friends he couldn't visit Mom without including Adele.

"I'd prefer a sip of wine." Adele crossed her arms.

"We're bored with tea." Mom sniffed and ran a hand over one side of her sleek, gray hair. "You know, Champ, the nice girl you should marry just left."

His mother repeated the same news from only minutes before, and Mark lugged the usual heaviness deep in his bones. He forced a half smile and furrowed his brow. Sometimes, his mother's chatter amused him. She was often happy and oblivious to any personal losses. Still, dementia was cruel, and he couldn't do a thing to ease its steady progress. Because she lived through the same experience, Tessa understood.

"Well, will you serve us tea or not?" Mom tugged on his sleeve.

"You asked for wine." She didn't know what she preferred. Dementia confused and exhausted caregivers, too.

"Wine? I don't even drink alcohol." Mom shook a finger.

He exchanged resigned glances with Bree, smiled reassurance at the women, and had searched for an acceptable beverage.

The morning after the Mexican dinner with Bree, Mark answered his office phone, and when he recognized the caller's voice, he exhaled enough air to blow out candles on a birthday cake. A thin strip of sunlight sliced the desk and radiated to the whole room. Tessa lit him in the same way. Throat gripping, he nearly couldn't speak. Now, he tightened his grip on the phone. His wish was granted. Tessa wanted to talk. "Hello, Miss Shore," he greeted her with teasing formality. Heart leaping, he swallowed and waited. He wheeled back from the desk and jetted to his feet.

"Hi, Mr. Delaney."

She responded in the same light tone, but then silence floated like mist. She called for a reason. Should he celebrate? He inhaled a shallow breath. What should he say? His brain dissolved to mush.

"How are you today?"

Her question lilted. Why did she call? He'd give anything to see her again. Office sounds from the hallway faded to a muffled hum, and only Tessa mattered. He paced to the window and stared at the sunny streets below. Heart pounding and hands vibrating, he hardly recognized himself. "Swamped but good. I'll run around the lake after work. How are *you*?" The small talk was a roadblock, planted in the way of the deeper connection he craved.

"I'm fine." She sighed. "Slightly homesick for Leadership Camp, but I'll get over it. I always do." Did she miss him as much as he missed her? With his graduation, he was no longer her student. Now, without guilt, she could forget the rule. He could reveal he was absolutely certain he loved her.

"Mark, I..."

Her hesitant start teased of something important. He pictured her emerald eyes, reflecting light, and her speckled cheeks, stretching into a smile. Gathering all his willpower, he planted his feet and remained still. All he wanted was to bolt to her office, blurt his feelings, and gently gather her into a never-ending embrace. Swallowing, he squinted at the light outside glinting off the windows across the street. Today was a glorious, summer day. With Tessa in his life, every day would shine.

"I wondered…"

"Yes?" He pictured a dramatic swoop with her free hand. While she formulated her message, she would sweep back her hair and purse her lips.

"If I drop by your office, will I interrupt any urgent work?"

Even over the phone, a nervous tension pulsed. "Nothing important." His urgent to-do pile could wait. He'd rearrange his entire schedule every single day to make space for Tessa. He'd turn his entire life upside down to spend as much time together as she would allow.

"I'm on my way."

Mark paced until she arrived less than two minutes later. "Your call was a nice surprise, and a personal appearance is even better." He smiled and searched her expression. He couldn't quite decipher the combination of wrinkled forehead, jutting chin, and demure smile. "You look very nice." Her yellow dress added more sunshine to the office. He forced his hands to his sides to avoid easing her close.

Tessa swung shut the office door. "I have a question."

His heart thumped, and moisture beaded under his collar. Should he anticipate or dread her words? He trusted she would treat his heart like glass, but she was strong and determined, and he couldn't predict where those qualities would lead. Definitely, she wouldn't interrupt work without a very good reason.

"Mark, I'm not your teacher, anymore. I refuse to worry about innuendo and accusations of favoritism in class." She threw high her arms, let them fall, and clasped them over her heart. "We still need to always stay professional at work. We can't interact at the office in a way that would make people raise their eyebrows. What we do outside of work…well…could be different. So…I wanted to ask…"

Vivid color filled her cheeks, and he burned with hope and desire. He steadied himself with a thigh against the desk. Time stopped, and the life-changing weeks he experienced replayed in a dizzying whirl. Could she possibly feel the way he did? Did she realize her invitation opened a door he feared might stay locked forever? "Tessa, ask me anything." He cupped her shoulders and searched deep into her eyes. "I love you." Burning heat sizzled from his chest to his cheekbones.

She widened her eyes, blinked, and melded the full length of her body against him. "Oh, Mark, I love you, too. More than you know. More than I ever dreamed possible."

Tessa adored him as much as he worshipped her! He tilted up her chin and nudged her lips with the most gentle of kisses. "Now, I believe you wanted to ask me something?"

She giggled. "You distracted me for a moment." She swept her gaze over his face. "Remember, we can never again connect this way at the office."

"I agree. Just promise not to throw me a look that demands a kiss." He chuckled and squeezed her shoulders. His pulse beat out of control. "Now, ask away."

"Would you join me for dinner some evening?"

She invited him on a real date. A gas flame didn't burn as hot as his torso. *Would* he? The depth of his feelings hammered in his heart. He'd never refuse anything she asked. Heat seeping through him, he drew a shaky breath and whispered next to her fragrant neck, "Tessa, my darling, without a doubt, I would love to join you for dinner...today and *every* day for the rest of my life."

Epilogue

Over the past four months, since the dinner date that launched their relationship as a full-fledged couple, Tessa intertwined her busy, complicated life with Mark's. She embraced adventures together, with and without their daughters and dogs. Following his lead, she grew to understand, support, and love him more each day.

A few months after Leadership Camp, HeatNow President Don Reilly complimented Mark's leadership skills and appointed him Vice President of Engineering.

Tessa toasted Mark with champagne and floated on a cloud of pride for days. His strength balanced her urge to control. With his support, she negotiated life's bumps in a more relaxed way.

Even an unexpected pregnancy caused more joy than concern. Ginger surprised everyone by secretly mating with Rufus, and, in a few weeks, she would give birth to an estimated ten puppies.

On a crisp, autumn day, Tessa ushered Ellie and Ginger into the care home for a Saturday visit. Anticipating Mark's presence, she tingled all the way up her spine. Among all the fun and sweet moments Tessa shared with Mark, frequent, joint visits to their mothers punctuated their weekend routine. Today, inside the cozy care home, the delicious aroma of fresh-baked bread filled the hallways and almost overtook the pine-scented cleaner.

"Will Mark and Bree and Rufus come, too?" Ponytail swishing, Ellie bounced along and squeaked her runners on the floor.

"They'll wait in the lounge with Grandma Adele and Rose." The two women were still fast friends but often slipped in and out of lucidity with the whims of dementia. "Tiptoe as quietly as a teddy bear, please." Tessa squeezed Ellie's hand. "Some people might nap in the afternoon."

Overall, Mom still enjoyed visitors, but arriving at the home, Tessa always held her breath. She couldn't guess in what state she'd find her mother. With any luck, today was a good day for both women.

Bumping Ginger's side, Ellie burst into the visitors' lounge. "Oh, goody, you're here."

Her gleeful, high voice filled the space around the muted sofas and matching chairs, and she ran to hug her grandma, Rose, Mark, Bree, and Rufus. Mark still spun a waltz in Tessa's heart.

Rising to greet her, he stretched to his full height.

Nearly gasping, she wanted to run her hands along the sides of his gray, plaid shirt to his faded, fitted jeans. The thrilling intimacy must wait. Fortunately, nobody else relaxed in the lounge today. While most of the residents enjoyed children and dogs, Tessa didn't want to test her luck.

Ginger flopped beside Rufus on the sage carpet, wrestled, and nipped.

"No, Ginger. Sit." She shook her head and pointed. The goofy dogs were cute but behaved like disobedient guests. Good thing Mom and Rose tolerated their playful antics.

"How's my favorite Chi—" Mom flailed a hand at Ellie.

"She's fine, Mom. Maybe you girls want to play a game?" Tessa changed the subject before her bewildered mother drew attention to Ellie's heritage. Ellie was as Canadian as the rest of the family, whether or not Mom understood the fact.

"Can we, Mommy? Do you want to play, Bree?"

"Pretty soon." Bree plopped cross-legged to the floor and stroked the dogs.

"Hello, dear." Rose gave a small wave. "What's your name, again? Are you Champ's girlfriend?"

"You've met Tessa, Mom. We've grown very close." He winked at Tessa and squeezed her elbow.

"Hi, Rose." Tessa smiled, raised a hand, and rippled her fingers in greeting. "I'm happy to see you." Sometimes, she recognized Tessa but often forgot details.

"She would make a good wife for Champ." Rose patted Adele's arm.

"Of course, she would. She's a nice girl, Rose. She's my daughter." Wearing a bright purple sweater, Adele leapt up and spread her arms for a hug.

"I remember now." Rose squinted and stared.

Tessa embraced her mother and then bent and clasped Rose's hands. "Your son is very handsome."

"He would make a good husband, dear," said Rose.

Rose was so right. He was everything she dreamed of in the right partner and more. Usually, she laughed off Rose's and Mom's determined matchmaking efforts, but today, she savored the moment. She flitted her gaze to gauge Mark's reaction and caught him exchanging a glance with Bree.

Bree stifled a giggle

Still quiet and shy, she embraced the role of surrogate, older sister for Ellie.

Mark shared that gradually Bree opened up and revealed more. The one time he took her to the cemetery where her parents were buried, he comforted her through her healing sobs. He recounted the childhood tricks he played on her oblivious mom, and she laughed and begged for more.

Today, Mark's trace of whisker shadow didn't hide the smug set of his jaw. He beamed a swirling energy she couldn't quite explain but made her slightly dizzy. "Okay, you two." Tessa planted her hands on hips. "What's up?"

"Why do you ask?"

Mark dropped his cheek muscles into a flat expression.

Tessa narrowed her eyes and examined his mock innocence. Definitely, he was up to something. "Oh, no reason." She played along. Suspecting Mark and Bree wouldn't contain their private amusement for long, she sank into a chair across from Mom and Rose. "Come, sit here." Tessa tapped a nearby chair for Ellie.

He retrieved a square, plastic container from the coffee table in the center of the seating area. "Bree and I packed cookies for a snack." He smirked at Bree and scanned the group.

"We baked them." Grinning, Bree leapt to a spot next to Mark.

"Champ baked?" Rose peered over her glasses.

"I make the best Saskatoon berry pie in Regina." Adele clapped together her hands. "Ask Tessa."

"Your fresh pie is delicious, Mom." Tessa's mouth

watered at the memory. Her mother's pie, prepared to the highest standard, earned boasting rights. No point in reminding her she hadn't baked in several years, ever since her memory declined.

Bree handed out pink napkins and served heart-shaped cookies to her grandma, Adele, and Ellie.

"How adorable." Squinting, Rose extended an arm and viewed a cookie from different angles.

"Mine says *Tessa and Mark.*" Adele furrowed her brow. "Are you two in love?"

Pausing in front of Tessa, Bree slipped the box to Mark and sank to the floor.

"Yes." He grasped it and peeked inside. "We love each other...and Ellie is the sweetest, four-year-old girl I know." Setting the container on the low table, he spun toward Tessa.

Giggling and fidgeting, Ellie nearly toppled off the chair.

Tessa's heart sped. He made a public declaration of his deep affection. His eyes burned with emotion and vulnerability. She could hardly believe he was the same man she met six months ago with his joy and sorrow packed inside as tightly as a locked suitcase. He would never be the most expressive person, but he now dared to reveal his feelings. In her arms, he bared his soul.

Now, heat rushed through her entire body, and she held her breath. Taking the cookie he offered, she stared at the words traced in icing and then at his tender expression.

The message in vivid pink teased. *Will you...?*

He took a deep breath and plunged to one knee.

"No!" She shouted at the gold, furry motion behind Mark's left shoulder.

He widened his eyes and dropped his jaw.

"Not you, Mark, the dogs." She slapped a hand over her mouth. Giggling and lifting his chin, she waved them away.

Ginger chomped and licked her lips.

Rufus devoured the leftover cookies.

"Oh, Mark, I'm so sorry I interrupted." She placed a hand over her pounding heart, and his gaze melted from wide-eyed alarm into gentle earnestness.

"Marry me? Tessa, my love, will you marry me?" He dug in a pocket and snapped open the lid of a small, velvet box.

"A thousand times *yes*," she shouted and flung her arms around Mark's neck and then admired the glittering gem. A hot rush of joy made her hands shake and her stomach twirl.

"Yay." Ellie shouted, leapt, and bounced in circles. "I get a daddy and a sister." She jumped onto Bree's lap.

Bree laughed and squeezed squirming, giggling Ellie.

"I told you he needed a nice wife." Rose squeezed Mom's hand.

"About time she found a good husband." Mom clucked her tongue. "Remind me of his name."

Through a haze of delight, Tessa scanned the circle of family and absorbed their joy. Rising shakily, she melted into Mark's strong embrace, tipped back her head, and gasped at the heat from his burning lips upon hers. Life could not get any better.

Acknowledgements

Thank you to all the readers who enjoyed my first book, LOVE TAKES FLIGHT. This time, you're in for a fun office romance.

I love and appreciate my supportive network of family, friends, and Saskatchewan Romance Writers who share their feedback and support. Author Donna Gartshore is always there to coach and cheer. Thank you, all!

As I write, I think fondly of my late dad, Ian Bickle, who was also an author and always encouraged me to read and write.

As well, thank you to my editor, Leanne Morgena, for teaching me so much as I brought to life this story of leaders at work and at home.

I welcome email from readers at
authormargotjohnson@gmail.com
or contact me on Facebook at Margot Johnson Author.

A word about the author...

Margot Johnson is the author of two romance novels: *LOVE TAKES FLIGHT* and *LOVE LEADS THE WAY*. She lives in Regina, Saskatchewan, Canada with her husband and golden retriever.

Contact Margot Johnson at
  Facebook: Margot Johnson Author
  authormargotjohnson@gmail.com